MUTAGENESIS

HUMAN REGRESSION

JORDAN ALLEN

This is a work of fiction. Names, characters, places, and incidents either are the product of the author's imagination or are used fictitiously. Any resemblance to actual persons, living or dead, events, or locales is entirely coincidental.

Copyright © 2024 by Jordan Allen

Cover illustration by Lucyan Carreira

ISBN 978-1-7394491-8-6

The sequel to

Mutagenesis: The New World

Contents

Chapter	Page
1: The Road North	1
2: Camlorn	14
3: Highwayland	27
4: Good Luck	39
5: Over the Fence	52
6: Street Cleaners	67
7: Unconnected	81
8: Harmonious Living	94
9: The Jewel of Namaah	107
10: One Half	123
11: The Fiend	134
12: Thick Flesh	146
13: Mercer's Mercy	161
14: Survival	174
15: Welcome Back	188
16: The Audience	204
17: Release the Hounds	218
18: Uncovered Evil	232
19: Reunion	246

Chapter 1:
The Road North

The mutant reared its ugly head from behind the rocks, smiling widely as it laid eyes upon its prey. It lumbered forward, its long arms dragging along the dusty ground peppered with patches of rough grass. All it knew was hunger; its humanity long forgotten. It had but a single desire, to feed. Living or dead, human or animal, it did not matter. Its appetite must be satiated.

Suddenly, its miserable life was snuffed out as a sharp knife pierced its skull. It dropped to the ground in a wretched heap with that sickening smile still fixed on its face. Its liberator knelt down beside it and prayed that the human soul who once inhabited the warped body was finally at peace.

"Another clean kill, Jason," said the man with the three-scoped eyepatch. His scopes rotated with a simple thought, and he scanned the area using his thermal vision. "It looks clear. Finish up here and let's get a move on just in case I've missed something."

Jason stood up and looked around. He did not doubt his friend's ability to detect mutants, frankly, it was one of his greatest strengths. No, he was looking to see if there was a building anywhere in sight. "Still nothing nearby, Sniper?" he asked the man with the eyepatch.

"I would tell you immediately if there was," said

Sniper as he scratched a German Shepherd behind the ears. The dog, Achilles, started licking his master's hand.

Two weeks ago, Jason, Sniper, Achilles and their friends, the mercenary group called Black Haze, had visited the remnants of Jason's desecrated hometown, Shackford. It had fallen to a mutant attack almost a year ago and Jason believed himself to be the only survivor left until he found the letter.

The letter had reignited a spark of hope in his heart. The two men and the dog made their way to the town of Fort Wood and, after a single night of rest, said their farewells to Black Haze then hit the road with a healthier stock of ammo and food. They had been scouring the many roads north of Shackford ever since.

Jason pulled out the letter for the fiftieth time and read it to himself.

Jason. If you're still alive and ever come back here, I've headed north.
It's scary to travel alone, but I know you'll find me eventually.
Please take care of yourself.

It was from a young lad, Kyle, who had escaped Shackford with Jason. He had fallen into the river while fishing and Jason presumed he had drowned after an unsuccessful rescue attempt. It had been a huge relief to learn that the boy was tougher than he seemed and managed to make his way back to Shackford alone.

"Will you quit wasting time with that stupid piece of paper and get a move on," demanded Sniper. He had said before that if he heard it read aloud again, he was going to burn it. "It's a highway he's heading to. You won't find any hidden code if that's what you're thinking."

Jason scowled and stashed the letter back in his pack. "I don't enjoy being miserable quite like you do, Sniper. It's nice to have something to keep you going in the wastes of humanity."

Sniper didn't say a word and led the way forward. The sun was high overhead in the once-great state of Texas. The men were so far from old civilisation at this point that you would almost forget that a mutant apocalypse had taken place a few decades ago. The remaining humans either roamed the land scavenging supplies and dodging death or they were holed up in one of the many settlements that had formed among the ruins.

Shackford and Fort Wood were two such places, but Shackford was no more. The crowning jewel of the local area, however, was New Dallas. Built deep within mutant territory where the former humans served as an unnatural defence. It didn't hurt that the city was also armed to the teeth and surrounded by many more literal walls.

For a few months, Jason had reluctantly called it home while held as a slave under Bartholomew Benedictus, a bar owner and Livelong distributor. The last thing the world needed was more of the drug that had birthed the mutants and destroyed the world, but Jason had put an end to Benedictus and then fled New Dallas with help from Sniper and Black Haze.

"There's something up ahead," said the gruff Sniper, pushing his dark hair away from his face. "It looks like a campsite. I can see smoke rising from it."

"Anybody there or have they moved on already?" asked Jason.

"Hard to say," replied Sniper as he climbed up a rock to try and get a better view. "We can edge our way closer and divert our path if we need to."

"Wouldn't we be better going around just in case?"

"Normally I would agree, but we're low on food and I don't want to go all the way back to Fort Wood to stock up then have to do this all over again. There's always the chance that it's somebody to trade with or they've left supplies behind."

The men approached cautiously, Sniper switching between his scopes to try and see from a distance what awaited them. He beckoned Jason forward silently and they pushed through the dry thickets leading into the camp. Achilles eagerly ran ahead and began sniffing around.

There was nobody here, at least not left alive. Three men lay sprawled across the floor, a bullet hole in each of their heads. Two of them were notably more armoured than the third man. The fire had not been smothered out; it had been left to burn. These men must have been alive as recently as this morning, but the flies were already starting to circle their abandoned corpses. It was a grim and unfortunate sight, but Jason couldn't help but be grateful that it did not yet emit a fouler smell.

"Mutants don't carry guns," said Jason as he started looking through the men's possessions to try and figure out who they were or what had happened to them.

"No," said Sniper, "they most certainly do not." He climbed yet another rock and scanned the surrounding area once more. A regular occurrence for a vigilant man like Sniper. He was a veteran of the wasteland and there was a reason he remained alive to tell the tale.

"Most of their gear seems to be here," said Jason. "A few ounces of silver, a couple of cans of food and a healthy stock of water. They weren't robbed, which is...strange."

Sniper shook his head and climbed down from the rock. "They weren't robbed as far as you can tell. Whoever did this may have taken something specific, so we can't rule it out. In any case, there doesn't seem to be anything nearby except for a few critters. We'll take a bottle of water each, a couple of cans and leave the rest. Looting leaves a sour taste in my mouth, but we need something to save us a long trek back to replenish our supplies. Any objection?"

"Not from me," said Jason as he looked at the less-armoured man's phone. By some miracle, there was a small bar of battery remaining. Jason sifted through, seeking any indication of who these men were. "This guy's name is Randall Everett. He has passport papers for a few places. There's New Dallas, Fort Wood, Harmony..."

There was something about the man's name that seemed familiar to Jason. He did not recognise the dead man, but the name...why did it ring a bell somewhere in the depths of his mind?

Sniper raised an eyebrow. "Harmony, eh? It's been a long time since I've ventured out that way."

"Is it far?"

"It's a little way north-east of Fort Wood. Imagine the Admah district of New Dallas, but larger and an entire town rather than a single sector. Scumbags everywhere, almost everybody is a cyborg and not a single man who lives there tells the truth unless he's paid to do so. It's best avoided if you can help it, but the jobs pay well and there is certainly no shortage of jobs. Gunderson and the Black Haze fellas operate out of there sometimes if they're strapped for funds. Gunderson's got family there so they're never stuck for somewhere to stay."

"I'll say a prayer for these men, and we can be on our way. We need to find Kyle somewhere in this forsaken county. I need to make sure the boy is alright."

"Go ahead," said Sniper. "We're going to lose daylight in a few hours. We'll find somewhere to take shelter and rest up. There must be an old house or town nearby somewhere. It's been a while since we've seen anything other than grass, rocks and weeds."

The two men trudged through the wasteland, called as such not because it was barren of life, but because so few humans dared venture across it. Their feet pounded the hard-packed dirt as they trekked onward, searching for somewhere safe to rest for the night. To them, shelter meant setting up barricades. Barricades meant they could risk resting simultaneously, a luxury they could not afford in the wilderness.

They pressed on as Achilles ran ahead, searching for a weasel or fox to feast on. Most of the larger animals that resided here a few generations ago had their numbers thinned out heavily by the mutants, who did not care what sort of flesh they could feed on. Although many suspected they had a preference for human meat.

"Lady Luck is on our side today," Sniper said as he stood by a ridge.

Jason caught up and looked over the drop. There was a small town no more than two hundred feet away with probably fewer than fifty buildings clustered loosely together. The streets looked mostly clear of mutants and the debris littering the road did not look like it had been moved in decades. This boded well for scavenging.

"Do you see what I see?" asked Jason. Sniper gave him a look and tapped on his eyepatch. "Fair point," admitted Jason.

A mid-sized Fresh and Fancy branch sat in the middle of the town, the large shopping cart signpost giving it away even from this distance. Nothing said supplies quite like a supermarket. If the men were fortunate, there would be an untouched aisle of canned goods ripe for the picking and if they were less fortunate, they may still be able to find somewhere to sleep peacefully.

"There's a way down on the left," said Sniper as he edged his way along the ridge. "I counted a dozen muties, all wunners and no toosies."

Mutants were categorised in three stages based on their size and strength, simply labelled as one, two and three. Black Haze had nicknamed them wunners, toosies and...come to think of it, Jason had never asked what they nicknamed stage three mutants before.

"Sniper," called Jason. There was no time like the present, he supposed.

"What do the Black Haze boys call stage three

mutants?"

"If we see one, I'll let you know."

"Come on, don't be like that."

Sniper laughed loudly. "Do you really care that much?"

"I suppose not, but I'm holding you to those terms. The second we find a single stage three, you have to tell me."

"Fine," said Sniper, unsure why Jason was bothered by it.

"I'm betting it's something like a threesie."

"You could have a dozen guesses and I bet you wouldn't even come close," chortled Sniper.

Jason wasn't sure whether that was a bluff to throw him off or not, but it only served to further pique his curiosity.

The men and the dog wandered through the streets, avoiding the mutants with the aid of Sniper's scopes. If they could restock and find somewhere away from the mutants where they could rest, they were at their safest. Much like in New Dallas, a wall of mutants was off-putting to those who may otherwise want to approach.

"This one is in the way," said Sniper, indicating a mutant who lay against a car at the back door of the Fresh and Fancy. "Want me to take him?"

"No," Jason said as he drew his knife. "I've told you before that I'm going to break your kill record."

"Then be my guest," smirked Sniper, genuinely pleased to see the young man having come so far since their first meeting.

Jason moved quickly and quietly toward the mutant, who lazily lay on the ground. It was conserving its energy, hoping fresh meat would cross its path one day, but that dream was now a dead end. It turned to face Jason and smiled as he plunged his knife deep into its eye socket. He pulled it back out and ran towards the heavy, metal doors with Sniper and Achilles right behind him.

"This won't budge easily," Jason said, rattling the

doors. "I don't think it's chained or blocked; it's just very stiff."

Sniper looked around, making sure no mutants had approached. "We'll have to bust it down. On three?"

Jason nodded and counted down. The two men barrelled through the doors, which burst wide open from their combined efforts. The intense heat from inside hit them in a wave, such was the nature of glass-covered buildings in the desert sun without air conditioning of any sort.

Sniper was surveying the area. "I'm counting about a dozen of them inside, but I'm losing thermal range. At least two of them are on the move towards us so keep your wits about you."

The two men crept through the sweltering corridor. Jason stopped to take a quick look around one of the back offices, but there was nothing worth scavenging. It was filled with mindless paperwork, mouldy old mugs of coffee and cloth dollars that had expired even before the end of the world had arrived.

A mutant sidled round the corner, keen to enjoy a meal that it had desired for so long. Sniper goaded it forward, unwilling to grant its wish for a snack. He raised his knife, and the mutant swung its arms wildly but was met by a sharp pair of teeth to the wrist courtesy of Achilles. Sniper used the opening and closed the gap, stabbing the mutant in the skull. The more bullets saved, the better.

A second mutant ran round the corner, this one a lot wilder than the previous. Jason ducked out of the way of a lunge and grabbed it from behind, thrusting his own knife into its temple with a thick squelch. He was both glad and saddened that he had become such an expert at this. To him, it meant that he was getting further and further removed from his old life. He knew a life of peace wasn't one that would come to humanity in his lifetime, but that was out of his hands, and he had to make the best of it.

Sniper looked at Jason as the mutant slumped to the

floor and they gave each other a nod of understanding and moved onto the main floor of the supermarket. As expected, the sun was beaming through the large glass windows covering the front wall where the entrance lay.

Above them was a smaller second floor with a balcony overlooking the aisles. Sniper signalled that he was going to go above while Jason cleared the mutants lurking about the mostly empty shelves down here. Achilles stayed with Jason as Sniper ran silently in search of the staircase, the hardened wanderer not needing an extra set of eyes to watch his back.

Jason rounded the corner into the once-frozen food section. Half of the freezers lay open, but they were so old and rundown that even a generator wouldn't have been enough to get them working again. At best, they could be torn apart for their remaining functional electronics. Achilles sniffed the air and growled softly, and Jason understood exactly what was coming. He held his knife in one hand and his pistol in the other, ready for the next mutant to attack.

As he crept towards where the dog was staring, the mutant emerged from the end of the aisle and Jason jammed his knife in its eye socket. He threw the brute into one of the old freezers and closed it shut; the less evidence to draw the attention of other mutants, the safer he was. Achilles sniffed the speckling of blood that had dripped on the floor and Jason wiped it clean with an old piece of cardboard that lay nearby.

Achilles leapt over Jason as he stood up. Two more mutants had crept up without the young man having heard. They dug their sharp nails into the dog, ready to take a bite out of the hound's side. Jason charged forward and tackled them to the ground, pulling Achilles free from their grip. He backed away, his gun at the ready as the mutants clambered back to their feet and immediately swung their abnormally long arms.

Pop. Pop.

Their heads burst open, and Jason turned to see Sniper on the balcony overhead with his rifle raised.

"Did you almost get my dog killed?" he shouted down with a savage look on his face.

"I *saved* your dog from getting killed while he was trying to save *me*," Jason replied.

"Fair enough," Sniper shrugged, looking around the lower floor from his safe perch up above. "In any case, it looks to be clear now. We'll scavenge what little left there is and rest up until morning."

"I don't think we'll get much food here."

"It doesn't have to be food. Screws, nuts, bolts, old world money. Whatever we can find that won't burden us will be good."

"Old world money?"

"Yes. Coins only because the metal can be melted down. I'm not so worried about the greenbacks in the office."

"It was all digital by the end, do you think there'll be many coins left to scavenge?"

"That's why we look. I've been around the block enough to know that many places did their best to flaunt the latter-stage Old World rules imposed upon them, particularly places outside major cities. Now quit yapping and get to it. I'll look around up here and you start down there."

Sniper slung his gun back over his shoulder and started the search of the upper level while Jason and Achilles prowled around downstairs. As he suspected, there was little sustenance to be found here outside of a single can of baked beans that had rolled underneath one of the shelving units. A lucky find, but it would only be enough for a small meal each.

Achilles started licking one of the rotten mutants by the door and Jason scolded him. Whenever Sniper was around, he wouldn't dare do such a thing, but with Jason? The cunning pup liked to push the boundaries of what he could get away with. Of course, Jason wouldn't let him away with some of his more disgusting habits, but it didn't stop Achilles from trying anyway.

"What did you find?" asked Sniper, joining his friend

and his dog a few minutes later.

Jason opened his bag and showed his haul. "A can of beans, a few of the screws and such that you mentioned along with a couple of empty glass bottles that we can fill with water when we next find the chance. How about you?"

"The beans ain't bad," said Sniper, surprised to see the can. "I grabbed a few shirts and jackets from the clothing racks. Could be useful if we get covered in mutant blood again."

"That does tend to happen," laughed Jason, looking at a couple of drips on his jacket from his earlier scuffle.

The duo and the dog headed for the old office in the back corridor. Jason barricaded the back exit to the Fresh and Fancy while Sniper rearranged the office so they would have cover on the off chance that they ended up in a shootout. Some of the more sheltered folks of the world would have called him paranoid, but not Jason. He had seen things fall apart even when the utmost precautions were taken.

When the two were satisfied they wouldn't be set upon easily, they sat down and heated up some dinner over a makeshift fire. All the while, Jason was thinking about the name he had read at the campsite-turned-graveyard earlier. Randall Everett. It bothered him. Who was he?

Sniper tossed aside the empty can of beans and Achilles wandered over and licked the remnants of sauce. "You're a disgusting mutt, aren't you boy?" he asked with a low chuckle, scratching the back of his pet's ears before turning to Jason. "Why do you look so miserable?"

"I'm not miserable, I'm thinking," Jason replied.

"Fair enough. Think away."

"I know the name Randall Everett from somewhere, but I can't place him."

Sniper sighed. "That sounds like talking, not thinking. If you were thinking, I wouldn't be able to hear it."

Jason ignored him. "He's definitely not from Shackford. He didn't work at the Third Circle. I don't recall his face, although I'll grant that the face of a dead man doesn't quite resemble the face of a living man."

"It could always be a name you heard in passing or it was written down somewhere."

That sparked something in Jason's brain. "It was written down somewhere."

"Where?"

"I don't know, but now that you've said it...I don't know, but I'm certain that you're right."

The two sat in silence as Sniper scratched Achilles, while Jason continued to search through his memories for where that name had been written. It was irking him, but he figured that it would come to him if he slept on it. The harder he strained his mind, the more he found himself making sillier leaps that made very little sense.

Suddenly, the silence was broken by a gunshot from within the building. Jason and Sniper drew their weapons and got behind an upturned table. Jason peered over the edge of it, keeping an eye on the office door, while Sniper used his scope to see who or what was nearby.

"There's a man coming this way," he muttered. "He's reloading his gun as he walks, but I can't see who or what he shot at. Appears to be fully human, no cybernetic parts."

The two sat in wait as footsteps began to echo down the corridor. The man started to whistle a slow, drawn-out tune. Perhaps it would have been a pleasant tune in another situation, but it filled Jason with a sense of dread. He knew that it was kill or be killed, and he took little pleasure in the thought of killing another human being.

"Where are you little piggies?" asked the man. His voice was calm and deep. "The Grim Reaper has come, and he doesn't like being kept waiting."

Jason and Sniper kept quiet as footsteps approached

the door.

"No? Well, let's just see what's in here then, shall we?"

Chapter 2:
Camlorn

16th April 2116: My cuts and bruises have disappeared in record time. I'm getting stronger by the day and the only trade-off is the occasional headache. Mutants still chase me down, but I'm not sure how long that'll last for. Will it ever stop? I don't know. It was a last ditch move of desperation, I know that, and it brings me great shame...yet, I'm certain now that I have the power to complete my task. Each and every one of them will die before I meet my end. I will make them wish they'd never been born.

*

As the handle twisted, Sniper unloaded a half dozen rounds into the man's chest. The man fell backwards, knocking his head against the concrete floor of the back corridor, and lay flat on the ground; he was completely out cold, but his chest was still heaving up and down. He was alive, for better or worse.

Jason's hands were shaking, and the sweat dripped from his brow. He glanced down at his gun, which was a blur before him, and his heart felt hollow.

"What the hell was that?" demanded Sniper.

"I...I don't know," muttered Jason. "I couldn't pull the trigger."

"That much was clear already; I was wondering why," said Sniper. He looked around the walls of the room, peering through them with his scope. "I don't think anything is approaching us yet, let's get this wise guy tied up so he doesn't try and pull any funny business."

"Right...yes, of course."

The man they had shot was a tall fellow, with jet-black hair and a wide frame. He was the sort of man you would imagine being a bodyguard for somebody much more important than himself, but there was a surprising warmth to his face that would lead you to believe he would smile...before he shot you in the head.

Sniper took the man's weapons—the gun he dropped during the fall along with knives hidden in both his waistband and right boot—and kept a lookout while Jason dragged the man into the office and bound his hands behind his back, and then tied both his feet and knees together tightly.

"Body armour," said Sniper, checking inside the man's ripped shirt. "He'll have a few bad bruises, but he'll live."

"That's nano cloth, no wonder he's alright. It's what Mr Kim fitted me out with back in New Dallas for the job at the Livelong factory. Where did this guy get it? It's expensive enough that Stefano would only rent it for our guys."

"I didn't know you knew Devon Kim, he's a friend of mine too," said Sniper, and Jason raised an eyebrow. "Not the time for that, alright. Maybe this fella is loaded or maybe he's just a very good thief. Who knows?"

Jason sat with the man while Sniper patrolled the Fresh and Fancy, ensuring that nothing was drawn in by the gunfire. Shortly after he returned, the man began to stir. He grunted uneasily and slowly opened his eyes.

"Good evening, gents," he said calmly upon laying

eyes upon Jason and Sniper. He glanced at Achilles. "Nice dog you got there. I'm glad you didn't stick him on me."

"Who are you?" asked Sniper.

The man smiled. "Not even a hello for a guy you shot? Not very well mannered, are you bud?" Sniper stared at the man, not indulging him. "Alright, alright. Name's Camlorn but call me whatever insulting name you please. I won't make a thing of it."

"What are you doing here?"

Camlorn laughed.

"Is something funny?"

"Why else would I be in a grocery store? I'm looking for supplies."

That's not going to fly here," said Jason. "You think we'll forget you stomping through here calling yourself the Grim Reaper?"

"I thought you two were piggies, it's what I call the mutants," chuckled Camlorn. Jason and Sniper glanced at each other, and Jason shook his head. "You don't believe me?"

"You don't survive out here without being cautious," said Jason. "I would think that I wouldn't need to tell you that, but when you run around all full of gusto, perhaps I do?"

"Where's your bag?" asked Sniper.

Camlorn, who had been rather quick with his responses so far, paused to think for a moment. Sniper thought he was thinking of a lie, while Jason thought he was debating whether to tell the truth or not. "I've stashed it elsewhere. It slows me down if I get into trouble. I was going to fetch it afterwards and load up whatever I could find."

Jason looked at Sniper. "I buy that," he said.

"I don't," spat Sniper.

Camlorn had a grim look on his face. "You can choose to believe me or not, but I won't tell you where it is. There are a few valuables in there that I am unwilling to lose. As much as it's clear that you do not trust me—

and you're not without good reason—I can also say that I do not trust you."

Sniper pulled Jason aside and whispered to him. "What should we do with him? I don't mind putting a bullet in his skull, but I suspect you won't allow that."

"I say we tie him up, leave his knife just out of reach, then get far away from here. It gives him a chance of survival and means we're in the clear too."

Sniper sighed. "Sometimes you're too much of a goodie-good for your own good, Jason. Mine too, if I'm honest."

Camlorn cleared his throat loudly.

"Yes?" asked Sniper, turning back to face the man.

"Pardon the interruption, eyepatch, but what was your friend's name?"

Jason walked over to him. "My name's Jason. What of it?"

Camlorn burst into laughter again, this time it wasn't fake or exaggerated. "Son of a gun," he said once he calmed down. "Hoo-wee! You wouldn't happen to be the same Jason that had a little run-in with a man named Bartholomew Benedictus?"

Jason's eyes grew wide. "How did you know that?"

"My friend, you're a legend around New Dallas these days. That took a fine brass pair to do something so bold. You pissed off a lot of folks with that and ol' King Mercer has been on the warpath since, finishing up the job. It's a pleasure to meet you, my friend. I would shake your hand, but...I'm a little tied up."

"You're from New Dallas?"

"Nah, I just pass through every now and again," said Camlorn, flicking his head over his shoulder and grinning widely. "Well, it's safe to say that I trust you just a little more than I did a minute ago. Any man who puts an end to Benedictus is a friend of mine. I'm sure I don't need to tell you the trade he was in?"

Sniper walked over to an old chair and sat down, bored of hearing about Jason's time in New Dallas, but Jason squatted down beside Camlorn; he was very much intrigued by the mysterious stranger now. "Livelong," he said.

Camlorn nodded slowly, a cunning smirk replacing the grin. "Heard you were one of his slaves gone rogue? Is that true?"

"That's right."

"Well, I trust you even more now, so I'll let you in on a little secret...but perhaps you know already?"

"What's that?"

"Benedictus was part of a group called The Regressionists. Does this ring any bells?"

Jason racked his brain but was drawing as much of a blank here as he did with Randall Everett. "Nope, never heard of them."

"Well, they're a bunch of kooks. Never heard anything like their nonsense before, let me tell you. Are you ready for this?"

Sniper was growing frustrated in the corner; he was only pretending not to listen. "You're not one to get to the point are you?"

"If there's a good story to tell, I best tell it right," said Camlorn. "The Regressionists believe that there's a way to turn mutants back into regular humans."

"That's impossible," said Jason, brushing off such an absurd notion.

"I told you they were kooks, right? Now, they say late stage one and beyond is too far gone. I mean, when a stage three is bigger than a house then there's no way that's reversible...but early to mid-stage one? They're certain that it's possible, and the word around their group is that they've found a way to do it."

From Sniper's mouth escaped a deep laugh of mockery. He stood up and approached Camlorn, squatting down beside him in the same manner as Jason. "How do they claim to do this?" he asked.

"They have a compound that they inject into people that they say neutralises the effects of Livelong, then they have a second one that they use to reverse the mutation process. The number of people they've suckered into the scam is...quite frankly, it's completely nuts. It's certainly made them sacks upon sacks of silver, more than you'd feel comfortable storing even on your digital wallets."

A lot of the major settlements in the former Texas area used silver for trade, but the ones who had working computer networks used a cryptocurrency backed by physical silver to save folks from having to haul their wealth around with them. There have been many concerns over the years about redeemability, but local groups regularly audit the banks to ensure they maintain a one-to-one ratio of silver to their cryptocurrency. That said, there have been many attempts to implement fractional reserve systems that landed a few folks a beheading.

Jason wasn't sure what to say. All he could think about was how all of this had been happening under his nose at The Third Circle. Benedictus's right-hand man, Stefano, probably had a hand in it too. He wondered if he hadn't killed the pair and remained in his former master's good graces, would he have been invited into The Regressionists? How would he have reacted if he *had* been invited? Benedictus was a man with a silver tongue and could be very convincing.

"Camlorn," said Sniper. "Let's say that we were very gracious gentlemen and decided to let you go. What would you do?"

"That's an easy one, Patch," said Camlorn, evoking a scowl from Sniper, "I'd get the hell out of here. I'm a busy guy and have places to be."

"Where?"

"I'm heading north for now, but that's all I can say. Nothing personal, but I don't think it's such a good idea to be telling you my business. I'm sure you don't want me knowing yours either, and I won't even bother asking."

Jason turned to Sniper. "I'm feeling generous today, how about you?"

"If you put me in a red suit, I'd be Santa Claus," said

Sniper dryly.

"Here's the plan, Camlorn," said Jason. "It's going to be getting dark soon, so we're going to spend the night here. We're going to keep you bound for now, but we'll be on our way tomorrow morning and leave your weapons somewhere on the main floor of the supermarket save for a knife which will be just out of reach for you here. You can cut yourself free, all of us get to walk out of here alive, and we don't need to see each other again."

Camlorn nodded slowly. "Seems like overkill to me, but I accept the terms...not like I've got a choice, I suppose. As long as I'm getting out of here alive, I'll not worry too much. There's just one thing I need to request before you take a snooze."

"What?" asked Jason.

"Somebody needs to take me out back for a piss."

*

Sniper finally stirred from his sleep, all the while Jason had kept a close eye on Camlorn. The black-haired man must have been awake the entire night, but he did not seem especially tired. Perhaps it was the nap he took after Sniper unloaded a few rounds into his armour, but it was eerie. He sat there silently, occasionally humming, occasionally trying to make small talk, but always alert save for the occasional winces that Jason put down to discomfort.

"Do you two do breakfast?" asked Camlorn, his stomach growling.

"Usually, but we're willing to skip today if you'd rather get out of here sharp," said Sniper, rubbing his hand across his face and then scratching his rough beard. Achilles stared up at him expectantly. "Alright," he said to the dog, "I suppose we'll have something before you decide now's the time to turn on me."

Sniper reached into his bag and pulled out one of the packs of jerky he had bought back in Fort Wood. Meat was a luxury out on the road, but he was wary that if it was out in the heat for much longer the flies would pick up the scent. He tossed a few scraps to Achilles who chewed them thoroughly, drooling all over the floor as he did so. Jason fed Camlorn, who joked that he was hungry enough to take a bite out of Jason's hand too.

"Mighty good of you to share," said Camlorn, with a seemingly genuine smile. "I'd offer you some of my own rations, but they're elsewhere. If I run into you again, I'll return the favour somehow."

After they had finished eating, Jason took Camlorn's gun and one of his knives and stashed them inside one of the broken refrigerators while Sniper set his other knife in the far corner of the room. It would be enough to give the men a chance to get clear of the supermarket before Camlorn rearmed himself.

"I'd say it's been a pleasure, Camlorn, but it's made for a more stressful night than I'd have liked," said Jason. Sniper simply gave Camlorn a nod and walked from the room with Achilles.

"Take care of yourselves, gents," said Camlorn, as Jason followed Sniper through the door.

The men and the dog hurried out of the small town, keeping an eye out for any more lingering mutants that lurked about the streets. Thankfully, the few mutants they did spot were too busy gnawing on an unfortunate coyote that had wandered in their path, leaving the north road out of town clear.

"You're not concerned that Camlorn said he's heading north too?" asked Jason.

"No," said Sniper.

"Why?"

"If I see him again, I'll just shoot him."

"He seemed alright to me."

"Of course, he seemed alright. He'd have to be a real dumbass to piss off the men holding him captive. He's a cunning one, that much is clear."

"I suppose the less said about him the better. Forget it and move on."

"Indeed," said Sniper, pushing ahead of Jason and keeping a close eye on the road ahead.

The duo marched diligently the whole morning as Achilles dashed back and forth into the wild grass, hunting vermin. Every so often, he would bring back the carcass of a rabbit or an armadillo; the rabbits tended to be mostly eaten, and the armadillos less so. It was a morning like any other and, thankfully, one devoid of mutant roamers on the road.

The old tarmac slowly faded into dust and dirt, leaving the men to wander across the plains and the hills as the sun peaked in the sky. The men and the dog walked for many miles, talking little and only ever stopping for a drink in the shade of an old billboard or tree. That was often the way of it. Jason would have been happy to talk most of the way, but Sniper only spoke if he had something to say. Talk for the sake of talk was a distraction from vigilance.

It was early afternoon before they finally took a proper rest. There was an old wooden barn that stood proudly down a lane and was in much better shape than the fallen-apart house it accompanied. It was a testament to the quality of building materials used before the fall of the Old World, as the barn had no doubt been more carefully constructed by the owners than whatever company had been contracted to build the house.

"We're clear," said Sniper, doing a once-over of the perimeter. "We'll take half an hour and then get back to it."

Jason lit a small fire and started preparing the rations. In the middle of the night, lighting a fire was a dangerous signal to any roaming mutants but during the daytime, he wasn't too concerned. It was rare to draw one in by the smell of smoke.

"How much further to the highway?" asked Jason as he finished his lunch.

"Not far," muttered Sniper, taking the time to enjoy his canned ham and soggy carrots. "Can I not just enjoy my lunch without the chitchat?"

Jason ignored Sniper's request to be left to eat in peace. "And you're positive that's where we'll find Kyle? On this highway town? It seems like a big gamble if you ask me."

Sniper didn't answer. Jason had asked him about their destination countless times and he was tired of having to constantly reassure the young man that he was certain this was the way to go. In truth, Sniper wasn't sure at all and just wanted Jason to stop bothering him about it.

"Look, kid," he said, "there is almost nothing on the road north except for Highwayland. Anything else would be a tiny group of people that don't want to be found. If you want to find Kyle or find out where he may have gone, then this is the way it has to be done. Understood?"

Jason nodded slowly. "I just pray that he found somebody to guide him there. He would probably be safer staying in the ruins of Shackford rather than travelling cross-country all by himself. He's a good kid, but he's always been a little on the nervous side when it comes to mutants and I'm sure what happened last year hasn't exactly helped."

"Yep," said Sniper. "Your hometown being ransacked, and your family being killed would traumatise even the best of them. But look, the way I see it is—"

Sniper stopped abruptly as gunfire broke out somewhere nearby. He ran up a rickety wooden staircase and onto a small ledge where he stared through a glassless wooden window frame and into the distance.

"What is it?" asked Jason from below, quickly packing away their supplies and making sure his gun was loaded.

"Caravan being attacked by some mutants," said

Sniper. "All wunners by the looks of it, a half dozen of them. The men are trying to protect their horse and wagon."

"What are we waiting for?"

"For them to pass by and leave us alone."

"What about the caravaners?"

Sniper chuckled. "I'm going to be a dead man because of your insistence on helping every straggler. Fine, let's go."

The men and the dog ran from the barn towards the commotion. Sniper stayed back and pulled out his rifle, taking very careful aim at the mutants pouncing upon the lightly armed caravan. Jason meanwhile charged headfirst into the fray, ensuring he wasn't in the way of Sniper's line of sight. Achilles clung close to Jason to protect the human he had grown so fond of.

The caravaners had already taken out two mutants by the time Jason had gotten close, but one of the mutants was grappling with one of the roaming traders and made for an easy target to pick off. Another bang later and Sniper had killed a fourth. A couple of wasted rounds from Jason, then a lucky shot to the head ended a fifth. Sniper put down the sixth after Achilles sank his teeth into its heel to hold it back from its would-be victims.

Once the chaos had ended, everyone took a moment to breathe a sigh of relief. The caravaners, of which there were four, thanked Jason profusely as Sniper made his way over.

"And you're quite the shot, yourself," said the leader of the caravaners to Sniper. "My name is Briggs and I'm forever in your debt."

"I don't do debts," replied Sniper.

"Your thanks is enough," said Jason sincerely. "We couldn't know you were getting swarmed by mutants and just leave you to it. It wouldn't be right to not help however we could."

"Well, it's mighty appreciated," said Briggs, shaking both of their hands in turn while one of the caravaners tossed Achilles a few scraps of cooked chicken to thank the dog. "Where are you headed?"

"We're making our way to Highwayland," said Jason while Sniper remained silent, not wanting to give away any information he didn't need to. "We've been on the road a while and we figure we must be getting close.

The caravaners all looked at each other and Briggs gave them a nod. "It just so happens that we're heading there too. It's part of our regular route. Funny how fate plays out, ain't it? You're welcome to travel with us. Safety in numbers and all that."

"For us or for you?" asked Sniper.

"Yeah, I gotta give you that one," said Briggs with a half-smile. "We're not normally so ill-prepared, but we lost one of our bodyguards last week to a stage two when we tried crossing a bridge thinking it would be an easy route. Didn't think we'd see any roamers wandering this far outside of civilisation or the ruins of former civilisation."

"If they can't find people to eat, they'll find animals," said Sniper. "Whatever they can do to feed and grow bigger, they'll do it. That's just in their nature."

"Then we'd best be out of here, don't you think?"

"Give us a second," said Jason, approaching Sniper. "You're a good judge of character. What do you reckon?" he muttered.

"They're better supplied than we are, we saved their behinds, and they are indeed going in the same direction as us. I'd not normally follow strangers, but I think we're safe enough here. That emblem on Briggs' jacket with the roof over a car is a Fort Wood symbol. I'd say we can trust them."

"Do you think we can get into Highwayland without them?"

"It doesn't operate off a passport system like a lot of the larger settlements with electricity to spare, so going with caravaners is probably our best shot without having to wear our Sunday finest and play nice."

Jason gave Sniper a nod and turned towards Briggs.

"Lead the way, Briggs."

"You guys are a hoot, gave it some real thinking there," he said with a bright smile. "We ain't got far to go now, so let's get moving while the sun's up."

The group of men, the dog and the horse started walking along the barely discernible road, covered in dirt and weeds as it was. Jason's resolve was strengthened further, knowing that he was one step closer to finding Kyle.

Chapter 3:
Highwayland

18th April 2116: Freedom never tasted so good. There's just something about the feeling of being on the brink of death that makes a man appreciate life that much more. Boy, could I use a drink. Just a simple run of the mill pisswater beer would do the job. The market was a bust, no surprise. If I get really desperate, I could always munch down on one of the piggies, but I'd rather not add degeneracy to my list of problems. Still, there's always something to find out on the road. Scavengers are so poor at their jobs that you can still come across houses untouched since the fall of the Old World. I'll find something. I always do.

*

It was sunset over the south as Jason, Sniper, Achilles and the caravan approached the collapsed ramp up to the broken highway that was adorned with houses and shacks of wood and tin. Jason wasn't sure if the ramp had collapsed with the passage of time or if it had been blown up by the residents to make it that much harder for raiders to invade their high standing oasis. One thing was for sure, Highwayland was quite the welcome sight in the otherwise hostile wasteland of wilderness and mutants.

"Let me do the talking," said Briggs. "These fellas know me and I'll be able to vouch for you. Otherwise, you'll be interviewed for a day solid and all your belongings will be stripped."

"We wouldn't want that," said Sniper, the long-range scope on his patch twitching to zoom in on the broken highway.

"Haven't you been here before?" asked Jason.

"It was in a former life," Sniper remarked.

Jason knew what this meant. At one point, Sniper had been part of King Mercer of New Dallas's army. The warlord-turned-king had often tried to recruit people from other settlements to serve him or to become a citizen of New Dallas, and sometimes the men he sent to the settlements did not play so nice if the offer was refused.

Sniper had left that life behind when his wife and son were murdered on the orders of a rogue Sergeant called Nathaniel Ezra. King Mercer had recently publicly executed a number of his most traitorous allies and Ezra was one of these, denying Sniper his chance at revenge. He refused to talk about it other than to explain to Jason that it had happened and Jason knew better than to bring it up again.

"Here we are," said Briggs as they approached the base of the highway.

There was an intercom hooked up to a concrete pillar and above them was a large hole in the highway, big enough for a few men and a horse to fit through but with no discernible way to reach it.

Briggs pushed a button on the intercom and a few moments later static came from it, followed by a man's voice. "Who goes there?" he asked.

"It's Briggs, Roberts, O'Hare and Thompson," said the caravaner. "We've got two fellas we picked up on the road with us. They helped us out in a tight spot, saved at least a couple of our lives most probably."

"Their names, Briggs."

"One of them calls himself Jason Cooper and the—"

"Jason?" came another male voice, this one much younger. Jason felt his heart leap, a feeling of both shock and relief that he hadn't experienced in some time. He knew that voice very well and it was most welcome to his ears.

"Kyle?" Jason asked at the intercom. "Kyle, is that you?"

"I can't believe you're here!" shouted the excited boy. "Paul, let him come up."

"What's the other guy's name, the one with the eyepatch?" asked Paul.

"My name is Felix Creighton," said Sniper. "I'm a scavenger and mercenary, but I'm not on any active jobs and I assure you that you'll have no trouble from me. If it would put you at ease, I will turn over my weapons as long as my scope isn't taken from me."

"That won't be necessary," replied Paul. "Briggs vouches for you and Kyle knows your friend. That's good enough for me. Stand clear and we'll send down the elevator."

Everyone backed away from the intercom and whoever was waiting above hooked up a large platform to a few hooks and lowered it through the hole—the pulley system making a horrible grinding noise the entire way—until it reached the ground. The intercom buzzed once more. "Briggs and his men can come up first, then you pair and your dog will come up on the second load," said Paul.

Once Briggs and his men had been pulled up, the platform was lowered for Jason, Sniper and Achilles. They stood on it and held onto a couple of poles that had been welded onto it to keep their balance as the pulley system was activated and they began to rise.

Jason and Sniper emerged onto the highway and much to Jason's surprise, Highwayland stretched for quite some distance with mismatched houses of wood, stone and metal sheeting along the way. There were makeshift farms growing crops, there were animals fenced into pens, and there were stores with their wares on display out in the open. The town must have been home to a few hundred people at least, even larger than Shackford had been in its prime. And all of that built atop an old highway in the middle of nowhere.

"It is you!" exclaimed Kyle, as Jason, Sniper and Achilles stepped off the platform.

Jason was deeply relieved to see Kyle, alive and well. He clasped the boy's hand and hugged him for a moment before letting him breathe. "If you ever fall into a river and nearly drown again, I'm going to kill you," he joked.

"I knew that if you were still alive you'd go back to Shackford one day," said Kyle, bouncing up and down. Jason had never seen him this animated before, even when he had found out that Jason was going to teach him how to shoot. He was clearly very pleased to see his old friend and mentor.

"How did you find your way here?" Jason asked him.

"One of the caravans gave me directions when they pulled me from the river. They said I could travel with them, but I didn't want to go without you. I waited at the cabin in the woods for a few days, but you didn't come back, so I left a note there and another in your old house."

"The three mutants?"

"All gone by that time," said Kyle. "I had to be very careful, but I knew that I couldn't just cower away in the woods for the rest of my life. You wouldn't have wanted that, right?"

"Right," said Jason, then Sniper cleared his throat. "Oh yeah. Kyle, I'd like you to meet Sniper and his dog, Achilles. We've been looking out for each other over the last year or so now."

"I'm your replacement," joked Sniper, shaking Kyle's hand as the boy stared at his scope in awe. Sniper made it rotate between the three modes with his mind and

Kyle looked even more astounded.

"It's nice to meet you, Mr Sniper," said Kyle, unsure of what else to say.

"Likewise, son. Jason says you're a good kid and I trust his word. I'm sure we'll get along just fine."

Briggs was talking to a man, presumably Paul, since Jason and Sniper had reached the top. Now that he had finished, the caravaner walked over to the pair. "Gentlemen, I've talked things through with Paul and you're good to go about your business here as you see fit. There's a bar a little way up the road that has a few beds you can take for a small bit of coin. We've got to get to our business."

"Thank you, Briggs," said Jason, shaking the man's hand.

"No, thank you both," replied Briggs. "We could easily have lost our lives to those mutants if you two hadn't stepped in. We'll be hanging about here until tomorrow before hitting the road, so if you see us about be sure to say hello."

Briggs and his three men headed deeper into the town, leaving Jason and Sniper to their own devices.

"We need to have a proper catch-up," Jason said to Kyle. "A lot has happened in the last year, for you as well as me."

"It'll have to wait until my shift is over," said Kyle. "I'm working as a guard here now. My aim has improved a lot, I'm pleased to say."

"I figured you'd leave most of the mutants down there to rot," said Sniper.

"Only if they're stage one roamers or a stage two," said Kyle. "No point wasting our ammo. If it's a lurker that hangs around and could be a risk to anyone coming into town, we'll lower someone halfway down and dispatch it. It's easier if you crack its skull with a brick first, it dazes them a little and keeps them in place because they're just waiting for you to come closer."

Jason laughed. He was proud of how far Kyle had come and amazed that the formerly soft boy had toughened up so much. It was something Jason had thought about himself too. Before Shackford fell, he wasn't afraid of the fallen land, but he was untested and naïve to some of the harsh realities of the New World. Now, everything out here, from scavenging for supplies to killing mutants on the daily, had become second nature to him, although Sniper had told him more than once that he was still untested and that if he was ever stuck out here alone then it would another story altogether.

"I'll meet you at Isabella's once I'm finished here," said Kyle. "I would let you hang around, but when I'm paired up with Paul...well, I don't think he'll let me get away with it. He takes this job very seriously and, to be honest, I can't fault him for that at all."

"Just right," said Jason. "It's best you take guard duties seriously after what happened back home. A good guard is the difference between life and death as we sadly know."

"I won't argue with that," said Kyle sombrely, thinking back to the family he had lost.

Jason and Sniper walked down the street, taking in the town. For a long, straight road, the citizens had been thorough in how they had put it together. The concrete barriers at the edge of the highway were fortified by more barriers of wood and metal, all of which were topped with razor wire. Jason was now confident that the highway ramps had been deliberately blown up to keep the citizens safe as the ramp that should have led down on the other side was also missing.

"This is one of the strangest places I've ever been," Jason said to Sniper.

Sniper shook his head. "After all these months I shouldn't be surprised that you're wet behind the ears, yet every time you open your mouth I'm shocked once more."

"Does everything you say have to be an insult?" Jason asked with a frown.

"Stop making yourself so easily mocked and I'll dial

back the snarkiness."

The two stopped at a shack with a wooden sign hanging outside with a very sharp, "Isabella's Bar and Inn," carved into it. The bar at the front was open-air, something that was much appreciated in the hot heat found year-round in these parts, and a barmaid sat behind it looking bored. She was a woman in her late thirties with black hair and a pretty face, but her skin was brown and damaged from too much time in the sun.

"Newcomers?" she asked, looking much more chipper than she had before.

"You got a couple of beds for the night?" asked Sniper.

"I've got one in the back for you and this one is welcome to share with me," she said, leaning toward Jason exposing her ample cleavage.

"No, thank you," said Jason, trying to avert his eyes with little success.

She giggled in a way that suited a woman much younger than her. "I'm just playin' with you, handsome. I'm Isabella, it's my name on the sign. Do you have physical or do you pay digital?"

"Either's fine," said Sniper.

"Physical it is," said Isabella, prompting Sniper to reach into his pack and pull out a couple of coins. He glanced at Jason, who did the same.

Jason wasn't trying to be a freeloader, but Sniper kept jabbing at him as if to imply he was. In fact, he had made quite a bit of money when he was a slave for Benedictus and had been fortunate enough that he could still use it. It was all thanks to New Dallas and Fort Wood both utilising a cryptocurrency backed by silver and having a terminal connecting accounts in each settlement. When they had last visited Fort Wood, Jason had visited the bank and withdrawn some just in case he needed it on the road.

"You two lookin' a drink?" asked Isabella once they had paid for their beds. Jason ordered a simple root beer while Sniper took a small glass of whiskey.

The pair sat by the bar, looking at the people in town going about their business. Highwayland was small compared to somewhere like New Dallas, or even Fort Wood, but it was relatively bustling, all things considered. The townsfolk always seemed to have something to do, whether that was tending to crops, picking up a few supplies from the different stores that sold all sorts of wares from bandages to bullets, or even just taking the time to talk with their neighbours. Jason missed having neighbours.

"It's a nice place, ain't it?" said a redheaded young man, sitting down at the bar beside Jason. "Just a beer, please Izzy."

"Who are you?" asked Sniper rather bluntly.

"Name's John," said the man, tipping his hat, "but most folks here call me Lucky Johnny."

"And why do they call you that?" asked Jason.

"Ain't it obvious? It's because I'm a rather fortunate fellow. Been attacked by hundreds of mutants, travelled from here to New Dallas to the Star Republic and back, yet I'm still here to tell the tale."

"What's the Star Repu—"

"I could name a hundred mercenaries that have done the same," said Sniper, cutting in.

"But have they done it alone with just a pistol to keep them company?" asked Johnny, with a smug smirk.

"Why are you bothering us?" asked Sniper.

"This one ain't the friendly sort, Johnny," remarked Isabella.

"I can see that," chuckled Johnny, taking off his hat. "I apologise for how I approached you pair out of the blue. It's clear that you'd rather be left alone to enjoy your drinks. I'll just sip mine in the peaceful silence and watch the world go by with you, how about that?"

"Don't mind him," said Jason, flicking his head in Sniper's direction as Sniper scowled. "My name's Jason. I'm a friend of Kyle's."

"Wait, wait, wait," said Johnny. "You're *that* Jason? The one who saved our Kyle from a mutant attack? The honour is all mine, my friend. Kyle is a good boy and a great service to our humble little island in the sea of mutants out there. I liked you before we even met, Jason."

"That's me," said Jason, embarrassed at being praised by this stranger. The friendliness was welcome, but Jason wasn't used to it these days.

"You know, I'm sure we'd become fast friends. Are the pair of you staying here for long?"

"Honestly, I hadn't thought about it," said Jason. "I wanted to make sure that Kyle was doing alright and I can see that he is. I'm sure it won't be too long before we hit the road again."

"And go where?" asked Sniper.

"Wherever you planned to go next," said Jason.

"I have no idea where that'll be. You want to keep tagging along until you're old and grey? You could always stay here if you want to go back to a life more similar to your old one."

Jason didn't answer. He was glad that Kyle was safe, but he still did not know whether or not his sisters, Lindsay and Abigail, had survived the fall of Shackford. He found no trace of them upon his return, but it was possible he missed them among the dead. In any case, he couldn't stay somewhere like this without knowing for sure that they weren't still out there somewhere.

"This is probably a bad time for me to be talkin' to you both," said Johnny, downing his beer. "Jason, we'll get a chance to speak later. There's a proposal I've got for you, should you be willin' to hear it. Nothin' untoward, I assure you, but we'll talk about that another time."

Johnny stood up, thanked Isabella, and took his leave. He was a strange man and Jason was curious about what this proposal could have been, a job perhaps? He and Sniper sat there in silence as night fell.

It was dark when Kyle finished his shift and headed to the bar along with a lot of the other guards across town who had been rotated out. Isabella kept trying to offer Kyle alcohol, but the lad had the sense to turn her down and stuck with water. Jason was pleased to see that he was keeping his wits about him even in a seemingly safe town.

"Have you two sat here all evening?" asked Kyle, pulling up a chair.

"Yup," said Jason while Sniper scratched Achilles behind the ears.

"Alright, let's waste no more time," said Kyle. "What have I missed the last...how long? Nine months? Ten? I've lost track."

Jason proceeded to tell Kyle everything, from the scavenging mission with Black Haze where he saved Sniper from a stage two mutant to his return to Shackford. Kyle's mouth hung open in shock and horror at various points of Jason's tale, particularly his abduction by a scavenger and slaver named Griffon, who subsequently sold him on, and his meeting with a stage three mutant in a Livelong facility in Outer Dallas. The young man's face bore a look of disdain anytime their fellow escapee, Cyrus, was brought up, even when he learned that Benedictus had ordered his death.

"He came through in the end," said Jason.

"If he hadn't betrayed us in the first place, things may have turned out very differently," said Kyle, still angry at the recently deceased Cyrus.

"You've got it turned around, Kyle. Cyrus was meant to betray us so that he could save me later. The Lord works in mysterious ways, and he gave Cyrus his chance at redemption. It took a lot of courage from him to put his life on the line for someone else."

"I suppose so," sighed Kyle, "it may seem different because you were there, and I wasn't. A part of me will always feel that sting when I think about him. He was ready to shoot us."

"What about you?"

"It's as I said earlier, the caravaners I ran into made sure I was alright. Once I had left you that message, I followed a map they'd marked and given to me. I got lucky if I'm honest. I had to hide out in empty houses and even had to climb a few trees to avoid the mutants on the road. Stayed in one of them all night once. I spied a fair few people on the main roads, but I didn't like the look of them so I kept my distance from others until I reached here.

"I spotted this place from a distance and knew I'd come the right way. I was tired, I was hungry, I was thirsty, and they were kind enough to take me in. They've treated me well and made sure I was trained up and put to work. There's nothing like having a sense of purpose again, and the shelter and protection doesn't hurt either."

Jason couldn't help but smile the whole time he was listening. "Who knows? Maybe one day we'll find a few others who were lucky enough to escape home."

"I hope so," said Kyle, sounding cheerful again.

"It's always good when there's a happy ending," said Sniper.

"Exactly," beamed Kyle.

Sniper let out a dry laugh and Jason thought it best not to inform the boy that Sniper was being sarcastic. He figured it was best to let the kid have some semblance of innocence left while he was young. He had grown up where it mattered over the time they had been apart.

Jason and Kyle chatted for a while longer and were just about to call it a night when there was suddenly a grinding sound coming from near the entrance to Highwayland.

"It's awful late for someone to show up in town, isn't it?" asked Jason.

"It is," said Kyle, standing up and heading over to see who was being let in at this hour.

Jason and Sniper followed, curious themselves. The pulley system started to move in reverse and the elevator was being pulled upward. Kyle was allowed through, but one of the guards held his arm up to block Jason and Sniper from coming any closer.

"Dangerous for civilians," he said sternly, waiting for the elevator to reach the top.

A figure rose through the hole in the highway and gave a big grin as he saw who was waiting for him. The tall man with the black hair and wide frame stepped onto the road and held his arms up to be searched. Jason was shocked to see that he had come all this way too.

"It's nice to have a few familiar faces here to greet me," said Camlorn.

Chapter 4:
Good Luck

20th April 2116: I broke every damn bone in my left hand no more than an hour ago. There was a strange numbness to the pain that I can't quite describe in writing. They always said I had a silver tongue, but never a silver pen. The most fascinating part about it is that ten minutes ago I could just about flex my fingers. It still ached like all hell, but I could do it. Talk about progress and recovery. You really have to give it to those Crown Pharmaceuticals sickos, they knew how to create something truly groundbreaking. If anybody reads this some years down the line, just know that I'm left-handed.

*

"Nice to see you back, Eric," said one of the guards. "You come from far this time?"

Camlorn gave him an innocent smile. "I was in New Dallas until recently, then I stopped for a bit of shopping on my way here. There's a big supermarket to the south that's filled with surprises."

"You staying long?"

"Not this time, Fred," said Camlorn, giving the guard a nod before walking over to Jason and Sniper with Kyle following closely behind.

"What a fine night it is, gents," Camlorn said to them. He clapped Sniper on the arm who pushed him off. "Easy now. We're all free men here in Highwayland. I don't see any reason for us to be on bad terms. I'm alive and well, you're both alive and well. We're all just peachy, ain't we? That wrong foot we got off on? I think we can both let it go."

Sniper stared coldly at Camlorn.

"Nothing, Patch?" asked Camlorn before turning to Jason and holding his hand out. "How about you Jason? We good?"

"As long as you give me no reason to doubt it," said Jason, shaking Camlorn's hand.

"Glad to hear it. Now, if you'll excuse me, it's been a long journey here," Camlorn paused and then laughed loudly. "What am I saying? We came the same way, so of course you would know that."

The mysterious man gave an exaggerated nod and walked down the highway and into the darkness. Sniper stared after him with his thermal scope and would not look away.

"What is it?" Jason asked.

"I'm not sure," said Sniper softly. "Probably nothing."

Jason walked over to the guard who had spoken to Camlorn as though he was a friend. "Excuse me," said Jason, "but who is he? You called him Eric, but he told us that his name was Camlorn."

"Well, he didn't lie," said the guard, surprised he was being asked about this. "His full name is Eric Camlorn, but he doesn't care which of the two you use. He's been here a dozen odd times over the years, but I don't know all that much about him. Friendly enough fella at the very least, doesn't cause no trouble."

"Is he a scavenger?"

"Couldn't tell you. He usually shows up here fairly

well-equipped and with coin to spend on supplies. That said, he used to travel with some girl, but that stopped a year or two ago."

"What was her name? Did something happen to her?"

The guard paused for a moment with a furrowed brow as though searching his memories for an answer. "I think it was Amanda...no, no, it was Angie, that was it. Couldn't tell you what happened, but there was a decent gap between his last visit with her and his first visit without her."

"And what—"

"Look, I appreciate you're a friend of Kyle's, Jason, but it ain't right that I start gossiping about somebody who's been nothing but nice to me. I'd prefer you go speak to Eric yourself if you want to know anything about him."

Jason nodded. "That's fair. Sorry about that."

He returned to Sniper, who had been listening in on the conversation. "There's something off about Camlorn," Sniper said.

"Should we just give him the benefit of the doubt?" asked Jason.

"No."

"He doesn't seem to have done anything wrong."

"He tried hunting us when he knew we were in the supermarket."

"With a plausible explanation for that."

"If you think so," scoffed Sniper. "Come on, let's turn in for the night. I don't want to waste time arguing about this."

Jason and Sniper headed to Isabella's, followed by a yawning Kyle. The young man bid them farewell and headed to a small house built for him by the townsfolk. It was a quaint little place, but Kyle was just happy to have a roof over his head in a place where death wasn't staring him in the face every day.

Jason stashed his pack in a trunk at the bottom of the bed, locked it and then tied the key around a string that he then placed around his neck. He made sure to keep his gun next to him as he slept, a habit that he had picked up since leaving New Dallas. He did not care that Sniper was so hung up on what Camlorn may or may not have been up to, all he cared about was that Kyle was safe and he had a moment to breathe before hitting the road once again.

*

"Wake up," said Sniper, giving Jason a shove.

"Eh?" grunted Jason. It was still dark outside.

"Camlorn's on the move."

"What are you talking about?" asked Jason, sitting up. "Have you been spying on him the last couple of hours?"

"Yes," replied Sniper, tapping his scope. "He's an easy man to follow with this. That fella's body temperature is running high, must be sick or something."

"I'm going back to sleep," said Jason, lying back down.

"Do you trust me?"

"What?"

"I asked if you trusted me."

"Of course. What kind of question is that?"

Sniper looked deadly serious. "If you trust me, then follow me on this one. I'm telling you, there's something wrong with this guy. If he doesn't pull anything shady tonight, I'll shut up about him."

Jason sighed, threw his clothes on and picked up his gun. He followed Sniper outside and the pair kept to the shadows as Sniper led them to Camlorn. Jason was hoping that they wouldn't get themselves kicked out of Highwayland before morning came.

Sniper jerked his head, to signal that Camlorn was around the corner. The pair leaned against the wall of the house they stood beside and listened as he began speaking to someone.

"Good to see you're still here, old friend," said Camlorn cheerily. "The last few times I dropped by, you were missing. We really should have had the chance to catch up before now."

"Eric," came Lucky Johnny's voice, "I don't know what it is you want from me, but I had nothing to do with what happened to Angie. It was—"

"You do not get to say her name," said Camlorn angrily, careful to keep his voice low. "Are you still with them?"

"What do you mean?"

"You know damn well what I mean. Are you still with them?"

"Eric, come on."

"Answer the question, Johnny!"

Lucky Johnny didn't say a word and Camlorn simply tutted at him. He then began to laugh a little, then a lot. Before long it turned into raucous laughter, loud enough to wake half the town. A few people came to their windows and one of the guards wandered over to see what all the commotion was.

"Is there a problem here?" asked the guard.

"No problem," said Camlorn, putting his arm around Johnny as though they were best friends. "I just wanted to wish my friend here good luck."

"Good luck?" asked Johnny. "In what?"

"In surviving this," said Camlorn, grabbing Johnny's head and suddenly twisting his neck with tremendous force. It cracked horrifically and Jason heard Johnny's body hit the asphalt as Camlorn and the guard drew upon each other. A single shot later and the guard joined Johnny on the ground.

Sniper leaned around the corner and shot Camlorn in the back, but the man merely stumbled a little. He dashed forward and ran for the far side of town, heading towards the dead end where the highway was further broken. Jason and Sniper chased him, shooting at the murderer.

"Sorry about causing a scene, fellas," called Camlorn as he sprinted away. "Sometimes there's no other way to make a point."

As they approached the dead drop, Jason grabbed Camlorn's sleeve and Sniper shot him once again, this time in the leg. Blood splattered everywhere and Camlorn tripped, the momentum threw him over the edge as Jason tried to hold onto him. Camlorn's jacket slipped off in Jason's hand and Camlorn fell sixty feet to the ground below and his body hit the rocks.

Jason looked over the edge and could see a bloody and broken Camlorn sprawled across the ground with a smile upon his face. A gruesome end for the man, but considering the murders he had just committed, it was a deserved end. Sniper had been right about him the whole time.

"Sad," said Sniper, peering over the edge. "His temperature is dropping, looks like he's a goner."

"Should we move his body?"

"That's something the folks here should be responsible for."

"I mean, you killed him."

"The fall killed him," remarked Sniper. "The lunatic looked like he was going to jump anyway."

"And if the mutants come for his corpse?"

Sniper paused before answering. "Alright, let's go get him."

The entire town was out on the streets, wondering what had happened. A few panicked residents were explaining to the others that Camlorn had attacked Johnny and the guard. Much to Jason's relief, they were portraying Jason and Sniper as heroes rather than accomplices.

Before Jason and Sniper reached the entrance, Briggs approached them. "Just what the devil happened here?"

"Camlorn thought it would be a smart move to snap Johnny's neck and shoot a guard before throwing himself off the highway," said Sniper. "Can someone lower us down while we drag his rotten corpse back up here? We'll explain properly once there's no mutant food lying beneath the town."

"Make it quick," said Briggs. "Tell the guards, I said it was fine and it should be alright."

Sniper gave Briggs a thankful nod and he led Jason to the elevator. The guard who had welcomed Camlorn in such a friendly manner before looked confused. "Where are you going?" he asked.

"To fetch Camlorn's body," said Jason.

"Eric...he's dead?" Fred asked, his face as pale as a ghost.

"Briggs said it's okay and to make it quick," replied Sniper.

The guard nodded, not even thinking about questioning whether Sniper was being honest. He called another guard over and they hoisted the elevator platform up, hooking it onto its chains. Jason and Sniper climbed on and were lowered to the ground. The pair hurried along underneath Highwayland, following the road above until it came to a stop.

"Where is he?" asked Jason, looking at the bloodstain on the ground, illuminated by the moonlight overhead.

"He was here," said Sniper defiantly. "That's his blood."

"There's no way he survived that fall. That's not possible, is it?"

"You saw his body as well as I did. The man was crippled and dying."

Jason was still holding Camlorn's jacket and started ruffling through the pockets. What he expected to find, he did not know, but there was a single piece of folded paper inside.

"You couldn't have taken his bag?" asked Sniper.

"I didn't take his jacket on purpose, I was trying to catch him."

"What does it say?"

Jason unfolded the paper. It was a long list of people's names, many of which were crossed out, but there were several names clustered towards the end that stood out to Jason.

~~Stefano Lombardi – New Dallas~~
~~Bartholomew Benedictus – New Dallas~~
Marcus Millar – New Dallas (FRC)
~~Andrew Vickers – Greystone~~
Jamison Hyde – Unknown
~~Randall Everett – Unknown~~
John McGaw – Highwayland
Benjamin Burnside – Carson Robotics
Jeremy Gregson – Harmony
Stephen Gunther - Harmony
Ivor Carlisle – Harmony (maybe ND)

"I don't believe it," said Jason.

"What?" asked Sniper.

"Stefano and Benedictus are both on this list and they've been crossed off."

"Because you killed them?"

"It must be. Randall Everett..."

"Wasn't that the name of the dead guy at that campsite the other day?"

"I know where I know him from!" exclaimed Jason, the penny finally dropping. "His name is here along with Ivor Carlisle. Carlisle owns a bar in New Dallas called—"

"Namaah," said Sniper, nodding slowly.

"How do you know?"

"He's got a place in both New Dallas and in Harmony."

"It says that right here on the list. Randall Everett was one of his men and I'd seen his name written in a notebook in Stefano's office. I think he had an appointment and was visiting The Third Circle, but I never met him."

Sniper looked at the list and tapped the name 'John McGaw' before looking up at the highway above. "I'll bet you any money that's Lucky Johnny."

"Camlorn is hunting these people?"

"Was hunting them."

"You still think he's dead?"

"I think somebody moved his body," said Sniper. "There's no way he was working alone. That's probably why he was so calm when we restrained him. I'd say he had backup waiting for him, watching us. They could be close by right now, but I can't pick up anything with any of my scopes."

"So what to do about this?" asked Jason.

"Nothing."

"Nothing?"

"Nothing."

"What about these people who could be murdered?"

Sniper looked confused. "You see the names on the list, right? Benedictus and his men. Carlisle and at least one of his. Do you honestly think these are good people? Why bother saving them?"

"And what about Johnny?"

"What about him?"

"He had friends up there, a place that took someone like Kyle in. Who's to say that everyone on the list is deserving of a broken neck or a bullet in the head?"

Sniper sighed. "You're starting to get a saviour complex, my friend. It's going to get you into trouble."

"It's not a saviour complex," scoffed Jason, "I just don't want the death of innocents on my conscience when I could have done something to prevent it."

Sniper sighed once more and slowly shook his head. "Fine, here's a compromise for you. We'll check out this Carson place, we'll even check out Harmony and a couple of names there. If it turns out that it's a bunch of scumbags, we leave it alone and go about our business. If some of them turn out to be upstanding citizens, then you can find a way to warn a few of them off."

"Alright, I'm in," said Jason.

"You're damn right because that's the best offer I'm giving you. I don't want to spend my hard-earned silver trekking back and forth aimlessly."

*

"Carson Robotics?" Briggs asked as he and his fellow caravaners were packing up to leave. "What in the world would you want to go there for?"

"Please, just humour me," said Jason.

Briggs gave him a puzzled look but didn't put up an argument. "It's a notorious place for scavengers. The outside is heavily guarded by mutants."

"Guarded?"

"Guarded," nodded Briggs. "It's like they've been rounded up and let loose there because they never seem to dissipate. I've heard many tales and rumours about what's going on in Carson and who could be hiding out inside. Anything from gangs of raiders to degenerate refugees."

"And do you know any way in?" asked Sniper.

"I don't know of anyone that does. If you ask me, trying to break in isn't worth the risk. If you can get past the mutants, you run the risk of somebody blowing your brains out before you find anything good to take...then you need to get out past the mutants again to escape."

"Fantastic," said Sniper.

"Can you mark it on this map of the area?" asked Jason.

"Hmm," said Briggs, looking intently at the map and pulling a cracked ballpoint pen from his jacket pocket. "It's past this woodland, but not after the valley...I think it's around here somewhere," he said, tapping on the map with his pen and then drawing a small circle.

"Thanks, Briggs," said Jason, getting a nod in return as Briggs rejoined his men and resumed packing the wagon.

Jason and Sniper stepped out of earshot while Achilles roamed back and forth. They had explained to the guards that Camlorn's body had disappeared, and it was chalked up to a mutant having eaten him already. A ridiculous notion by any stretch of the imagination, but Jason and Sniper didn't have any better theories outside of having an accomplice dragging him off somewhere.

Kyle approached Jason and Sniper with a small bag. He threw it into the air and Jason caught it. "What's this?" Jason asked him.

"A few extra supplies," said Kyle. "A couple of cans of food, two flasks of water and a half dozen lighters that still work. I hope it helps."

"If these are yours, we can't accept them," said Jason trying to pass the bag back.

Kyle smiled at him. "After everything you've done for me, it's the least I can do for you. I wouldn't be alive if you hadn't saved me in Shackford and gotten us to that cabin. I prayed you were still out there every day and you were."

"You should name your first kid after him," joked Sniper.

The young man chuckled. "I'll be naming him after my dad should I be lucky enough to last that long."

"Thank you, Kyle," said Jason holding the bag up. "I meant it, this is great."

"Do you want some other good news?" asked Kyle.

"If there's good news, I'll take it," said Jason.

"The guard that Camlorn shot? He's going to be alright. It'll take some time for his leg to heal up and he won't be doing much running for some time, but he'll live to tell the tale. Camlorn must be better at snapping necks than he is at shooting people."

Jason looked at Sniper, who shook his head. "Can't count on that being the case," said Sniper.

"Once you've done whatever you need to do, make sure you come and visit," said Kyle. "With any luck, I'll have expanded my house and you won't have to take a bed at Isabella's. She's a bit...I dunno. I don't want to speak ill of people here, I've been treated well."

"How about Lucky Jonny?"

"He was friendly enough, but a little odd. If you get him talking long enough, he'll start talking to you about something called...what was it now? Did he say Recursionists."

Jason and Sniper exchanged a glance. "Kyle," said Jason, "was that by any chance Regressionists?"

"Yes! That was it. I don't know what Recursionists is, my mistake."

"That's who he was hunting," said Jason. "It can't be a coincidence that he brought it up to us. He said Benedictus was one and he'd probably just finished slaughtering Everett and his men before we arrived last week. They're all part of this group."

"Probably," shrugged Sniper. "We'll see when we find this Burnside fella and ask him. That's assuming he'll talk to us...or the mutants don't eat us."

Kyle stood there confused, but Jason reassured him that it was nothing to worry about. "Just make sure that if somebody else asks you about The Regressionists, you let them know you don't want any part of it."

"Understood," said Kyle, clearly not understanding the *why* of this advice, yet he trusted Jason enough to know that it was in his best interest to abide by it.

"It was nice meeting you Kyle," said Sniper reaching out to shake the young man's hand.

"It was nice meeting you too," said Kyle, shaking Sniper's hand and then tussling Achilles' ears. The dog sat there silently, enjoying the attention.

"You take care of yourself, alright?" Jason told him.

"You too," said Kyle. "I hope you find Lindsay and Abigail before we next meet."

Jason gave him a nod and a small wave, then headed towards the elevator with Sniper and Achilles. He had no idea when he would next see his young friend, but the relief to see him alive and well was still keeping

Jason optimistic. If Kyle survived then so too did his sisters, he was sure of it. He just needed to find them, but for now, Carson Robotics awaited him.

Chapter 5:
Over the Fence

24ᵗʰ April 2116: Lost my temper a little yesterday. At the very least, that's one more name crossed off the list. Shame about the guy who took a bullet to the leg, but he's lucky I didn't put one much higher. I can't let anyone kill me after everything I've done to get this far, but I still feel bad about hurting the poor fella. It won't be too long before reaching Harmony and I may have to step into a confession booth if it hasn't been taken over by yet another brothel. Can't keep a good thing good for too long these days. Could you ever? I suppose I'll never know because the Old World is forever tinted with rosy glasses, even at the end when it had fallen to pieces.

*

They stood there with that happily vacant look on their faces, their eyes dead and white and their skin stretched and raw. There must have been nearly a hundred of them surrounding the perimeter. Their necks, arms and legs were long and rigid, a sight wholly unnatural but a sight far too familiar in the world. Mutants.

The words Carson Robotics were painted on a section of the large building ahead. It appeared to be a factory of some kind. The glass windows were murky, not having been cleaned in over sixty years—before the collapse of the Old World. It was a monument to the past, surrounded by the enemies that dragged the world into its grim present.

"Briggs wasn't lying," muttered Sniper from atop the old telephone pole he had climbed. "If you want my advice, I say we turn back. Out here we have plenty of space to create distance, but if more are inside..."

"You can go and I'll do it myself," said Jason from just below Sniper's position on the pole.

"Have you developed a death wish or something? What's gotten into you that this is so important?"

"I told you before that—"

"I know what you told me about preventing murders, but I don't believe that's your true reason."

Jason climbed down from the pole and back onto the ground where Achilles awaited the two men. Sniper hopped down too as Jason was looking through his bag for something.

"Your grandfather's gun won't help you much," said Sniper.

"I'm not looking for that," said Jason, pulling out a hand grenade. "But it's nice to know you're not using your scope to look through my bag. I respect that you respect my privacy."

Sniper chuckled. "You grabbed that back in Highwayland?"

"I figured there would be two ways we can go about this. Round up the mutants and try blowing them to pieces or using it to lure them away."

"You've never used a grenade before, have you?"

"No."

"A single grenade won't be blowing up a dozen of them, never mind—"

"I bought five of them," said Jason pulling out a few more and stuffing them in his jacket.

Sniper laughed again, he started to think Jason had become a bit of a lunatic, but he appreciated the effort. "That's better, but you'll not be able to take out all of them that way."

"I don't need to take out all of them, I just need to take out enough of them that we can get past the fence."

"Alright, clearly you have a plan. Enlighten me."

"Happily," said Jason. "We're facing north towards the entrance, right? I'm going to head east and fire a warning shot to draw a few away while you head west and draw others away. I'm going to blow a few of the stragglers to bits and you can pick some off from a distance with your rifle. When they start getting too close, we circle back around here and approach from the centre. Anything that comes close in the meantime, takes a bullet."

"I've got a better plan," said Sniper.

"What's that?" asked Jason.

Sniper raised his rifle, rotated his eye scope to his zoom lens, took aim and fired a bullet straight through the skull of the nearest mutant standing almost two hundred yards away. Dozens of them stirred and wandered towards Jason, Sniper and Achilles' position as Sniper began to shoot more of them.

"Are you insane?" asked Jason.

"Head around to the far side and fire a round every now and then. I'm going to pick a few of them off one by one until they're thinned out enough for us to push on through. I don't want you using those grenades in case you blow one of us up or we get impaled by shrapnel. If things start getting ropey, Achilles will help you flank them. Get moving."

Sniper took aim again and shot another mutant, getting more attention from the other spread out mutants who began to converge as they headed towards the telephone pole, all while Jason ran off to the side to distract them.

Jason kneeled beside a large rock and took careful aim into the crowd approaching Sniper, pleased to see them indeed falling one by one, but less pleased to see more and more coming. As they fell, they started to pick up speed and broke into a run. This was Jason's time to strike.

He shot into the cluster of mutants three times, landing hits on their arms which did little more than annoy them but annoying them was all that was needed. A bundle of them broke off and started to run towards Jason. As they grew closer, shooting them became much easier and Jason took out two of them before he was forced to back off.

He ran at a slow but steady pace, knowing that he would burn out faster than they would. He spun around and shot three more times, aiming for their gangly legs. One lucky shot to a kneecap and the mutant at the front of the pack stumbled, causing a half dozen of its abominable friends to come tumbling down on top of it. The others were not to be deterred and ran around them; they were still gaining on Jason, little by little.

As the mutants began to close in, Achilles leapt at one, biting into its neck and tearing a large chunk from it that he threw aside. The mutant let out what could only be disguised as a cackle as it fell to the ground, alive but unable to raise its head enough to keep its balance. The dog began running circles around them and Jason killed a half dozen more, then glanced over at Sniper to see if now was the time to make a break for it.

In the not-too-far distance, Sniper flicked his hand towards the building and Jason sprinted past the lunging mutants, now a much thinner crowd than before. He and Sniper's paths converged as Achilles continued to weave between the brutes, taking some of the heat off the two men.

"It's chained up," said Jason, as they drew closer to the gate.

"I know," said Sniper, shooting a mutant in the leg as it attempted to grab him. He slung his rifle over his back and drew a handgun. "There's a missing section of barbed wire on top of the fence, just to the right of the gate. We're going over, not through."

Jason, Sniper and Achilles were almost there, but the army of mutants was almost encircling them and they were still massively outnumbered. Jason killed a mutant lurking by the fence as Achilles bounded forward to distract more mutants. Sniper ordered his dog to climb over then spun around to cover him. Achilles did as told and the dog leapt up high, scrambled over the fence and landed at the other side. Jason followed, throwing himself up and over.

Clumsily landing beside Achilles, he turned to aid Sniper but another mutant came between the grizzled man and the fence. Jason shot the beast in the back of the head, causing one of its eyes to explode and splatter blood all over Sniper. With the final monster in his way dead, Sniper pulled himself up and landed on the ground to join Jason and Achilles in relative safety.

The mutants were not done yet, and they all charged towards the fence unwilling to let a meal escape. Jason and Sniper didn't want to waste any more bullets that they already had so they bolted for an emergency exit to what appeared to be the factory floor.

"It's locked," said Sniper, giving the door a shove. He glanced briefly upwards, but Jason didn't waste time seeing what had caught Sniper's attention.

"Stand back," said the young man, lowering his shoulder and taking a run at it. He rammed into the door and forced his way inside. As the door swung open, it slammed against the inner wall and shook vigorously. The two men and the dog hurried through and closed the door behind them.

"Quick," said Sniper, throwing himself over a railing and grabbing a box from a bench on the other side. "Take this and start piling. I'll grab a few more for you."

He tossed the box to Jason, who caught the heavy load and dropped it in front of the door. Between them, the two men piled up a few more make the door as immobile as they could. With any luck, the mutants would give up if they were able to break through the fence, but blocking the door was their safety net. Once the door was thoroughly barricaded, the pair leaned against the wall, took a deep breath and began to laugh.

"I would have appreciated more warning before you started shooting," said Jason.

"You would have spent too long trying to come up with a more detailed plan," said Sniper. "Sometimes you need to think less and act more."

"You're usually much more calculated than that."

"It's not the length of time spent on the plan, it's how effective it will be. It got your adrenaline pumping, didn't it? And here we are, still alive to tell the tale."

Jason chuckled and finally took in his surroundings. The room was dimly lit by the daylight oozing in through the grimy windows which cast a yellowish tint upon the murky metal of the factory. Crates of robotic parts lay abandoned and various mechanical contraptions sat in an unfinished state on motionless conveyor belts, never to be completed. Jason could confidently say that the power was suddenly cut one day, decades before he was born, and hadn't been switched on since.

"We're being watched," said Sniper, pointing at a door that sat at the end of a metal walkway well above them.

"Is that a camera?" asked Jason, looking at a small orb with its lens pointed straight at them.

"There was one above the door outside too," said Sniper. "In fact, there were quite a few of them out there. There are eyes all over this place."

"Are you sure they're operational? This factory looks dead."

"Positive," said Sniper, tapping his scope and turning around to look outside. "There's a sliver of heat coming from within them, even the ones in the yard. I can't see far enough with this to know if there's anyone in here with us, but somebody, somewhere can see us."

"And the mutants?"

"They didn't come through the fence," said Sniper.

"Those dumb dumbs tried climbing, but they kept getting in each other's way. We're lucky there isn't a toosie out there or it would probably have brought half the fence down and we'd be being chased through the halls right now. Those boxes in front of the door wouldn't stand a chance."

A grim smile crept across Jason's face. There was nothing he loathed more than the sight of a stage two mutant. After all, it was thanks to three of them that he had lost everything. His family, his home, his people. If Kyle hadn't survived, it would just be him alone in the world. Well, that wasn't true, he thought to himself. He had Sniper, he had his friends from Black Haze, and Lyra was alive and well in New Dallas as far as he knew.

"Are you going to daydream all day or shall we get moving?" asked Sniper, taking a swig of water from his flask. He then headed towards the staircase that lead to the walkway over the factory floor. Achilles followed his master closely while Jason checked to make sure his gun was loaded.

"Hang on, I'm coming," he said, following the man and his dog up the stairs.

The factory floor was silent except for the clanking of footsteps as the men ascended. The walkway split into two directions, one leading toward a small control room and the other to the door where the camera sat. It had followed them the whole way, confirming Sniper's suspicions.

Sniper stopped before it. "We're looking for a man named Benjamin Burnside. We're not here to cause trouble, nor do we want to take anything from you or this facility. We're here to give him a message and nothing else." There was no reaction from the camera, not that Sniper expected one.

Jason pushed the door open and walked into the dark hallway. A couple of feet later, the lights came on, nearly blinding him. Once his eyes adjusted, he could see that the hallway was pristine. It reminded him of the Crown Pharmaceuticals facility where he had been sent to recover vials of Livelong by Benedictus. It had the same intense minimalism that was so common in the final decades of the Old World. However, for such an old building, this section had been remarkably preserved even compared to that Livelong facility.

"There's someone else here," muttered Sniper, looking through one of the walls.

"Just one person?" asked Jason.

"As far as I can—dammit!"

"What?"

"They're using something to run interference with my scope. I can't see a damn thing out of it."

Sniper raised his eyepiece ever so slightly, revealing his real eye hidden behind it. He was careful in moving it so that the wires that reached under his eyelids and past his eyeball weren't moved much. They were fairly secure, but he was paranoid about disrupting them as it was a complicated process to have them reattached. He squinted and blinked a few times as his eye adjusted to seeing naturally.

"I guess we're going in blind," he said, raising his pistol and moving along the corridor softly.

Jason followed, keeping a careful eye on any paths to the side. He glanced through the doorways of the rooms as he moved along, all of them appeared to be clean and organised. Whoever was staying here had been keeping on top of things, perhaps to stave themselves off from boredom. What he wondered was how the dwellers were sustaining themselves. Where was the food coming from? Was there a functional water pipe?

From somewhere close by, Jason could hear a faint rubbing or scraping sound. Sniper nodded up ahead, signalling that he heard the noise too. He raised his hand to Achilles who stood perfectly still while the two men crept along. Sniper leaned gingerly around the corner and then stepped out; his gun pointed at his target.

"Son of a bitch," he said, keeping his gun steady. He

sounded more relieved than he did angry. "Jason, come on out. I'm sure if you need to shoot, you won't choke this time."

Jason stepped out with his gun also raised. His mouth dropped in surprise at the sight before him. The person making the scraping sound was vigorously cleaning the floor with a worn metal sponge, giving its best effort to remove a bloodstain. The cleaner itself was the shape of a woman with a body of metal, its screws and hinges slightly rusty. It wore pieces of synthetic skin that stretched across parts of its body, most of which had long worn away, and a wave of black hair fell from its tanned head. It was dressed in a pristine blue dress with white flowers patterning it and a dark blue ribbon tied around its waist. It was an android.

The android kept cleaning, paying no attention to Jason and Sniper. Sniper cleared his throat. "Excuse me," he said.

"I am cleaning," said the android in a distorted feminine voice. "I must keep this place clean for when Master returns and you have cause enough disruption."

Jason was dumbfounded. He had heard from his grandfather about men and women made of metal; androids made in the image of humanity. It was a poor attempt to play God and resulted in the creation of an unnatural lifeform. It was incredibly jarring to see, even more so than the mutants he had grown desensitised to through the course of his life.

"Will you stop to talk to us?" asked Sniper, not moving his gun even though the robot appeared unarmed.

"Are you going to kill me?" it asked, looking up for a second before continuing its scrubbing.

"I've wasted enough bullets on the way in here, so I'd prefer to not do so. We're here looking for someone."

"I am the only one here," said the robot.

Jason finally managed to pick his jaw up and spoke. "Does the name Benjamin Burnside mean anything to you?"

The android stopped scrubbing and looked up once more. "Yes. That is Master's name."

"And what is yours?" asked Jason.

"Emilia."

"Emilia, we have reason to believe your master is in danger. Can we speak to him?"

"Blonde man," said Emilia, "it is as I said, I must keep this place clean for when Master returns. He is not here."

"Whose blood is that?" asked Sniper.

"I do not want to talk about it."

"Is that your master's blood?"

"No. Please, leave me alone."

Emilia started scrubbing harder than ever. It was clear that it was bothered by their presence but seemed unable to do anything about them. Jason realised that it was not a machine in the sense that it operated in a strictly mechanical fashion. It had a personality of sorts, something that let it simulate human emotions. He thought that perhaps he needed to take a different approach.

"Emilia," he said, lowering his gun. "We're not here to cause problems for you or your master, we're here to warn him that somebody is coming to kill him. We're here to help."

Emilia looked up again with no discernible facial expression across her synthetic features. "What is your name, blonde man?"

"Jason."

"Jason, I am inclined to believe you, but I should not speak to you without Master's permission."

"Are you sworn to protect your master?"

"Yes."

"Then surely, if you believe me, then it would be in service to your master to speak with us?"

Emilia paused for a moment and then stood up. "I will spare you a few minutes if it is in service to my master."

"Who knew you had such a way with the metal

ladies, Jason," muttered Sniper, finally lowering his gun too.

"Emilia," said Jason, taking out Camlorn's list. "There was a man who sought to kill everyone mentioned on this piece of paper. He's dead, but we believe he was working with others, and they'll eventually come here to kill Benjamin."

"Someone already arrived to kill my master yesterday."

"Is that whose blood this is?"

"Yes," confirmed Emilia, without a hint of remorse in her distorted voice. "He said his name was Camlorn."

Jason and Sniper looked at each other in surprise. "Did he give you a first name?" asked Jason.

"Eric."

"There's no way it's the same guy," spat Sniper. "He was on the brink of death when I last looked at him. His limbs were broken, and his body was gone within five minutes. Somebody moved him, there's no way he got up and walked away."

"Come with me," said Emilia, turning away and walking down the corridor. The android walked with a slight limp, as though one of its legs was longer than the other.

Jason followed the robot and Sniper whistled for Achilles to come along too. The four walked through the maze-like facility where everything was immaculate.

"Do you maintain this place by yourself?" asked Jason.

"Yes," said Emilia. "I have been here since the Old World fell. I have had company on occasions, but it is only Master who has been kind to me."

"How are you still operational?" asked Sniper.

"There is a large stash of batteries in this facility, most of which were intended for androids like myself. They're designed to not break down for a century, but their energy depletes after three months so I must recharge them regularly."

"How?"

"There are solar panels on the roof that were once used for Bitcoin mining before this place became a robotics facility upon mining being outlawed. They fell into disrepair, but Master brings me parts to help fix them. It is a losing battle with the parts being more difficult to scavenge, yet my only option is to persevere. One day I will run out of power for the final time."

"And you can't just leave in search of more?"

"I am not a combat android; I am a personal assistant. And, you have seen the world, would I be accepted in human society?"

"No," admitted Sniper. "Androids are few and far between out there, most of your kind stopped functioning long ago. You're very lucky to have a set-up like this."

"If the world is ever righted, perhaps I will be reactivated one day, but I do not hold out hope for that."

Emilia led them to a room with large monitors where they could see everything the cameras around the facility could. The screens showed largely empty rooms and corridors, including one that showed Camlorn's bloodstain. A half dozen monitors revealed the outside world and the many mutants wandering or standing idle. The mutants had largely abandoned the fence on the outside and continued to dwell around the perimeter of Carson Robotics.

"Solar powered?" asked Jason, nodding toward the screen.

"Yes," said Emilia. "Unfortunately, powered by a generator that I am not strong enough to drag around behind me to keep me alive."

"Was that a joke?"

"Yes and no," said Emilia. Jason was surprised that she was even capable of humour.

The android disconnected a wire and plugged it into a port on her forearm. She rewound a video feed showing the field of mutants until it showed a man running through them, merely shoving them out of the way. He did not bother to kill them, even as they scratched and tore at him. One of the mutants took a bite out of his shoulder, but he snapped its neck and continued until he got to the fence, where he threw himself over with ease. As he grew closer to the camera, it was clear who the man was.

"It *is* him," said Jason in surprise. "That's Camlorn."

"There's no mistaking it, that's him alright," agreed Sniper.

"How is he alive? Is he a cyborg?"

"No, I'd have seen that when I looked through him. He's very much a human."

"I have more to show you," said Emilia, resetting the outside video feed to the present and rewinding the feed that showed the bloodstain. "My protocols allow me to defend myself should someone make a threat against me or my master. When Camlorn arrived and demanded to see my master, I questioned him and...I don't know how to put this next part in simple terms you."

"He's got a big mouth, right?" asked Jason.

"Yes, but that is not what I am talking about. He talked about a group called The Regressionists and demanded to know if my master was still affiliated with them. He said that if he was not, there would be no trouble. I told him that I did not know, and he said that it doesn't give my master good odds."

"And you killed him?"

"Please watch," said Emilia, gesturing towards the monitor.

It now showed Emilia running through the hallway with her typical limp and a gun in hand as Camlorn took long strides after her, not even bothering to jog. He looked as casual as could be. He yelled something, but the camera did not provide any audio. Emilia suddenly turned and pointed the gun at him, shooting him three times between gaps in his body armour. Camlorn touched the bullet holes in his torso and looked at the blood. Emilia shot him four more times before he finally dropped to the ground. As blood started to pour out of

Camlorn's motionless body, Emilia ran away.

"I locked myself in a safe room, somewhere impenetrable," she said as she sped through more footage.

Jason muttered quietly. "I guess that's the end of that—"

Emilia returned the playback speed to normal Camlorn suddenly started to stir on the monitor, surrounded in a pool of his own blood as he was. He clutched his wounds and stood up weakly, dragging himself down the corridor where Emilia had run. He was clearly very weak, but he was also very much still alive.

"This guy's superhuman," said Jason, astounded by what he was seeing.

"That means back at Highwayland, he did just get up and walk away by himself," said Sniper. The look on Sniper's face was one that Jason was not familiar with, it was a look of fear.

"He gave up and left the Carson Robotics facility," said Emilia. "I am not sure where his next destination is, but he headed eastwards."

"To Harmony," said Sniper, nodding. "That fits with the next person on his list. He couldn't be too far ahead of us."

Jason stood there silently, running everything over in his head. He felt like there was something he had missed as he tried to lay out everything he had seen since he first met Eric Camlorn. The man had no fear because he was seemingly unkillable. He was hunting a list of men, among them a number of sinister individuals because they are part of The Regressionists. Why?

"Emilia, is there a way out of here that you can show us so we don't need to deal with the mutants again?"

"The mutants are my protection," said Emilia. "I cannot reveal one way or another if there is another route. Not to anyone. If it wasn't for the mutants, I would be dead already and my home would have been stripped bare, leaving me to rust away for the rest of time."

"Not even in the service of your master?" asked Sniper.

"I can do you one favour and distract them for a moment, but that is all. I will shoot one of them at the far corner of the fence so most of them gather there and, that way, your path over the fence and back to the road will be much easier. You have killed many of my protectors already, so I would kindly request that you simply injure them if you must shoot them."

Jason's face suddenly grew pale. What Emilia said had put the missing piece in place for him. Sniper noticed the aghast look Jason bore. "What is it?" he asked.

"I can't believe I didn't see it until just now," said Jason.

"See what?" asked Sniper.

"I know how Camlorn survived his fall, I know how he can take bullets and get up and walk away a minute or two later."

"Will you quit babbling and just tell me what you're talking about?" snapped Sniper, growing impatient.

Jason looked Sniper dead in the eyes. "Camlorn injected himself with Livelong."

Chapter 6:
Street Cleaners

28th April 2116: Beep beep, boop boop. That stupid bucket of bolts can say whatever she wants about that weirdo pervert Burnside, but I know fine rightly that she knows where he is and where his allegiance lies. I could have busted my way into her little safe room eventually or maybe even waited her out, but I've had delay after delay and setback after setback. No more. Sometimes you've just got to let the small fish slip away and go for the big fish. Maybe in Harmony I can pick off a few minnows that didn't even make the list.

*

The midday sun shone brightly overhead, as it always did in the walled city of New Dallas. The streets of the Renaissance district were bustling with activity from guards changing shifts, citizens buying assorted goods from the street vendors and the crying beggars who were being shooed away.

Lyra served up two plates of cooked prairie dog and long-grain rice to an old couple who had spent their entire wait bickering. They were not arguing about the food, it was something to do with the man spending some of their savings on ammo rather than a new shirt to replace the tatty one he was wearing.

"If I'm not armed well, one of those mutants will be wearing my skin for a shirt," he had said.

"Well, he would be all the uglier for it," his wife had told him.

Lyra took their silver and gave them a small handful of change back. She looked down the street towards the Admah district, reminiscing about when Jason would come to visit her on his rare days off. It had not even been two months since he asked her to leave New Dallas with him, but it felt like much longer. She could not go, of course, what would happen to her father without her? Even still, she missed him and wondered where he was now.

"Afternoon, Lyra," came a man's voice, startling her. "Caught you in a daydream, have I?"

The man sat down along with another man who had accompanied him. They were both dressed in black combat armour and were armed to the teeth, both members of the Mercer Guard.

"I'm in a world of my own, Smith," Lyra said with a small laugh. "The usual for you boys?"

"Sounds good to me," chuckled Smith.

"Can you throw in a root beer with mine, darlin'?" asked the other guard.

"Sure thing, McCullough," said Lyra, grabbing a large hunk of armadillo meat, slicing it into small steaks and throwing it onto her pan.

She served the men their drinks—fresh water and a root beer brewed at Sanderson's Sarsaparilla a few blocks away— and laid out their plates while the meat was cooking. She flipped the steaks and began to load their plates up with rice she had cooked in the pot an hour ago. Once the steaks were ready, she scooped them onto the plate and served them hot.

"Looks fantastic as usual," said Smith, cutting his steak and wolfing it down.

"Long shift today, fellas?" asked Lyra.

McCullough washed down a mouth of rice with his root beer before answering. "We're having to pull extra hours while the Street Cleaners are out on their...erm, how should I put this...special missions?"

The second Lyra heard Street Cleaners, she knew where this was going. It was an open secret that King Mercer had assembled a task force of men whose job it was to weed out corruption within the city. Drug dealers, bribers of guards, whatever misdeeds that could be identified, the Street Cleaners would ensure that the corrupt either cleaned up their act or they would disappear in the night.

"Are resources stretched that thin now?" asked Lyra.

"Surely, you've noticed it yourself?" asked Smith. "Half the trade that used to come into the city bypasses the checks they're meant to undergo."

Lyra smiled cunningly. "I make sure my suppliers are legit, Smith. You said it yourself that only half the trade bypasses the checks, mine has always come through the proper channels so nothing gets disrupted in my humble little stall."

Smith chuckled. "And it's a good thing too because half the businesses around here are being disrupted, often through no fault of their own. I don't think the big boss realised just how out of whack things had gotten over the last few years."

"Isn't that why so many of his advisors were publicly executed?"

"I'm not saying they didn't deserve it but it seemed...impulsive? They were scumbags, sure, I get that..."

"But they had roles to fulfil and now there's a void that's getting filled while other problems are arising," said McCullough, at which Smith nodded.

"There was order in the corruption," said Smith. "It was far from perfect, but would you rather that imperfect order or the chaos of the world beyond our walls? I spent many a year out there wandering, scavenging, killing, but New Dallas is a dream in comparison."

Lyra leaned closer to the guards. "So what *does* happen to the men who disappear?" McCullough's eyes widened but he didn't say a word while Smith looked uncomfortable. "I won't tell anyone, swear."

Smith leaned in closer too. "Keep this hushed, alright? The Street Cleaners kick their door in and then toss them into a cell until they choose to straighten up. If they have to pay them a second visit, they're taken up to The Drop and thrown to the mutants."

"The Drop?" asked Lyra, looking horrified. "They're thrown down the chute while still alive?"

Smith nodded. "If they're lucky, they die from the fall. A small number of them are not lucky and wind up with a bunch of broken bones while the mutants swarm in and feast on them."

Just then, another customer arrived that Lyra had to serve, ending the horrifying conversation. As she prepared a rat skewer, the guards finished their meals and left their silver on the counter. She said a quick goodbye to them before they headed back to work.

The rest of Lyra's working day passed in a fairly uninteresting manner. Each time there was a lull in customers, she returned to her favourite pastime of people-watching. There was always a new, weird sight to see but it only entertained her for a few minutes before she started looking for a new one.

As the sun began to sink behind the lingering Old World skyscrapers, the dinner rush came in. She threw together meals at a speed others would find startlingly fast, but it was second nature to her at this point. When the crowd dissipated and departed to their homes, hobbles and whatever bars would take them, she packed up the leftover food, put the earnings for the day in her bag and locked up the stall.

Lyra headed straight to one of the three public banks in the city, walking past the familiar armed guards who gave her a small nod. She could name every single one on rotation, that familiar she was with this branch. After depositing her earnings, she walked back outside. Today was a Tuesday, so she had no need to contact her suppliers. Everything was covered already and there would be fresh deliveries in the morning.

The young woman stood still on the street as people passed by, her gaze focused on the gate between Renaissance and Admah. She must have been standing there for at least five minutes contemplating whether or not to satisfy her curiosity or head home, but she finally made up her mind.

Lyra walked towards the large barricade where two guards stood at the ground, two guards stood on posts on top and two more were doubtless at the other side of the gate. They were armed and armoured, ready to handily remove anyone who caused a disturbance; if any district would bring trouble, it was Admah, so there was no shortage of guards on watch here.

"Have a good evening," said a guard, handing Lyra's passport back to her and admitting her through. To think Jason had his slave brand scanned any time he wanted to pass through a gate was a horrifying thought to her. The constant surveillance of Benedictus must have been a nightmare for him to live through, but she often wondered if her New Dallas passport was that much different.

Compared to the general populace of New Dallas, the people of Admah were shabbier, gaunter and others...well, they were degenerates. You could see them coming a mile off, their deformed faces and maligned skin were hard to cover up, although some tried their hardest using synthetic skin and makeup. The idea of eating mutant flesh was so foreign and disgusting to her, yet she couldn't help but pity some of them. Those who chose to have children of their own were also cursed with that horrible fate and those children were not to blame.

Lyra continued walking until she reached The Third Circle. There it was, no different than when she had last laid eyes on it. Standing at the top of the small set of stone stairs were two guards, both looking more hardened than even those of the Mercer Guard. One of them noticed her staring.

"Hey, you," he shouted at her.

"Yes?" she asked.

"If you're not coming in or looking to be one of the regular girls, get out of here."

Lyra turned to leave but stopped herself. "Can I ask you something?" she said to the guard.

He looked puzzled. "I suppose so. Go on, out with it."

"If Mr Benedictus is gone, how come the bar is still open?"

The man smirked a little. "We're under new management," he said. "Damn lucky too, that slave almost cost all of us our livelihoods."

"Jason Cooper, right? Did you know him?"

"Yeah, I did," he muttered. "Was a real nice guy, you know? Never caused trouble for any of us, always eager to lend a hand. Took a beating he didn't deserve and the second he could move again...bang. Took out four men."

"Four?"

"Four. Him and some guy with an eyepatch. Shot the boss, the big boss and two of...right, that's enough. Stop distracting me and get out of here."

"Okay, I'm sorry," said Lyra, bowing her head slightly.

She walked away, heading back home. She knew about the deaths of Bartholomew Benedictus and Stefano Lombardi; she didn't know there were two others. They might not have been Jason, right? It must have been the guy with the eyepatch. She had only seen him briefly, moments before Jason asked her to come with him out into the wild wasteland. It was strange that Jason had never mentioned him before, who could he have been?

"Help..." groaned a voice from the alleyway beside her.

Lyra peered in and could see a man sprawled out on

the ground in the shadows. There was blood splattered all across the asphalt beside him. She looked around the street and nobody else seemed to notice or care that he was hurt. It must have been a trick and she wasn't going to let herself fall for it. Lyra started to walk away.

"Please...help..." the man moaned in agony.

Lyra looked back and couldn't help but feel pity. Against her better judgement, she cautiously entered the alley only to be grabbed by a pair of arms from behind a rust-eaten dumpster. The man on the ground leapt to his feet and helped his friend pull her deeper in and around the corner, where nobody on the street could see her.

"Let go!" Lyra shouted as the men threw her to the ground. She skinned her arm on the broken concrete as she landed.

"Goodie, goodie," said the one who had faked being hurt. Lyra could see now that they were degenerates. "She's a beauty, ain't she Collins?"

"She'll do rightly," said the other degenerate with a terrifying smile stretched across his wretched face.

"Before we get goin', let's see if she's got any silv—"

With a bang, the man fell dead. Before Collins could even turn around, he too was greeted by a bullet. A man in the shadows held his rifle steady, making sure they weren't getting back up before walking towards Lyra.

"Jason?" she asked.

"What?" asked the man, coming into clearer view. He had black hair and wore dark clothing that looked like it was poorly disguised body armour. Whoever this man was, he was not Jason.

"I'm sorry, I thought you were somebody else...thank you."

"Come on," said the man, putting his arm under Lyra's and pulling her to her feet. "You're not too badly hurt are you?"

"No, it's just a graze," she said, gently prodding her wound. It stung a little, all it needed was to be cleaned and wrapped for a couple of days. "Who are you?"

"Wilson," said the man bluntly.

"Is that your first name or last name?"

He didn't answer, he simply led Lyra back onto the street and to the district gate. He nodded to the guards, who opened the gate for him without the need to scan anything. He and Lyra passed through, and he walked her all the way back to the front door of her apartment complex.

"Be more careful from now on," he said, shooing her inside.

"Are you not going to tell me who you are?" she asked.

"Wilson."

"I know, you said that already, but that doesn't tell me anything."

"Consider that a conscious choice."

"Were you following me?"

Wilson sighed. "Yes, now go inside."

"Who sent you?"

Frustration was starting to creep over Wilson's face. "Go inside and stay out of trouble. The streets are not safe these days, you hear?"

"You're one of *them*, aren't you?"

"One of who?"

"One of the Street Cleaners. You're working for King Mercer. Why is he having me followed?"

"Inside."

"Tell me why I'm being followed."

"Have a good evening, miss," said Wilson, refusing to let Lyra pry any further. He walked away and out of sight as Lyra stood there confused.

Shaking her head, Lyra headed inside and climbed the staircase up to the fourth floor where her apartment lay. She knocked on the door and waited. It wasn't long before a shuffling could be heard from inside and a man's voice answered her.

"Who is it?" he asked in a sing-song sort of way.

"Food delivery for Mr McConnell," replied Lyra, cheerfully. She was rattled by her near mugging but kept her usual optimism on display.

"I'm not paying, I was expecting you five minutes ago," he chuckled.

"Then you're not getting your food," said Lyra slyly as the man opened the door.

Standing before her was her father, Cormac McConnell. His sandy hair was greying, and his eyes were clouded over, having long since lost his sight, yet a smile was spread across his face knowing that his daughter was home. She embraced him and gave him a kiss on the cheek before heading inside and unpacking the food.

Their apartment was as bare as most, having little time or reason to buy more than the most essential of scavenged furniture. What they did prize, however, was an old record player and a dozen records of old jazz albums and compilations. They couldn't have named a single artist or song, the cardboard sleeves having faded to a murky off-white, but they could hum each track by heart.

As Lyra dished out their dinner, her father put on one of the records. Immediately Lyra recognised it was the one they had nicknamed Kickin' Bobby from a time she misheard one of the lyrics as a child. They named all of the singers and songs in a similar fashion; it entertained them to no end, their naming game, almost as much as the music entertained them.

"Oh boy, he's a-kickin' today," said Cormac, shimmying around the room, careful to avoid the two tattered armchairs and the chipped and scratched coffee table.

Lyra giggled watching him make a fool of himself but she knew he acted this way for her. He was bored and miserable most of the day at home by himself, how could he not be? Yet he would still throw everything into making her smile. She loved him dearly.

"It's the second week of the month," he said, making his way over to the table and exaggeratedly sniffing the air. "So today is...hmm...it must be armadillo?"

"Bingo, Daddy," said Lyra.

Cormac sat down at the kitchen table effortlessly, having memorised the house layout down to every inch. It was not always this way as he had struggled to adjust to losing his sight when he first had his accident, but in the time since, his other senses had heightened including his spatial awareness. In his home, he was anything but impaired.

The two began to eat as Lyra brought him up to speed on her day, much as she did every day. When she started talking about what Smith and McCullough had told her about the Street Cleaners, her father let an uncharacteristically grim laugh escape. "That takes me back," he said.

"It does?" asked Lyra.

"Oh boy, it sure does. You would be too young to remember but when we arrived here with your mother, the entire place was in turmoil and it was half the size that it is today. Every no-good lowlife and scum-guzzling dirtbag was looking for his piece of the pie and ol' Mercer was ruthless in establishing order in this place. Never a day went by where you didn't see some poor sap with his brains spread across the road. It was so crazy that we all took bets on which sorry son of a gun would be next."

Lyra looked down at her armadillo uncomfortably, thinking about what she had witnessed when Wilson had saved her. "Things were that bad, huh?"

"I don't know if I would call it bad. Gruesome, sure, but a lot of those guys had it coming. Sometimes to make law and order an institution you have to be ruthless. Mercer certainly was that back in the day before things calmed down. Once he had his men in place and the silver started weighing down their pockets, this place was locked in solid."

"Even with this place locked down, you still lost your sight."

"What are you talking about? I can see just fine," said Cormac, pretending to eat with his knife instead of his fork. "In all seriousness, Lyra, it's just one of those things. I've cursed pretty much everyone under the sun for that grenade, but it won't do any good. With time, I've realised that it was just one of those freak accidents. I was never the target and whoever set it off will probably go straight to hell for it. It wasn't anything to do with Mercer, if anything it's because of the order he instilled that things aren't way worse for us."

"When I think about what some people have been through, we don't have it so bad, do we?" admitted Lyra.

"We're doing alright," said Cormac. "We're doing alright."

"Do you miss it? Seeing the city?"

"Nah, the city is as ugly as it gets," laughed Cormac. "The only thing I miss is seeing your beautiful smile...although I'm sure you're rolling your eyes at this very minute."

He was right, she had rolled her eyes at the nice comment, but she did it with that same smile he loved upon her face.

"You still ain't heard a thing from that Jason boy?" asked Cormac after polishing off every last scrap of his meal.

"Not a word," said Lyra.

"A real shame," sighed Cormac. "You really should have accepted his offer and gone with him when he asked you, you know?"

"And what about you?"

"You told me he said I could come too! It would have been a great road trip until we found somewhere to stay."

"How are you supposed to travel blind?"

"It would have been worth a shot, eh? Now that's something I would like to see again one day, the open road. If I can't see it, I'd at least like to smell it. The air out there is different...it's cleaner. Back to the point, however, he seemed like a good fella."

Lyra sat quietly for a minute before answering her father. "The more I think about it, the more it weighs on me what he did. Killing people, I mean. At first, I thought someone like Bartholomew Benedictus had it coming, but..."

"He did have it coming," remarked Cormac.

"Maybe, but who are we to be judge, jury and executioner?"

"You need to get out of your own head, little missy. Don't despair over evil people going to the grave. Feel for those they've harmed on their way to it."

"You're right, you're right," said Lyra sombrely. "It's too late now anyway. I'd give anything to talk to him and hear his side of things."

"Call it God, call it fate, but things have a way of happening exactly how they're supposed to. I suspect one day he'll come knocking on that door and we'll hit the road with him. Pull all our coin from the bank then go somewhere quiet where we can live out our days. I thought peaceful places like that were all long gone until you told me about that hometown of his, Shackforge."

"Shackford," corrected Lyra.

"Doesn't matter what you call it, it sounded like a paradise."

"You *do* remember how it fell, don't you?"

"Three stage two mutants," said Cormac. "Trust me, I know more about mutants than you do, Lyra. I've seen my fair share on the road. Kept you and your mother safe from hundreds of them when we were travelling with the caravan. Louisiana was filled with those smilers, let me tell you. Freak accidents like what happened to his town cost you a lot, I'm more than aware, but they also help you learn. Wherever that boy is to settle down, he'll make damn sure it's fortified far greater than Shackford ever was."

"It's like I said, it's too late now."

"It's like *I* said, things happen how they're supposed to."

"Daddy, you have no way of knowing what's supposed to happen."

"When I lost my eyesight, I gained the power of

foresight."

"Come on now, you are not psychic," scoffed Lyra.

"I could be," said Cormac holding his fingers to his temples. "Psychics are very real and we're very powerful."

"Then don't go spreading it around, all psychic technology is banned in New Dallas. The Mercer Guard will throw you straight in the cells or throw you out of town."

"I'll tell them you supplied me with the tech and get you thrown out with me."

"So we'll just hit the road together, me as your babysitter? Keeping you safe from mutants, raiders and who knows what else?"

"Nah, just give me an automatic, stay behind me and I'll lay to waste our entire surroundings. Spare no mutant, no raider, no nothing."

"I'm glad you included the part about staying behind you or I'd be a goner and you'd be wandering in circles until you starved."

The father and daughter had a good laugh throughout their rambling conversation as the record continued to play in the background. They cracked open two bottles of Sanderson's Sarsaparilla and kept their conversation cheerful for the rest of the night until Cormac decided to turn in. After one last jab from Lyra about him being tired from doing nothing all day, he headed to bed.

Lyra walked over to the window of the apartment and watched the now-quiet street below. It was illuminated by a couple of dim streetlights, kept low on purpose to save the city's power. There was still the occasional straggler wandering past, and even a group of scavengers who rolled into town on a pair of horses but there was little else going on. It was a normal night in New Dallas and she was glad of the peace after what had happened earlier in the evening.

As Lyra's eyes started to glaze over, a gunshot rang out in the night from somewhere across the street. It alarmed her for a second before she realised what it meant. The Street Cleaners were doing their jobs. The young woman's lips curled into a smile.

Chapter 7:
Unconnected

5th May 2116: I ran into one of them erratics this evening. Big, gangly fella who was busting a few dances moves along the plains. Strange, strange creature. Freaked me the hell out, that's for sure. If I'm unlucky enough to go full stage one then survive until stage two I hope I don't end up like that. I wonder just what it is that makes erratics the way they are. Could it have something to do with the person they once were or is it just an insane run of bad luck? Whatever it is, I hope to the Lord above that I don't meet that fate.

*

The sky over the ridge ahead was clear and bright even though everything else above was a dark sheet that hung over the land. Jason, Sniper and Achilles pushed themselves onwards to the top of the ridge where they finally spied their destination. Harmony. If Camlorn was anywhere, it would be here.

The town was protected by twenty-feet tall solid metal fences around its perimeter and whatever houses once stood surrounding it had been smashed to pieces to keep a clear line of vision for the guards inside. It almost reminded Jason of a much larger, heavy-duty Shackford, but while his hometown had made every effort to keep things quiet and dim at night, Harmony gave no such care. If anything, it stood as a beacon to everything in the wasteland, inviting them to enter or dare to try.

"Mutants are lining the walls," said Sniper, his scope zooming in on the iron and steel panels. "If we're quiet, we shouldn't attract any attention, but I'll keep an eye on things."

"Are you sure the guards won't shoot us?" asked Jason.

A faint smile crept onto Sniper's face. "Sure? No. Fairly confident is how I would put it."

"That makes me feel great, doesn't it?"

"Relax," said Sniper. "I'm not worried about the approach. Just make sure you bribe the guard nicely on the way in or he might just leave you out here all night. That'll really put the brakes on our hunt for ol' Livelong Camlorn."

Jason and Sniper had talked about Jason's theory at length and Sniper was fully onboard. The strange heat signatures Sniper had picked up when he had seen Camlorn fleeing from Highwayland was enough evidence to convince him.

"He's probably in there waiting for us."

"He has no idea we're following him, Jason."

"I wouldn't be so sure with this fella. He's astute and he's resourceful. I reckon he could have broken himself free when we had him tied up at the market but he decided to see if he could win us over before anything else."

"I don't think he had taken the Livelong at that point," said Sniper, pausing for a moment. "Or at the very least he had only taken it recently."

"Well, perhaps we can ask him that when he comes for Mr Gregson," said Jason. "If he hasn't gotten to him already, that is."

"Well, we can worry about that later," said Sniper, walking down the ridge and toward the old road that led into Harmony.

Jason followed, his hand clutching his gun firmly. After everything that had happened on the road recently, he wasn't as well stocked for ammo as he would have liked. He had to make sure that he replenished his stash before leaving Harmony or Sniper would have to do all the heavy lifting with his rifle while they made their way to their next destination.

"The wunners haven't spotted us yet," muttered Sniper as he picked up the pace. "Come on."

The pair dashed down the road with Achilles clinging close to his master. Sniper kept his eyes all around, looking from side to side and over his shoulder. Jason meanwhile kept his eyes focused on the chain fence ahead where a large gate lay.

As the two men and the dog approached, the door fired up and opened for them. A much sturdier inner door also opened and two guards walked out with their rifles pointed at Jason and Sniper while another guard pulled the chain gate to the side and let the travellers enter, closing it behind them.

"Passports?" asked one of the guards with the rifles.

"Right here," said Sniper, pulling out his phone and passing it to the guard who had let them through the gate.

The guard took it from him and walked over to the wall where a computer terminal was hooked up under a shelter. He pulled out a thin cable and plugged it into the bottom of Sniper's phone. The guard tapped on the keyboard a couple of times before the screen flashed green.

"You're good, Mr Creighton," said the man, handing Sniper's phone back to him. "How about you?" he asked, turning to Jason.

"First time," said Jason, holding out his phone. "However much it costs, I'll pay."

"New fish, eh?" sniggered the guard, nodding to his

fellow guards who smirked in return.

"It's been a quiet night for us," said one of the guards with the rifles. "Slow business means a pricier passport. I think a hundred ounces ought to do it."

Sniper stood silently, letting Jason handle the extortion by himself.

"Fifty," said Jason, standing his ground.

"Not going to cut it," said the guard, pointing his rifle towards the gate. "I'm sure you won't mind spending the night out here until our shift changes. Whaddaya reckon, boys?"

"A hundred doesn't split evenly between the three of you and neither does fifty," said Jason. "Twenty-five for each of you, all in cash without transfers. No digital trail for your bosses to worry about. Sound fair?"

The three guards all looked at each other and the one standing by the monitor nodded. "Works for me," he said, plugging Jason's phone in and installing passport papers for Harmony. "You happy enough if I take the details from your New Dallas passport?"

"Fine by me," said Jason as he looked through his pack and started counting his silvers.

After Jason was set up, the guards patted him and Sniper down and looked through their bags to check for any contraband. Jason didn't bother to protest when they confiscated his grenades, assuring him that he could have them back when he left. After that, the guards brought Jason, Sniper and Achilles inside the walls and told the two men they were free to do as they pleased.

The town of Harmony lay before them, a glowing town of neon and noise that was less cramped than Fort Wood but much denser than New Dallas. Every fourth person that Jason saw had some sort of cybernetic enhancement, from a bionic eye to a limb replacement. It was a far cry from being an android like Emilia, yet it still evoked fear in Jason. He couldn't explain it, but it gave him a sick feeling in his stomach. He could overlook Sniper's augment as it was removable and didn't involve sawing off a body part, but this was something else entirely.

"You overpaid," said Sniper as they moved out of earshot. He didn't give cyborgs a second thought, being a borderline cyborg himself.

"What do you reckon I could have talked them down to?" asked Jason.

"Probably ten a head, thirty in total. They'd get in a lot of trouble for turning away business and losing tax revenue for Harmony."

Jason said nothing, silently seething at not being more firm with the guards. To distract himself, he looked around. There were open-air bars nearby and traders peddling their wares, even at this hour. As busy as it was, Jason could only imagine how packed it would be in daylight. When Sniper compared this place to Admaah in New Dallas, he was not exaggerating. Jason was certain that a group of five women standing along the roadside and chatting with hapless drunks were prostitutes. There was even a man nearby sticking a needle in his arm and giving a satisfied sigh. It was open debauchery and, if it was a sign of things to come, it was on an unprecedented scale. At least Admaah knew when to reel it in for fear of Mercer ever deciding to crack down.

"Degenerates are allowed here?" asked Jason upon spying a man with a hideously deformed face.

"If they've got money, they're welcome," said Sniper. "This place is organised chaos run by some of the filthiest money-grubbers you could imagine."

"Who?"

"I couldn't tell you their names, but the figurehead of this place is called Barton Wyatt. He's what they call a *president*."

"I know what a president is."

"Yes, and he isn't *really* one."

"Ah," said Jason, understanding what Sniper was getting at.

"We'll head to Papa's Silver Dollars," said Sniper.

"Folks there usually like running their mouths. If you're feeling like a good time, you can try out this old arcade machine they've got."

"Arcade machine?"

Sniper nodded. "Big screen with buttons. You can make a guy with a sword beat up a tiger. Lotta fun if you don't want to throw back some whiskeys with me."

"We don't have time for games!" said Jason.

"Alright, suit yourself," said Sniper with a shrug.

"You don't sound overly concerned about finding Camlorn."

"I am concerned. Not as much as you, I'll admit, but people take Livelong all the time. It's a sad fact, but it *does* come with some benefits before the horrible side effects. You saw Camlorn survive that fall and being pumped full of lead and he's walking around more or less fine. In desperate times, some people will turn to that rather than take a noble death."

"I know you're right...but I hate that you're right."

"I don't like it either, but let's get a move on and we can grumble about the sad state of the world once we've wrapped up this whole ordeal."

Jason agreed and they moved on through the streets. Along the way, they were accosted by more women on street corners—they wore fewer clothes the deeper into town the men went—as well as the merchants who hadn't closed up shop for the day. Jason was given rapid-fire sales pitches for all manner of cybernetic augmentations, weapons and drugs that would supposedly make all of his dreams come true, so naturally, he ignored every one of them.

"Papa's Silver Dollars," said Jason, pointing to a bar up ahead with a lone guard sitting outside on a stool sipping a beer in front of the rundown building that was barely fit for purpose.

"Did the fancy luminescent sign give it away?" asked Sniper.

"It looks like a dump."

"It is."

Sniper ordered Achilles to wait outside the bar. The inattentive guard didn't even bat an eyelid as the two men strolled inside, visibly armed. Nothing of the sort would have flown in New Dallas. Jason remembered back to his days of the Third Circle where he would do pat downs on the regular to check for weapons. It was a rare exception for an armed man to be allowed inside the bar.

The inside was fairly dim with half of the overhead lightbulbs broken or fused. There were a dozen tables scattered across the room, only half of which were occupied. At the counter were two men playing some sort of game with dice and passing silvers back and forth to each other. The bald barman was watching intently as though this was the most interesting thing he'd seen all week.

Sniper walked straight up to the barman. "How you doing, Rigel?"

"Eh?" asked the barman, squinting to try and see Sniper clearly. "Snipe, that you? Been a while."

"It has indeed. I've been on the road for some time and haven't had much chance to come visit."

"Not much changed around here, no sir."

"What about these Regressionists I'm hearing about?" asked Sniper.

The two men playing their dice game stopped rather abruptly to take a look at Sniper, then resumed playing but it was clear to Jason that they were listening in.

"Alright," said Rigel. "Maybe some things have changed a bit. What you heard about 'em?"

"Only that they've found a way to revert the mutation caused by Livelong. Any truth to that?"

"You looking into them? Got some business?"

"Nothing like that. It's a personal curiosity, that's all. You know much else about them?"

"Can't say that I do, Snipe. I've seen a few of them in here but they don't bring any trouble."

Sniper tapped his knuckles on the counter and eyed the two men with the dice. "That's a shame, I was hoping to be put in touch with one of their members, a Jeremy Gregson."

The men suddenly stopped playing again and one of them turned to Sniper. "Jeremy?" he asked curiously.

"Do you know him?" asked Jason.

"What's it to you?" asked the man.

"A friend of ours from Highwayland called Lucky Johnny told us if we're ever about Harmony, he's the man to speak to."

The man glanced at his friend before looking back to Jason. "You know Johnny?"

Jason nodded slowly. "Met him a few times, shared a few conversations. Nice guy."

"Alright, good enough for me," said the man with a shrug. "If you're looking for Jeremy, he runs a demonstration every night at nine. Head down to Walnut Street and look for a building with a red door. Tell the man outside that Nolan and Pace sent you and you'll be allowed in."

"What time's it now?" Sniper asked.

Rigel checked his wristwatch. "A little after eight thirty."

"Alright, we best get moving," said Sniper. "Mind if I leave Achilles here until we come back?"

"I'm sure Julian outside won't mind the company," chuckled Rigel. "Could you make sure your pup growls a few times to keep him awake?"

"Much obliged," said Sniper as he turned to leave.

"Thanks, gents," said Jason to the two men who nodded and returned to their game.

The two men walked from the bar and Sniper ordered Achilles to remain behind for a while. He guided Jason down the street, already knowing where to go.

"That was one hell of a coincidence, wasn't it?" remarked Sniper.

"Unless The Regressionists have scouts or recruiters posted all over town just waiting to hear somebody asking the right questions. Would they be that widespread?"

"That's what I'm thinking. The tentacles go deep into the bowels of this place."

"They're going to make us hand over our guns, aren't they?"

"Probably, but we shouldn't start something unless we absolutely must. Go along with it."

Walnut Street was a quiet place with very few lights save for a couple of houses with lanterns turned on for the night. Electricity was saved for the bold part of town, the place that would catch the most attention. Regular folks trying to live had to be more cautious and ration what they could.

Jason and Sniper walked up the street until they found the building with the red door where an armoured man was leaning against the wall next to it. Jason glanced at the sign up top that had faded over the decades. He could just about pick out the word 'Theatre' from the faint remnants of the lettering.

"Can I help y'all?" asked the doorman.

"Nolan and Pace sent us," said Sniper. "Something about a demonstration at nine."

"You're cutting it fine, fellas," said the doorman, opening the door for them.

"You want our weapons?" asked Jason.

"Nah, you're all good," said the man, slapping his palm against the wall twice. "Take the door on your left when you get inside."

A confused Jason and Sniper walked on in. The room was dark but it was clearly an old lobby. The men walked over to the door the doorman had mentioned and headed through. Suddenly, the sound of a small, murmuring crowd greeted their ears. It was indeed a theatre, but there were no more than a hundred seats in here, of which only fifteen or sixteen were taken by an assortment of guests.

On stage, there was a computer terminal, complete with a large monitor. It was hooked up to a few sensors which sat unconnected on a table beside an empty chair.

Jason and Sniper took their seats at the back of the small crowd and watched without saying a word. Jason could hear the faint whir and twitch of Sniper's scope as he scanned the back rooms for activity.

Less than a minute later, Sniper gave him a small nudge and three men walked onto the stage. Two of them wore white lab coats while the other was shirtless. The shirtless man sat in the chair with a faint smile on his face while one of the coated men stood beside him, holding a small red case in his hands. The other man in the white coat walked to the edge of the crowd and held out his hands. He had wispy, greying hair and a thick brown beard that couldn't hide his toothy smile.

"Welcome, welcome," he said to the crowd. "What a fantastic turnout we have tonight, I do say. My name is Doctor Jeremy Gregson and with me is Doctor Stephen Gunther. Assisting us tonight with our wondrous demonstration is the ever-brave and ever-trusting Wyatt. Give him a hand."

There was a smattering of general applause. Jason and Sniper joined in, not wanting to draw any unnecessary attention to themselves.

"Tonight, my friends, we are going to perform what can only be described as a miracle for you. You have no doubt heard from our men out on the ground that we can reverse the mutation process and this is only a partial truth. So far, we can reverse the effects of Livelong before the stage one transformation occurs. While we have not yet cracked the code for the reversal of a stage one mutant, we are consistently working on doing just that. One day, my friends, we will achieve it."

There was another small round of claps. Jason, however, wasn't buying a word of what this man was saying.

"Doctor Gunther, if you will," said Gregson, holding out a hand.

Gunther opened the red case he was carrying and took out a vial of purple liquid that was attached to a syringe. He handed it to Gregson who approached

Wyatt, still sitting cheerily on the chair.

"What am I doing?" asked Gregson, setting the vial on the table. "Wouldn't it be better to show you what's going on inside our friend's body?"

Gregson took the various sensors and connected them via clips and needles to Wyatt, who winced slightly at the needles being pushed into his skin. Gregson turned on the monitor and a bunch of incomprehensible readings showed up on the screen for the audience to see.

"Do you see this vibrating section?" he said, pointing to the centre of the screen. "That is Wyatt's blood flow and the numbers beside it shows the content of Livelong in his bloodstream. It currently says zero but it won't stay that way for long."

Gregson lifted the needle as Wyatt twisted his arm so that his bicep was facing Gregson. The doctor pushed the needle into Wyatt's muscle and watched the monitor. A few seconds later, he pressed the plunger and the purple liquid disappeared. A full dose of Livelong now making its way through Wyatt.

"Watch the monitor," said Gregson as the numbers started to climb. "The Livelong count is rising, isn't it? It's at two for now and that's as high as I would recommend letting it get. Shall we see what we can do about that?"

Gunther passed Gregson another syringe with a clear liquid inside. Gregson injected it around the same spot on Wyatt's bicep and seconds later, the number on the monitor started to decrease.

"And there you have it, folks," said Gregson standing up. "The Livelong amount is reducing as we speak and within a minute, it will have been completely neutralised. Sadly, of course, the positive effects will disappear with it, however, we do not *need* to inject the neutraliser right away. If you have any further questions, I will stick around for a small question and answer session, and you too can learn how to get involved in our movement."

A couple of people stood up to leave, while others remained seated. Sniper was one of the ones who stood up and Jason followed him out the door. Neither said a word until they were clear of Walnut Street, but Sniper was clearly holding something back.

"What did you see?" asked Jason once he was sure nobody was around to listen in.

"A great big scam," said Sniper angrily. "Those sensors weren't hooked up to anything."

"You're sure?" asked Jason.

"Positive. Not a single wire or piece of copper gave off the slightest heat reading. That monitor was playing a recording. Did you notice how Gregson glanced at it to wait for the right time to inject?"

"It *was* all a great big lie then."

"Yes," said Sniper, walking ahead.

"Where are you going?" Jason asked him.

"Going to go get drunk at the bar. Camlorn can blow each and every one of their brains out for all I care, I'm done. I'll see you in the morning and we can get the hell out of here."

Jason stood on the street alone, not sure what to do with himself. It was clear now to him what The Regressionists were up to. Selling people Livelong so they can then sell them a fake cure and make themselves very wealthy. Benedictus's involvement made perfect sense to him; a greedy man with a lust for power and control would love nothing more than to convince people he could make them superhuman with no downsides.

Pulling out Camlorn's list, Jason couldn't help but feel disgust for each and every name on it. They were sick and twisted people, poisoning others and condemning them to a fate worse than death all for their own benefit. The entire rotten organisation deserved to burn to the ground and if Camlorn was going to do it, Jason wouldn't stand in his way.

Feeling angry and lost, Jason wandered back to the noise of the centre of town where people were getting more raucous and the swinging music they played more obnoxious. He walked along, trying to find somewhere with a seat, but something on a noticeboard caught his eye and made him stop in horror.

"Oh no," he muttered as he pulled a sheet of paper from the board.

It was an image of his own face. At the top of it was a bounty notice and at the bottom was a value of three hundred silvers. He was a wanted man in Harmony and here he was ignorantly wandering the streets. Jason looked at the small print in the corner.

Present proof of death to a representative of Ivor Carlisle at Namaah to receive payment.

"Well, well," came a familiar voice from behind Jason. "If I didn't know better, I would say you were following me. Speedy one, aren't you, Jason? You managed to beat me here."

Jason reached for his gun and spun around, once again face to face with Eric Camlorn who bore a wide grin.

Chapter 8:
Harmonious Living

10th May 2116: Home, sweet Harmony. What a dump this place is, but I gotta admit that I've missed it just a little. Cheap beer, cheap bullets and the dirtiest street food you could ever hope to find. I've been to, what, twelve settlements in my lifetime? And Harmony is both the worst and the best. As long as I keep myself clean, I shouldn't spook anyone too badly. Keep it quiet as I go about the cleanse. It'll see me through this place.

*

Jason held his gun pointed at Camlorn, but the man continued to smile. Jason wasn't even sure why he was pointing it at him and the people nearby were starting to take notice.

"Considering that bounty," said Camlorn calmly, "you may want to lower your weapon. I don't think you need any more attention, my friend."

"Sorry," muttered Jason, lowering his gun.

"Why are you following me?" asked Camlorn.

"I'm not anymore. I've been to Carson and met Emilia and I've even been to a Regressionist demonstration. Do whatever you want to that group, I don't care."

"Ah, you've seen the light, have you?" said Camlorn, bumping a drunkard off his chair and then sitting down on it. The drunkard got up and stumbled off, not quite sure what had happened.

"They're scammers selling people Livelong and a fake cure," said Jason. "Scumbags of the highest order and preying on the gullible."

Camlorn laughed. "You've only scratched the surface, Jason. There's so much more to these freaks than a single meeting will tell you."

"You played dumb about them when we first met. You suggested they actually believed their own claims of being able to reverse the effects of Livelong."

"I did."

"Why?"

"It wouldn't have helped my situation to start getting too wild with the conspiracies, would it? You may not have killed me, but I'm sure ol' Patch would have been more than happy to stick his dog on me and let the mutt feed."

"He's not as cold as you believe."

Camlorn shrugged and took a sip of the drunkard's beer. "I'll take your word for it," he said, gesturing towards the empty chair beside him. "Sit with me for a while."

Jason sat down, leaned back against the table and stared out into the street. He was at a loss. He had found Kyle and he had given up the hunt for Camlorn, now he didn't know what to do with himself. He didn't have the first clue how to go about finding his sisters, particularly after so long. What use was it being out here and surviving if he couldn't do some good along the way?

"Did you take it?" Jason asked Camlorn without looking up.

"Yep," said Camlorn, nodding slowly. "I ain't proud of it but needs must."

"What are those needs?"

"Killing every one of them bastards involved in that damned cult. I'm telling you, Jason, these guys are bad news. Sounds like you saw it yourself with Benedictus, otherwise you wouldn't have blown his brains across his office. The rest of them are just as culpable."

"Tell me then. What is it that they really want?"

"Take a guess."

"Profit and power."

"That's too broad, my friend. Give me something a bit more specific. You're a smart guy, think about it for a minute."

Jason did just that. He stared at the sky, at the almost invisible stars obscured by the misty light of Harmony reaching upwards. He focused and tried to drown out the noise with his own thoughts, remembering everything he had seen and heard since first meeting Camlorn barely two weeks ago.

"It's two-pronged, isn't it?" said Jason. "The first prong is the profit from selling the Livelong and the fake cure. The second is that they can have an obedient army of super soldiers doing their bidding because they believe they can be cured should their mutations start to go a step too far."

"I had you pegged right," smirked Camlorn, "but there's more to it than that."

"Enlighten me."

"The people at the top of this hellhole world thrive *because* it is the way it is. They don't want the mutants to disappear. For every one dead, they want to see two more take its place. Too many dead mutants means people start to branch out and start to make something for themselves again. They can't be under the thumb of scumbags like Benedictus, Carlisle and that entire crew that sit like kings on top of a world of ruin. That thought horrifies The Regressionists and the chaos outside the walls means they can control what goes on inside the walls. The people? Well, they're naïve. They'll cling to whatever lie is fed to them because it gives them hope for a better future. An end to the chaos and a return to a world that they've never even known. What they're doing goes beyond even that...horrific."

"The masses of mutants wouldn't be easy to wipe out even without more of them being born."

Camlorn took another swig of the beer. "No, but maybe a century from now things will be different. A shame I won't be around to see it, but maybe you'll be lucky and have grandkids who will."

"I'm not cut out for this world," said Jason despondently. "I thought I could do whatever it takes to survive, but I lose a part of myself each time I kill a man."

"How many have you killed?"

"Four," said Jason. "Each of them may have deserved it, but I don't know if I have it in me to kill again. I froze in the supermarket when you crept up on us."

"Maybe that wasn't you losing your soul, rather it was you keeping it."

"What do you mean?"

"Do you believe in God, Jason?"

"Yes."

"Could it not be possible that he held you back? You weren't allowed to shoot me because killing me means that The Regressionists continue to get away with their racket. I don't think it's an accident that we were both in that little town nor was it an accident we were both heading to Highwayland."

"And now we're here," said Jason.

"And now we're here," agreed Camlorn.

The two sat in silence for a minute, Jason staring into the sky and Camlorn drinking the beer. Suddenly, Camlorn closed his eyes and clutched his head while trying to stifle a grunt of pain.

"How long have you got left?" Jason asked.

"I would guess six months maximum before I go full stage one," said Camlorn with a grim smile. "I was hurt pretty badly a while ago, not long before we met, so I took a full vial. I'm good and sturdy now, but a microdose would have been preferable had the choice not been out of my hands."

"I hope you see your mission through," said Jason.

Camlorn reached into his jacket and tossed Jason a pair of sunglasses before standing up. "At least cover your eyes so it's harder to recognise you. I'll tear down whatever posters I see along the way."

"Where are you going next?"

"You've got the list; you'll work it out. Maybe I'll see you there tomorrow. Who knows? Perhaps that'll take care of your bounty trouble too."

Jason reached into his jacket and passed Camlorn his list back. "Here," he said.

"Keep it," said Camlorn, tapping his temple with two fingers. "It's all up in here anyway."

Camlorn walked down the street and into the crowd of the night. Jason couldn't help but feel bad for the man. He was on this crusade against evil alone, but on the other hand, he had a purpose. He had a reason to keep going rather than letting himself succumb to the inevitable mutation that was slowly creeping up on him.

Jason put the sunglasses on and reached into his bag. He tore up an old t-shirt and tied it around his neck like a makeshift neckerchief. He then pulled it up to cover his chin. As ridiculous as he felt, he still didn't stand out half as much as the cyborgs.

He stood up and walked through the town, making sure to swerve out of the way of the prostitutes who were trying to grab hold of his arms. He found a food stall where a chef was shaking a batch of egg-fried rice around in a wok. Suddenly aware of how hungry he was, Jason sat down to eat.

"Rice?" asked the chef with barely a glance at Jason.

"How much?"

"Dollar," said the chef.

"Quarter dollar," said Jason firmly, not content to be ripped off twice in one day.

"Sure, kid," said the man, grabbing a small plate from under the counter and dumping a portion of rice

Jordan Allen

onto the plate for Jason. He slid it across the counter and tossed Jason a spoon that looked as though it could have used a wash.

Jason clasped his hands together and bowed his head in prayer, thanking the Lord for his meal. He picked up the grimy spoon and pulled down his neckerchief so he could shovel the rice into his mouth. It was a far tastier meal than anything canned he had eaten on the road over the last few days.

As he was finishing, a man in a brown Stetson hat sat down beside him and ordered a serving of his own, paying a quarter dollar too. He stared at Jason as he waited for his food before starting to laugh.

"Something funny?" Jason asked him.

"Hoo," said the man with a whistle. "Boy, do you think you can hide yourself with a pair of shades in a town of cyborgs?"

"Beg your pardon?"

"Jason Cooper, you're the talk of the town in bounty hunting circles. I know a few folks who've hit the road looking for you and here you are just sitting having your dinner out in the open with a piece of plastic as a disguise."

"If you're looking to claim the bounty then—"

"I come in peace," said the man, holding up his hands jokingly. "Name's Mal. I'm a big fan."

"You're a fan?"

"Big one, yes," said Mal, pulling out a cigar and lighting it up with a match. "You mind?"

"As you please," said Jason.

Mal took out the cigar and pointed it at Jason. "You took out one of my favourite Livelong suppliers. Dries up my line of work on account of smashing them vials is a big earner in some circles, but I'm not going to complain about a bit of clean up in this world."

"It's a drop in the ocean," remarked Jason.

"Maybe, maybe," muttered Mal as he set his smoking cigar on the table and started eating his rice with an even grimier spoon than the one Jason had used.

"You're a bounty hunter then?" Jason asked him.

"Yep," said Mal, "and there's no better place to be for a bounty hunter than sweet, sweet Harmony. In a town where half the population is a criminal, it keeps me busy and paid. Mind, sometimes it's hard getting the payment from clients. What brings you here?"

"I was looking for someone."

"Find 'em?"

"Yes."

"Now you're leaving?"

"I'm not sure."

"You've got a pair of brass ones, Cooper," said Mal with a chuckle. "If I were you, I'd make myself scarce before you get recognised by someone less kind than myself."

"I might do just that. I can't say I like this place too much."

"Ah, it's not so bad once you get used to it."

"How long does that take?"

"Couldn't tell you. I was born and raised in this town. Mind you, it was a lot smaller when I was knee-high. That said, there's always something new around every corner so it keeps things interesting...for better or worse."

Jason let slip a laugh. "That's not very reassuring, Mal."

"Ain't supposed to be reassuring, it's just me voicing an observation."

"Speaking of interesting. You know who put this bounty on my head, right?

"Of course," said Mal, stopping to puff his cigar. "Carlisle of Namaah. Grade A filth that crawled out of a cesspool and decided to heap on some more dung for good measure. He's a real nice guy, a class act."

"You've met him before?"

"Seen him from a distance. Had to take out a few of his customers and he didn't so much as bat an eyelid."

"You did it in the club?"

"Nah, the alley outside. Two of his guards just stood

there and watched and let me back inside to have a drink after."

"Never paid enough to go after him?"

Mal laughed uproariously, catching his cigar as it fell from his mouth. He adjusted his hat once his laughter faded a short while later. "You think anybody would dare try and kill him? The man is as well-connected and guarded as you can get. If you so much as point a gun in his direction, you'll have fifty bullet holes in you before you can even pull the trigger. It's a crazy notion."

Jason stood up. "Thanks, Mal."

"Eh?" he replied in confusion.

Jason held out a hand and Mal shook it, still with a look of bewilderment on his face. "I think I've found the direction I needed."

"Glad to be of service," said Mal with a shrug. "You seem like a nice kid. I'll do you a favour and tell a few of my friends you're on the road heading south."

"I'd appreciate that."

Jason pulled his neckerchief up once more and headed down the street, making his way back to Pa's Silver Dollars where he hoped Sniper was. It was going to be tough to convince him to watch Camlorn's back when he made his move against Carlisle, but that was exactly what Jason was going to do. People like Mal would clean up the streets for the right price and Jason was going to do it because it was the right thing to do, even if he was fighting an uphill battle.

As Jason approached the bar, Julian the doorman gave him a nod. "Brawl's goin' down inside, chum," he said, scratching behind Achilles's ears.

"And you're not doing anything about it?" Jason asked.

"Naw, I'm only paid to deal with the wild'uns outside."

Jason hurried inside to see what the commotion was and spotted Sniper staggering around and throwing jabs at Nolan as Pace tried to keep the two apart. Rigel was watching from the bar while cleaning a glass, a smile on his face. It seemed as though the rest of the patrons were entertained, and this free show worked just nicely for the portly bartender.

"Sniper, what's going on?" asked Jason, pulling Sniper back.

"Gotta teach 'em a lesson," slurred Sniper, exhaling more whiskey fumes than air.

"Get this deadbeat out of here," demanded Nolan.

"Shut it," Jason told him, trying to keep Sniper from flying off the handle.

"Yeah, shut your filthy mouth, you scum," said Sniper.

Nolan threw Pace aside and lunged at Sniper, but Jason grabbed the Regressionist by the jacket and punched him in the jaw, knocking him onto the bar where he then slumped to the floor and landed in an awkward heap.

"Holy smokes, you killed him," said Sniper with a chuckle.

Nolan grunted on the ground and Pace pulled him up. "Come on, Nolan," said Pace, leading his dazed friend away. "Let's get out of here."

"Come back and I'll shoot ya both," Sniper called after them.

When they disappeared, Jason forced Sniper to sit down at the bar. He wasn't sure what to say as anytime he had seen Sniper drink alcohol, he controlled himself remarkably well. Seeing him in this overtly intoxicated state shattered the illusion of the man who was so calm, calculated and in control. It made him seem more human compared to the hardened wasteland wanderer that he was used to. Jason didn't like it much.

"What happened?" Jason asked as Sniper ordered another whiskey.

"Just a minor disagreement, s'all," said Sniper flipping a silver coin to Rigel and missing his mark entirely. The coin pinged off a glass and fell to the floor.

"That's enough," said Jason, snatching the whiskey that Riger slid over before Sniper could throw it into the back of his throat. "Get up and let's head outside for a while."

"Gonna catch up to those deceivers, eh?"

Jason took Sniper outside and into the alley where they could talk without worrying about being overheard so easily. It didn't hurt that there was no alcohol to be found there and the other bars were nicely out of sight. Maybe it would keep Sniper from getting into a worse state.

"I don't see 'em," said Sniper, looking around. "What the hell we doin' here?"

"You're a mess," said Jason. "How did you get into such a drunken stupor?"

"I just don't like people like them tryna take 'vantage of folks, alright?"

"That's all?"

"S'all."

Jason didn't buy it. There had to have been countless occasions when Sniper had ignored wrongdoings simply because he decided it was none of his business. He had certainly talked about a few of them and the hunt for Camlorn was something he had been less than enthusiastic about when it seemed like Camlorn was another lowlife killing innocents.

"You know, I met him earlier tonight," said Jason.

"Who?" asked Sniper.

"Camlorn."

"That damn name again!" yelled Sniper, kicking an empty glass bottle. It flew down the alley and smashed into the wall, shattering into dozens of pieces and littering the alley with its shards and fragments.

"And it turns out I've got a bounty on my head," said Jason, letting out a dry chuckle.

"You don't say?" asked Sniper, sounding surprised. "I wonder who's got it out for a goodie two shoes like you, J. I suppose...I suppose that answers my question, don't it? Scum and crooks everywhere, there's going to be someone you've pissed off. One of Benedictus's buddies, no doubt."

"Carlisle."

"Ah...ah yeah, of course. It had to be him, didn't it? Toss his body on the pyre and set it alight. Burn all these bums alive and teach the rest of 'em a lesson. No mercy, I say!"

"That's one way to deal with them."

Sniper leaned against the wall and slid to the ground. He reached into a pouch on his belt and pulled out a gold band. He stared at it intently for a short while, then closed it in his fist in frustration. Jason walked over to him, but he didn't know what to say. He knew who Sniper was thinking about right now; his dead wife, Maria.

"It's all just so...damn...pointless," said Sniper. He looked up at Jason. "Why am I still alive? Everything is just...it's pointless."

Jason shook his head slowly. "I was starting to think that way for a little while. Why did I get to live while my parents and brother died...my sisters lost somewhere in the world, probably dead in a ditch or a mutant's stomach. Pointless was the perfect word for it, I thought."

"Sounds dead on target to me."

"No," said Jason defiantly. "I wanted to live, but I didn't know why I deserved life over anyone else. I was wrong to think that way because while there's still some good in the world, I can be there to stop evil from squashing it under its bloodstained boot. I can do something to preserve that little bit of innocence that hasn't been snuffed out under the weight of this cruel, cruel world."

Sniper sighed then threw his head back and let out a guttural laugh. "Your optimism is torturous to listen to sometimes, you know?"

"I don't care. If you truly still care about this world and doing something that would make your family proud, you'll come to Namaah with me tomorrow. We'll help Camlorn put an end to Carlisle and eliminate some vermin."

"I dunno..."

"What sort of world would you have wanted your son, may God rest his soul, to grow up in?"

"A better one than this...a much better one than this. Thomas deserved the best."

"Why can't we help make it that way?"

"Jason, you fool...we're only two men. Two men! Two men in this damn world with no power to right the injustices that occur every single day. Every. Damn. Day."

Jason reached into his bag and pulled out his grandfather's revolver, which David Cooper had nicknamed Camelot and pointed it at the wall opposite. "It's amazing how a little piece of metal can be bent into a tool of both peace and destruction. It can bring about the end of an evil man just as easily as it can an innocent one. I don't think I would mind using it to kill an evil man if it would save the life of an innocent man. I think it's worth it."

Sniper yawned and then dragged his hand across his face. "Alright," he said.

"Alright?"

"Alright," he repeated. "If anything, it'll at least get that there bounty of yours removed if the man who placed it ain't there to pay it. We'll see...we'll see if it does some good on top of that."

Jason put his grandfather's gun away again and thought for a moment before speaking. "We're going to need a way to get inside with weapons. If it's anything like The Third Circle, only certain folks will be allowed to bring their guns in."

"Not a problem."

"How so?"

"There's a gal who lives here in Harmony, Miranda, and she'll be able—"

"Able to what?" asked Jason, wondering why Sniper cut himself off so suddenly.

"Sorry, not feelin' so good right now."

Jason stood up and pulled Sniper to his feet. "You

can sleep it off so you're in a fit state to aim tomorrow. Come on."

"Damned Regressionists," spat Sniper as the two men headed back into the streets.

Chapter 9:
The Jewel of Namaah

15ᵗʰ May 2116: Benny boy, you sly old dog. Of all the places to find you, it would be here. Emilia may have kept that rusty trap of hers shut, but boy did you sing like a hummingbird. I don't reckon I'll get the chance to stroll into old Fantom and even at that, it would be my last day on Earth if I did. My goodness, it's very, very refreshing to see someone turn on The Regressionists whose name isn't Eric Camlorn. Still, it's a damn shame that there aren't more of us turncoats after everything they've done.

*

Sniper led Jason through the streets of Harmony, pausing every now and then to take a swig of water. Jason knew he was hungover and miserable, but Sniper did him the courtesy of not complaining about it. There was no doubt in Jason's mind that his friend was highly embarrassed by his drunken state the previous night, but Jason gave Sniper a similar courtesy in not bringing it up.

"Sniper," said Jason then gesturing towards a

market stall that was serving up helpings of rice and eggs. "Do you want breakfast before we go meet your friend?"

Sniper shook his head. "Nah, I'm good. Feel free to get a plate, but I'll be keeping my distance. Something about the smell this morning..."

"I'm good too," said Jason, ignoring the rumbling in his stomach. Breakfast was a luxury these days, but Jason still couldn't help but want for it. The rate at which he was bleeding silver meant that it would remain a luxury that he would pass on for the time being.

The two men walked through the crowds of people, many of whom were bickering about prices and many others were too drunk to even notice them. It was astounding to Jason that so many people were inebriated so early in the day, yet there they were. Even in the hustle and bustle of Harmony, Jason kept his face as hidden as he could manage in fear of being recognised.

Jason ducked out of the way of a man who was tossed across the street by a guard. He was about to keep walking, but Jason took pity on the man and pulled him to his feet before running to catch up with Sniper. The two headed into a less busy side street where most of the litter from the main street seemed to have been tossed. A little way down there was a signpost that read...

"Gunderson's Munitions?" asked Jason, presuming an association with the leader of Black Haze.

"Different Gunderson," said Sniper flippantly before opening the door.

The two walked inside the shop which was dark and lit by three glowing orange lights that were spread across the ceiling. It may have been brighter at one point, but someone had welded metal plates to the windows. Considering the amount of weaponry stored in here, Jason was not surprised.

He looked at the different display cabinets and cages and spied everything from basic pistols to what could only be described as portable canons that would take off your entire arm—these ones were very much outside his budget. There were grenades and gadgets aplenty, from the more mundane sonic knives used to cut through metal to strange mechanical spheres that looked as though they would fold out; into what, Jason could only guess.

"Felix, Felix, Felix," said a woman who was leaning against the counter. She had a shock of curly blonde hair and wore a brown hat with a wide brim. Her face was stunningly beautiful, yet it bore five obvious scars across her cheeks, chin, and forehead and possibly even more that could not be seen in the poor light.

"Miranda," said Sniper, giving her a curt nod. "How've you been?"

"All the better for seeing your face, sugar," she said, standing up and stretching back, showing off her slim and curvaceous figure. She strolled around onto the shop floor, her boots clopping against the broken ceramic tiles. "Just what is this creature that you've brought me today?" she asked, looking Jason up and down.

"His name's Jason," said Sniper.

"How do you do," said Jason, reaching out his hand.

"Well," she Miranda, shaking Jason's hand. "Is this the same little critter that my father told me about?"

It irked Jason to be called a little critter, especially by a woman who couldn't have been much more than a couple of years older than he was. Even still, he bit his tongue knowing that this was Gunderson's daughter. He had a great deal of respect for her father, Gunderson having agreed to bring him along on a scavenging mission when he was just a stranger and even helping him escape from New Dallas.

"That's him," said Sniper.

"You look just like your poster," said Miranda, winking at him.

"You've seen that?" asked Jason.

"Most of the town has, but most of them are too high

in the sky to notice. It's the ones who are down to earth that you'll want to watch out for, sugar. Got some very good bounty hunters in this town and they'd shank you and vanish before you could as much as look in their direction."

"That's partly why we're here," said Sniper.

"Partly?" asked Miranda, raising an eyebrow.

"The other part is less simple. We need to smuggle some weapons into Namaah—

Miranda laughed loudly.

"So we can kill Ivor Carlisle."

Miranda laughed even louder. She kept laughing and, when she finally stopped, she gave them an incredulous look. "You're for real? You want to bring the man who killed Benedictus into his buddy's bar to kill that same buddy when Mr Cooper here has a bounty on his head courtesy of that buddy?"

Jason and Sniper looked at each other. "Yes," they said in unison.

"Well, it's a good thing you've come to Miranda because anybody else in town would rat you out in a heartbeat."

"That's exactly *why* we came to you," said Sniper with a sly grin. "You've never been afraid to poke a bear."

"It's why I'm so beautiful," said Miranda, drawing her hand across her scarred face. "In any case, I'm sure I can find a way to help you."

"This might help you to help us," said Sniper, holding out a small black box.

"A Visage Mirage...where did you get that?" asked Miranda, holding it up and looking at it closely.

"Devon Kim in New Dallas," said Sniper.

"Kim gets all the best gear," said Miranda, the jealousy evident in her voice. "Can't you put the VM on him yourself?"

"I'd rather not stick it in the wrong part of his brain," said Sniper, startling Jason.

"In my brain?" he asked.

"Yes," said Sniper briefly before continuing to talk to Miranda. "You've fitted one of these before, surely?"

"Once, but that was about three years ago and it took two tries to do it right," said Miranda, pressing a small button on the VM that made a set of spring-loaded needles burst out.

"I don't want that thing being plugged into my head," said Jason, taking a step back.

"You saw how effective a disguise it was for me in New Dallas, right?" Sniper asked him.

"I did...but..."

"But?"

"It's not so effective against cyborgs, of which there are many more here in Harmony than there are in New Dallas," said Miranda. "That was what he was going to say, I'm sure."

"Let's go with that," said Jason, nodding his head.

"Do you want to help your new best friend Camlorn or do you want to let him get torn to pieces by Carlisle's men?" asked Sniper. "Livelong or no Livelong, he isn't immune to a bullet in the head. The small price to even the odds is to put a few needles in yours."

"Livelong?" asked Miranda, folding her arms and raising another eyebrow. "What the hell have you two been getting up to out in the wild, wild world?"

"It's been a strange year," said Sniper, "but we're hoping we can reel in the craziness come January."

Jason sighed. "Fine, I'll do it."

"Oh goodies," smirked Miranda, holding her arm out and gesturing towards a room in the back. "Step into my office, Jason."

Miranda walked over and locked the front door as Jason and Sniper headed into the back room. Several cybernetic parts were lying loose on the floor in here, some of which had enough bullet holes in them that they were almost broken in two. Jason thought it best not to question what Miranda used this room for and sat down on one of the two chairs near a large device on a wooden table. The device was fitted with over a dozen magnifying lenses of varying sizes.

Miranda entered the room shortly after locking up outside and sat down with the VM in her hand. "How did Devon put this on you before, Felix?" asked Miranda.

"He just put it to the side of my head and pushed," said Sniper.

"Which side?"

"Right."

"Jason, turn around."

Jason stood up, rotated his chair and then sat back down again. He had the sinking feeling that his initial hesitancy was warranted, and he should have listened to his gut, but something kept him from speaking up.

"Alright," said Miranda, looking into one of the magnifying lenses and holding the VM up to the side of Jason's head. "Alright, alright, alright," she repeated quietly without moving.

"Is your hand shaking?" asked Sniper.

"No!" snapped Miranda before leaning around to look Jason in the face. "Don't listen to him, hun, he's screwing with us. Look at that smug face of his, he thinks it's hilarious."

Jason glanced at Sniper whose face was as deadpan as ever without a hint of a smirk.

Miranda got back into position and lined up the VM. Jason heard her take a deep breath as she pushed it into the side of his skull. He felt the needles sink through the bone like butter. He had expected it to come up against some resistance and cause him some pain, but it felt like light pressure that lingered after Miranda removed her hands.

"First time, woo!" she called, clapping her hands together. "Let me just turn this on."

She pressed a button on the side of the VM and Jason felt an unusual tingling. He looked around at Sniper who nodded slowly. Had it worked?

"You were more handsome before," said Miranda, clicking her tongue. "Something about the blonde hair and blue eyes just worked for me."

She retrieved a mirror from the corner of the room and held it up for Jason. Jason looked into it expecting to see something radically different, but he looked just as he always did.

"I don't look any different," he said.

"No?" asked Miranda, looking into the mirror. "You look different to me."

"It's working," said Sniper assuredly. "You've got brown shaggy hair, freckles and a scar on your neck. You won't be able to see it for yourself, even in a mirror. It's our brains the psychic field is affecting."

"I can't even see the VM anymore," said Miranda, tapping where she knew it to be.

"Cost me an arm and a leg," said Sniper. "I'm glad it still works."

"Did you warn him about the cancer?" asked Miranda.

"What?" barked Jason in horror.

"You'll be fine if you keep it turned off until tonight and then turn it on to head into Namaah," said Sniper, but Jason still looked worried. "Relax. That only happens if you wear it for long periods of time."

"That's not exactly something to relax about, is it?"

"Don't worry about getting sick twenty years from now, worry about not getting shot before the day is done."

"Alright," said Jason, feeling slightly better. "That is a good point."

"Your turn," said Miranda.

"What do you mean, my turn?" asked Sniper.

"Your eye scope."

"Not happening."

"Do you want to get in without suspicion or not?" asked Miranda. "I can give you some weapons that you can sneak through if you aren't searched too thoroughly, but if you draw attention to yourself with a device like that then there's no way in hell they won't give you a good and deep search. I'm sure that's the last thing you would want."

"I suppose so, but—"

"But?" asked Jason with a big smile.

"Shut up, you," replied Sniper, walking over and pushing Jason off the chair. "Make it quick," he told Miranda.

"Oh goodie," she said, reaching down for a toolbox that she slammed down on her table, "brain surgery in the morning."

"Don't make it sound so dramatic," said Sniper. "I expect this to be done good and quick. No mess, do you understand?"

Sniper lifted his scope revealing his left eye and the wires that ran behind his eyelid, connecting the scope to his optic nerve and even further back to his brain. Miranda held his eye open wide while pulling the upper eyelid out.

"Jason, there's a flashlight in the toolbox," she said, "will you shine it here for me?"

Jason opened the box and retrieved the flashlight. He turned it on but it flickered twice before petering out. After bashing it on the table a couple of times, the bulb lit back up and remained shining and stable. He held it up to Sniper's eye and shone it where Miranda had asked.

"Hmm," she said. "I'm not sure if I'll be able to do a clean job with this in such a small amount of time."

Sniper's cheek started twitching as the bright light made it hard to keep his eye open, even with Miranda holding it. "I didn't cheap out with this," he said. "If you can get just far enough back, there are detachable clips. It means that it can be removed without surgery while the main connectors remain attached."

"That makes my job a lot easier then," said Miranda with a wink. "I'm not as well trained in this sort of thing as Roland is, so you'll probably have a black eye tomorrow."

"I'll live," said Sniper dryly.

"Jason, suction cup and eyedrops," said Miranda.

"This may take a while, hun."

*

"Stop staring at me," said Sniper, scowling.

"I can't help it," said Jason, "you look so different without the scope."

"I look the same."

"Of course, you would say that. You've seen yourself without it before. I've only seen you move it up or aside. This time it's completely gone."

"Boys, boys, boys," said Miranda, shaking her head. "Can we get down to business before sundown?"

"Yes," said Jason, looking away from Sniper who continued to glare at him.

"Namaah has had problems with people smuggling weapons in before," said Miranda. "There have been at least fifteen murders in there in the last five years, so they've got a blanket ban on weapons unless you have special permission. You do not and *will not* get that permission without a lot of sway or silver. The windows are barred and tightly sealed, so I won't be able to pass you anything from the outside. It'll have to come in through the front door along with your fine selves."

"Our options?" asked Jason.

"You've got two of those," said Miranda. "The first is that you smuggle something in between your butt cheeks. A tad unsanitary and more than a little uncomfortable, but most bouncers and guards wouldn't dare put their hands there."

"That's a last resort," said Jason.

"Fair enough. Limited storage space too. The second option is that you conceal weapons in your boots. Now, you may think that they could be searched...and you'd be right, but not if you hide them *within* your boots."

"What do you mean?" asked Jason.

"So handsome, yet so simple," tutted Miranda before

reaching underneath her counter and pulling out two pairs of platform boots. "These boots are a little special something that smugglers love, but folk won't ever think to look here. Feast your eyes on the secret of these shoes."

Miranda turned the boot upside-down and pressed a small button. Upon the button clicking, the outsole flipped open while hanging onto the rest of the boot by a discrete hinge. Inside there was just enough space for a small pistol and some spare ammo, but that might just be enough.

"A much better alternative," said Jason.

"It's not great if it turns into a warzone," said Sniper, "but it's as much as we can expect with only a couple of hours of preparation."

"That's the way it goes most of the time," said Miranda. "Daddy is much better at the smuggling side of things, but if he's on the road, this is as much as I can do for you."

"Thanks, Miranda," said Sniper, reaching into his back for some silver to repay her aid with.

"I'll take half of what you were going to pay," said Miranda with a smile. "I wouldn't be such a great gal if I didn't help out a friend, would I?"

"Alright," said Sniper. "Much obliged."

"Thank you, Miranda," said Jason, getting a sly wink in response.

"We should lay low until it's showtime," said Sniper. "Miranda, is it alright if we hang out in your back room so this mug doesn't get spotted by an unsavoury sort?"

"Of course," she said, nodding her head towards the room and heading over to the front door to open up again. "Make yourselves at home back there, but don't touch anything."

*

"I can't help but think that everyone knows me," said Jason as he and Sniper walked through the streets of Harmony in the middle of the evening.

"VMs will make you paranoid like that when you can't see the difference for yourself," said Sniper. "It takes seeing someone else putting on a face filter a few times before you start to believe it. If it makes you feel better, I feel like I'm wandering around buck naked without my eye...naked and blind."

"I'm glad you're neither of those things," said Jason.

A few moments later they rounded a corner and spied their target. Namaah. It wasn't anything to write home about from the outside, another building with another neon sign; they were endless in this town. What made it stand out was the goons posted out front with their heavy body armour and the large rifles they held. It gave Jason a flashback of his days on door duty at The Third Circle.

"Gents," said Sniper, walking up and holding up his arms.

"Any guns on you, scruffy?" asked one of the door guards.

"Just that," said Sniper, nodding towards his holster. "And there's a knife in my boot."

The guard retrieved them and stashed them in a large crate by the door. He patted Sniper down and nodded him inside.

"How about you?" asked the guard, staring at Jason and making him feel as though he could see his true face.

"Pistol, but no knife," said Jason, holding out his arms and letting the guard take his gun.

"Take off your boots," said the man.

"My boots?"

"Your boots."

"Alright," said Jason, trying not to panic.

The guard looked inside each boot as though checking to see if there was a knife hidden here as there was in Sniper's boot. He passed it back to Jason and nodded him inside. Jason barely waited to get his boots back on his feet before following Sniper in.

While it had been unimpressive on the outside, Jason couldn't help but be surprised at what lay within. There was a large, varnished bar on the left where a hundred different brands of alcohol sat on the shelves with another dozen on tap. There was a large stage at the back of the room with a walkway down the centre that led to a pole where a girl was dancing topless with two baton-wielding guards standing close by to deal with any unruly patrons. Surrounding the walkway were tables upon tables from which the dozens of patrons were ogling the woman and flipping silver coins to her. Up above was a balcony cloaked in shadow, but Jason had a sneaking suspicion that this was where the VIPs were brought, and the best girls were later taken to dance for them personally.

"Where to?" asked Jason loudly, trying to be heard over the pulsing music beating against his head.

"To the bar," said Sniper, leading the way and sitting down at the bar where a scrawny bartender was wiping glasses. "Two root beers," Sniper said to him.

"Root beers?" asked the man, seemingly not used to a non-alcoholic request.

"I want to see the girls clearly for as long as I can get away with," said Sniper with a lecherous grin that did not suit him as he passed a couple of silvers to the bartender.

As the barman fetched the drinks, the two men turned to survey Namaah. Their eyes darted across every nook and cranny, taking in the doors for the bathrooms, any windows, the small staircase near the back of the stage. Anything and everything they could use should they need to make an escape. There was no room for error lest they have a longing for a bullet in the back.

"Fellas," came a familiar voice as someone pulled up a seat beside them. "Quite the evening, isn't it?"

"Camlorn," said Sniper, giving him a small nod.

"Nice to see you."

Camlorn let out a hearty chuckle. "Ain't that the greatest thing I ever heard," he said. "Last time we met, things were less than favourable. I'm guessing the mysterious stranger beside you talked you around then?"

"Who knows?" asked Sniper. "I only met this guy this morning."

"How does the new face feel, Jason?" asked Camlorn, pretending to poke him in the cheek.

"It doesn't," replied Jason.

"Yeah, yeah, that sounds about right," chuckled Camlorn.

"When's it showtime?" asked Sniper.

"You don't want to catch up before we talk business?" asked Camlorn.

"No," replied Sniper.

"Fair enough, my friend," shrugged Camlorn before turning to the bartender. "Three shots of your finest bourbon. Well, maybe a reasonably nice one. Finest may be cutting into my wallet a little too much."

"I don't drink," said Jason, as the bartender lined three glasses up on the bar.

Camlorn waited for the bartender to pour three shots and then grabbed all three glasses in one hand. "They're a bribe to get the best seat in the house. Grab your own sackless drinks and come on."

Camlorn led Jason and Sniper across the floor of Namaah and towards an occupied table at the side where there was a full view of the girl dancing, the staircase to the balcony and the balcony itself. There were three other men already sitting there, but that didn't deter Camlorn who pulled up a chair.

"Gentlemen," he said to them as Jason and Sniper stood back. "I would be much obliged if you would give us this table for a couple of hours. I've heard from a reliable source that the Jewel of Namaah is dancing tonight and these seats give us a fantastic line of sight. As a token of goodwill, here's a whiskey each on my dime."

Camlorn slid the glasses to the men who looked at each other, shrugged and wandered off without a word with their new drinks in hand.

"It always pays to ask nicely," said Camlorn.

"You weren't so nice to us in the grocery store," said Sniper.

"Patch...or the man formerly known as Patch," said Camlorn, pointing to Sniper's now-visible left eye. "That was all just a big misunderstanding, and it would be best for all of us if we left the past in the past. I'm a dying man, so letting bygones be bygones is important, ain't it?"

"You say that, but here we are following that list of people who have crossed you," retorted Sniper.

"That's different," said Camlorn, his smarminess suddenly gone.

"Who's the Jewel of Namaah?" asked Jason.

"A beautiful girl," said Camlorn. "Carlisle picked her up about half a year ago and she's soared into the hearts of all the men in town. You oughta see her Jason, she's this smoking redhead with a body to die for. If I hadn't been married for ten years, I would—"

"Let's get down to business, Camlorn," said Sniper. "Why did you want this seat? Why the view of the stage, the stairs and the balcony?"

Camlorn smiled and sat silently for a moment. "The stage is incidental," he said. "The stairs and the balcony are what I really want to see. You'll notice every now and then that a guard wanders down to bring the dancer out back. These women are all slaves and kept on a fairly tight leash for their own protection. The patrons here have been known to get...rowdy. In any case, the guard that moves the girl will take her backstage and that'll be a good chance to follow and slip up top to the balcony."

"Where Carlisle will be?" asked Jason.

"Carlisle would never miss one of his prized jewel's shows," said Camlorn. "He's got a lustful eye, that rat. Even if he's personally had each of his girls a dozen times over, he watches his favourites dance while licking his lips from start to finish. If he's in town, and I'm confident that he is, he'll be up there and we'll see that ugly mug of his looking down."

"There are a lot of guards here," said Sniper, "and I would imagine even more upstairs."

"Yes, indeed," said Camlorn. "I don't expect you two to get involved unless things start looking dicey. You're my support once we get this show on the road, alright?"

"Works for me," said Jason. "You've got a weapon?"

"Sitting on it right now," said Camlorn.

The music started to die out and the lights faded. "Showtime," said Camlorn.

Sniper pointed to his boot and leaned under the table to retrieve the gun he smuggled in. Once he had done so, Jason did the same. As he sat up, a man dressed in a red sequined jacket and black bowtie walked onto the stage and spoke to the crowd.

"Gentlemen, and to the one or two ladies in the audience. Today is a beautiful Saturday night in our fine town and do you know what that means?"

"Jewel! Jewel! Jewel!" chanted the crowd while Jason, Sniper and Camlorn sat and watched in silence.

"Let's not keep you fine folks waiting," called the host, "bring her out!"

With that, he hopped off the stage and disappeared as a light from above shone upon the walkway. Jason watched the stairs as a young red-haired woman in lacy crimson underwear and a black butterfly mask was half-dragged down the stairs by one of the guards. She took a deep breath and walked onto the stage, where the light followed her. The music started to pick up and she started to dance and touch herself as she moved. The men all cheered and whistled, but Jason felt immense pity for the young woman. While the men watched her with lust in their hearts, Jason couldn't help but notice the slave brand on her right hand and he felt a twinge in the brand that was forever seared into his own left hand.

"I don't see him," said Camlorn, sounding irked.

"Off! Off! Off!" yelled the men as the woman danced.

She blew a kiss to them and reached around behind her back, but then hesitated and brought her hands back around to the front. The men cheered at the teasing and she placed her hands upon the butterfly mask that sat upon her face. She took it off and threw it into the crowd. Jason immediately stood up and made his way to the stage.

"What the hell is he doing?" asked Camlorn.

"Jason!" called Sniper as Jason walked away from them.

He stopped in front of the stage and the guards moved to make sure he didn't go any closer. The Jewel of Namaah was now looking down at him, distracted by the strange man who had approached and who was staring at her in awe. Jason lifted his hand to the VM and turned it off, revealing his face to her and the rest of the people in the bar.

The girl suddenly stopped dancing upon seeing who had approached as Jason continued to stare up at her with a look of horror on his face.

"Jason?" she muttered, but Jason could not hear his sister's words over the noise.

Chapter 10:
One Half

15th May 2116: I didn't think I'd be making a second entry today, but boy is it a doozy. Walking down the street and who do I see? Why it's young Jason Cooper, temporarily free from the burden that is Captain Patch. Didn't think I'd lay eyes on him again, list or no list. I was right about him when we first met, he's a good fella. Maybe he'll be able to win Patch around and we'll have a peachy time dealing with Carlisle together. Truth be told, it would be nice having somebody you once had to watch your back for now watching your back for you.

*

Jason stared at Abigail and she back at him as the crowd grew restless. They booed and jeered, telling him to sit back down and asking for their desired Jewel of Namaah to resume her dance. They were enjoying the show and this stranger with a changing face had ruined it.

"Dance!" called one of the guards, pulling out a baton and beating Abigail on the back of her leg. He drew it back a second time, but...

Bang.

The guard dropped to the ground as Jason splattered his brains across the walkway. Namaah was suddenly in chaos, and everyone leapt to their feet, grabbing their own guns or scurrying away far from here. Jason watched as the other stage guard collapsed dead, courtesy of a watchful Sniper.

Camlorn hurled a smoke grenade into the crowd and dashed towards Jason, trying to pull him back. Jason fought against him, but Camlorn's Livelong-enhanced strength was too much to overcome. He reached out and just managed to grab Abigail's arm. He pulled her off the stage and dragged her along with him.

Everything was a blur for Jason as Camlorn released him to kill a few men in the way. They all ran for the door through the smoke and panicked crowd. There was gunfire everywhere and Jason wasn't sure if it was someone coming for him or Camlorn and Sniper trying to protect him, but either way, there were dead bodies littering the wooden floor.

"Come on!" yelled Camlorn, slapping Jason across the face and bringing him back to his senses. "Pull yourself together or we're all dead."

Camlorn led them out and through the busy night streets of Harmony. Jason, Sniper and Abigail all kept close ranks as they followed the mutant-to-be. They weaved through the crowds of drunkards and lollygaggers with the sound of gunfire still following them. One of the men in the street fell dead, the unfortunate straggler hit by a stray shot intended for Sniper.

Camlorn ushered them all into an alleyway and up to a rusty metal door. He tried to open it, but it wouldn't budge. With a heavy grunt, he slammed his fist against it, breaking most of his fingers and forcing the door wide open. He rushed everyone inside what appeared to be a rundown old shop as Camlorn barricaded the door with everything he could lay his hands on.

"Excuse me," he said to a scruffy old man who was puffing away at a pipe and watching curiously from the counter.

"I ain't lookin' for trouble," he said more nonchalantly than Jason would have expected.

"What the hell are we supposed to do now?" asked Camlorn, furious that his plan had been ruined before it had even begun.

"Follow me," said Sniper, taking the lead.

He ran to the front door and everyone followed close behind, neither Jason nor Abigail having uttered a single word since they left Namaah. Once Sniper had gotten them moving, Jason knew where he was taking them. They moved into another alley and Sniper banged on the door of Gunderson's Munitions, nervously checking over his shoulder in case they were still being followed, but all seemed to be clear for the time being.

"Miranda!" he called out and suddenly the door clicked and swung open.

"Inside," said Miranda, ushering all four of them into the shop and locking up behind her.

She pushed the group into the back room where she had removed Sniper's eye scope earlier that day. Everyone took a second to breathe, relieved that they were now somewhere safe, but they didn't feel much better for it.

"What the hell did you do?" an enraged Camlorn yelled at Jason, grabbing him by the jacket. "How can we expect to get close to Carlisle again with the scene you caused back there? Who's Miss Fiery Red to you that you'd screw us over for her?"

Jason shook his head, tears filling his eyes as he avoided his sister's gaze. Camlorn released Jason and then rubbed his eyes with his index finger and thumb to calm himself down.

"Things went south, huh?" asked Miranda, trying to break the tension.

Sniper ignored her and took off his jacket. He walked over to Abigail and placed it around her to cover the underwear that she was wearing. "You must be Abigail," he said to her, looking her dead in the face.

"Y-yes," she said weakly.

"My name's Felix," said Sniper. "I'm a friend of your brother's."

"Jason?" asked Abigail, touching Jason's arm, but he couldn't bear to turn around.

"Brother..." sighed Camlorn, holding his head in one of his hands. "Of all the damn places your sister could have been, Jason. Sorry I lost my cool, bud. I had no idea."

"It's fine," muttered Jason. "Thanks for having our back even after I ruined everything."

"Yeah...yeah," said Camlorn, nodding his head. For once, he was lost for words.

Miranda walked over to Abigail and put her arms around her shoulders. "Let's get you cleaned up, shall we?" she said, steering Abigail out of the room.

Jason, Sniper and Camlorn stood in silence that was only broken by the sound of Miranda and Abigail's footsteps on the wooden stairs. Jason ran a hand through his hair and inhaled deeply. He wasn't sure what he felt right now, but it was a strange concoction of relief, fear and anger. He wanted to scream and smash down a wall, but all he could do was let out that deep breath and stand there without words to share. He glanced at Camlorn, thinking he saw a tear in the man's eye, but it vanished upon looking back.

"What's done is done," said Sniper, the first one to speak. "I think it's safe to say priorities have changed a little. Camlorn, regarding Jason's sis—"

Camlorn shook his head. "Patch, you don't need to say a word about it. We do desperate and irrational things when we see something horrible happen to a loved one."

"I'm sorry I ruined your shot at killing Carlisle," said Jason.

Camlorn shrugged. "I'll find another way."

"Can't you skip over him and move on to someone

else on the list?" asked Sniper.

"No," replied Camlorn firmly. "He's one of the ones that can't be passed over. The things that man is involved in...fellas, your brains would explode and splatter over the Namaah stage just like that guard Jason nailed."

Jason and Sniper didn't laugh at the failed attempt at a joke.

"What I'm saying is that he's involved in something truly heinous. In any case, Namaah is probably going to go quiet for a few days. I'm guessing Carlisle will be making his way to New Dallas before long. Funny how you don't seem to get this level of craziness there, but hey ho. I suppose I'll hit the road and see if I can get there before he does."

"You're leaving already?" Jason asked him.

Camlorn walked to the door and looked over his shoulder. "When you're a man marked for death, you can't waste a second. I've got very little time left to do what I need to do. I'm sure you would understand if I were to explain it to you, but I think you've had enough for today. If you're ever in the neighbourhood, I'm always open to assistance...just don't mess everything up next time."

"Don't go mutating before you reach New Dallas," said Sniper.

Camlorn held up his hand with the fingers he had broken on the door and flexed all of his digits one by one without as much as a wince. "There are perks," he said before heading out.

Sniper followed him and made sure that the door was locked before returning to Jason.

"Sniper..." said Jason, not knowing where to start.

"I'm with Camlorn on this, Jason," he said. "No need to apologise. I don't have a sister, but I'm sure I would have reacted the exact same way if I'd seen her up on that stage."

"Where could Lindsay be?" Jason asked with a weak voice.

"That's a question for Abigail when you get the chance to talk to her, isn't it?" said Sniper. "I'm not a miracle man, as you well know, but to have just stumbled upon her in Namaah like that...it was a damn miracle."

"God is great," said Jason, his words quivering as he spoke them aloud. "God is great."

"Seems to be, yes," said Sniper.

A single set of footsteps beat against the wooden stairs and Miranda appeared seconds later. She leaned against the wall beside the door with her arms folded. She nodded to Jason. "Your sister wants to speak with you alone."

Jason slowly walked across the room towards the door. As he passed Miranda, he turned to her. "Thank you," he said, at which she smiled and gave him a silent kiss on the cheek.

Jason headed through a small door at the side of the shop floor and climbed up the stairs. With each step, a new question entered his mind. He didn't know what to say to Abigail and didn't want to bombard her with everything on his mind after the horror she had no doubt been through.

In the upstairs, corridor there was an open door to a kitchen, another to a bathroom and then one closed door at the far end. Jason headed towards it, awkwardly twisted the doorknob, and then pushed it open. He walked inside and saw Abigail sitting on a bed, now dressed in a pale green shirt and a pair of brown trousers; they must have been some of Miranda's spare clothes. She looked like the young, innocent girl that Jason had always known.

Upon seeing his face, she burst into tears. Jason walked over to her and wrapped his arms around her, pulling her in tight. She wept into his shoulder for a few minutes and Jason let his younger sister cry without saying a word.

"I...I thought I would be there forever," said Abigail, finally pulling herself together to say something. "You can't imagine what it was like being a slave in a place like that Jason, you can't—"

Jason held up his left hand to her and showed off his own burn scars. "There's always a way out," he said to her, "and I was yours."

Abigail smiled weakly at him and dried her eyes with her fingers, not wanting to wipe her tears on Miranda's clothes.

"I don't know what to say," said Jason. "I can't even imagine where to begin...Lindsay?"

"I don't know where she is," said Abigail breathlessly. "It's been so long now, but she was alive when we last saw each other."

"We'll take it from the start, alright?" Jason said, relieved that both Lindsay and Abigail had survived the massacre in their hometown. "What happened on the night Shackford fell?"

"Not long after you and Bill left to go see what the gunshots were, Mom and Dad woke up and got us ready to go. Dad was going to take us to the church, but suddenly Mom wanted to rush back home to grab something...I don't even remember what it was, but it probably wasn't anything important. Dad told us to keep going and barricade ourselves in, but we never saw either of them again."

Jason shook his head. "I found Mother when I went back to our house to look for you," he said. "I was attacked by one of the mutants and Dad saved me at the cost of his own life. Bill..."

"I know," said Abigail sadly, remembering her oldest brother. "I saw his body near the gate when we left town."

Jason's heart dropped. "You were still there," he said in horror. "You were still there when I was running for the forest. I left you behind. Bill died in front of me...so you were both still there."

"You can't blame yourself for anything," said Abigail, taking Jason's hand. "We escaped the church by sheer luck. For all we knew, you were still somewhere in town.

It's just the way things happened on that dreadful night."

"How many of you got out?" asked Jason.

"There were seven or eight of us, I think," said Abigail. "There was Lindsay and I. Andrew Blanchard, and his sister were with us. Jocelyn and her parents...maybe her cousin too? I'm not sure if she was with us when we got as far as the road. Some of it is a little hazy. In any case, we headed straight for the road and went East to lay low until we had a chance to get back into the town, but that didn't work out well for us at all."

"Why?"

"There was an old shack we found that we stayed in for two days, but we had no weapons, food or water. Lindsay and I decided to leave and fetch some from the river. We had planned to bring it back in a couple of old pots we found, but when we returned..."

"Dead?"

"No, they had all vanished. It had only been a couple of hours, but they had all vanished without a trace. We never saw any of them again."

"Slavers, maybe?"

"Or they decided to come and get water but got lost. Maybe they were caught by mutants somewhere on the road? It's impossible to say."

"Then what did you do?"

"We waited," said Abigail. "We knew there would be a trading caravan heading towards Shackford sooner or later, but we didn't know when. We got lucky and it came two days later. They were kind enough to give us some food and a knife. They pointed us in the direction of another settlement a few days away called Fort Wood, but we never made it that far."

"I was there," said Jason, with a pang in his heart. "If you had only gotten there, we may have found each other much sooner."

"Lindsay and I thought that we could make it there alone, but we kept finding mutants lurking near old houses and abandoned towns. We were forced to go off the road many times and eventually, we were found by a group called the Red Commandos."

"Mercenaries?"

"Mercenaries...raiders...slavers...whatever you want to call them. They found us hiding in an abandoned farmhouse. They seemed alright at first, but there was something off about them. When they tried to grab me, Lindsay stabbed one of them and they turned violent. We were beaten so hard we could barely stand up and then they brought us both here...to Harmony. I haven't left town since."

"Did they...did they..." Jason couldn't get the last word out, but the look on Abigail's face told him she understood.

"No," she said, "they didn't rape us. They thought that a pair of virgins would double our value and that was far more important to them. They had a much harder time convincing the man at the auction house that we were twins because we're not identical, so I was bought by Ivor Carlisle's men, got my slave brand and I haven't seen Lindsay since."

"My old boss was a pal of his," said Jason. "Lots of business dealings about who knows what, probably Livelong."

"Bartholomew Benedictus," said Abigail, her eyes growing wide. "It was you, wasn't it? You were the one that killed him."

"It was me," confirmed Jason. "How did you know about that?"

"Carlisle hasn't stopped talking about it since."

"He talks about it? When?"

Abigail winced. "Please, don't ask me that."

Jason didn't need her to answer to know when. The way Camlorn had spoken about Carlisle and his favourite Jewel was enough. Jason also knew that if he ever came face to face with Carlisle, that monster would be dead before he had a chance to as much as open his mouth.

"I'm going to get you out of here, you hear me?" Jason told her. "I don't care what it costs me, how long it takes or what I have to do to get it done. I'm getting you out of here."

"I believe you," said Abigail, hugging him tightly once again.

"We're not the only survivors, you know. Kyle made it out too and he's keeping himself busy in a town not too far from here. That's where we'll go once we're out of Harmony."

"Kyle?" asked Abigail, releasing Jason. "One of the kids you were teaching how to shoot?"

"I got him out of Shackford, but we were separated for a while. I finally tracked him down a couple of weeks ago and he's doing well. He's being trained up as a guard in this place called Highwayland. Shackford had walls, but Highwayland has height to keep the people safe. There won't be any stage twos climbing up to where they are, I assure you."

"That sounds nice," said Abigail, her voice lighter than it had been all night.

"It's one of the better places I've seen out in the world," said Jason. "Maybe we can be happy there? We can't get back what we've lost, but we can build something new."

Abigail smiled. "I would like that," she said. "Can we pray? I've been too ashamed of everything I've had to do to speak to the Lord, but I think...I think it's time."

"Of course," said Jason.

The two fell to their knees on the floor and clasped their hands together. Jason recited the Lord's Prayer aloud while Abigail sat silently in prayer with him. They stayed quiet afterwards, their heads bowed low in further prayer. It was the calmest Jason had felt in weeks, having finally found one of his lost sisters. He knew that he had to track down Lindsay somehow, but getting Abigail out of Harmony and to somewhere safe was his top priority and he asked for the Lord's guidance to do so.

There was a knock on the door as Jason and Abigail finished their prayers. "Come in," Jason said.

Miranda walked in, looking glad to see the pair with smiles on their faces. "You can both stay here for a while," she said. "I've got my business to run, so I'll have to open up the store below, but you can keep upstairs and do as you please until things cool down. Sniper's away to fetch Achilles. We'll come up with a plan over the next couple of days and see where we go, alright?"

"Thank you, Miranda," said Jason.

"Sure thing, hun."

Later that evening, Jason and Sniper set up their bedrolls in the hallway while Abigail took the bed and Miranda slept on the floor. Jason was tired, but he struggled to fall asleep. As relieved as he was to have found Abigail, he knew that tracking down Lindsay would not be an easy task. He was at the very least grateful that he now had a lead to go on. She was sold at an auction, and where there was an auction, there was an auctioneer who could be made to answer a few questions.

Chapter 11:
The Fiend

17ᵗʰ May 2116: Back on the lonesome road once again. Friends are like a bullet hole for me now. Easy come, easy go. All the same, I'm glad that Jason found his sister. Didn't know that much about the guy let alone his family. Sometimes when you're so wrapped up in your own world, you forget that other people have their own craziness going on. Maybe fate will strike once more, and we'll see each other again once he and Patch get themselves out of Harmony. It's not a question of if they'll get out, it's only a question of when.

*

The sunlight shone through the upstairs window of Gunderson's Munitions and Jason stood staring out through the glass and between the bars, missing the outdoors. Even the alcohol-tinged scent that permeated throughout the streets of Harmony would be nice. It had been a week since he had left the confines of the small upstairs apartment, and he felt like he was wasting time that he could have dedicated to tracking down Lindsay.

"It won't be long," said Abigail who was sitting on the floor while she looked through a decrepit Old World magazine. The tattered old paper looked as though it would crumble to dust if she held it just a little too tightly.

"I know, Abi," said Jason, but it didn't make him feel any better. He had more freedom in The Third Circle than he did here.

"You should be grateful," said Sniper.

"I am grateful," replied Jason irritably. "What are you getting at, Sniper? Why would you think I'm not grateful?"

Sniper didn't answer. He started throwing a broken chair leg down the hall for Achilles to fetch. The dog was the only one of the four of them that had been outside lately and, even then, it was a brief walk with Miranda in the early morning before the town woke up and she had to open the shop.

Jason couldn't fault her for the amount of help she'd given them since they arrived in town. He couldn't even begin to fathom how he would repay her and she refused to take any silver, even for the food she'd been supplying them with. He would find a way somehow, even if that meant coming back to Harmony once Carlisle was dead—whenever that would be.

"Would you kill me if I switched on the VM and went for a walk?"

"No," said Sniper, scratching his lengthening beard, "but the bounty hunters might if you get yourself rumbled. Don't forget that the psychic emittance is short-range. Even if a guard spies you from a watchtower through a scope, you'll look just as you always do."

"I think it would be a terrible idea," said Abigail.

"We need to find out from the auction house who bought Lindsay if we're to have any hope of finding her," said Jason. "That's a lot easier done while we're still in Harmony than it is once we're on the road back to

Highwayland."

"Then go do it and shut up about it," said Sniper. "Just keep in mind that your bounty has doubled after our little escapade in Namaah."

"My bounty is doubled and now you have a bounty too," said Jason. "It's all fun and games in this dump of a town."

"It ain't so bad if you keep out of trouble."

"Trouble always finds *me*."

"I'm not so sure that's true."

Jason had made up his mind. "Alright, I'm going. I'll be back before you know it."

"Don't let Miranda catch you or she'll flip her lid."

"It's a good thing she isn't back from fetching lunch then, isn't it?"

Abigail sighed. "Just be careful, alright?"

"I'm always careful," said Jason, switching on the VM and appearing to her as a different man.

"I'm not so sure that's true either," said Sniper, throwing the chair leg for Achilles once again.

Jason walked past the dog, who was growling and shaking the wooden stump vigorously. He proceeded down the stairs and exited the empty shop. He hurried from the side street quickly, worried that Miranda would round the corner any second and yell at him for being reckless. It would no doubt have been deserved, but he could not pass up the chance to get a lead on Lindsay's whereabouts.

He walked down the busy main street and straight past a circle of men who were kicking a screaming young man. The screaming teenager insisted he was not a thief, but it didn't stop the assault on him. A single guard was watching, but he wasn't doing anything to stop the beating and Jason's mind was too focused on his goal to give the poor guy a second thought. As soon as the young man's cries were out of earshot, the scene vanished from his mind.

Jason was suddenly aware that he had no idea where he was going. There could be ten auction houses in town for all he knew, and he wouldn't have been able to identify a single one. He decided it was best to ask for help and the closest person that looked like they may have indulged in a slave auction or two was a man with a cybernetic arm and a large grill of metal teeth that he was sharpening with a rusty file.

"Excuse me," said Jason.

"Eh?" said the man, stopping filing for a moment. He looked annoyed and Jason was starting to regret speaking to him, but he remembered Camlorn's approach to getting the table he wanted in Namaah.

"I'm new in town," he said, taking out two silvers and holding them up to the man. "I'm trying to find a decent slave auction and a finger pointing me in the right direction would be appreciated."

The man took the two silvers and held them up. He smiled a wicked metal grin and nodded to Jason. "Sure, sonny. Ol' Grinner will tell ya all ya need to know. Are ya lookin' for a worker or a woman?"

"Woman," said Jason.

"Ah, yeah. It'll be Verdugo's ya want if yer lookin' for the best in town. If ya don't mind a bit of a mutt, then ya can always try elsewhere. Baron Dutch himself uses Verdugo for his own harem, ya know?"

Jason didn't care to ask who Baron Dutch was. "Verdugo's it is," he said.

Grinner pointed down the street. "Head that way until ya reach the crossroads, then take a right. Head half a mile down further, then take a right at the fork. It'll be on the street a little ways down."

"Thanks for the info, Grinner," said Jason. "Have a nice day, friend."

"I shall," said the cyborg as he pocketed the silver coins.

Jason walked and he walked, careful to make sure that he didn't take any wrong turns. At the crossroads, he took a right. He walked until he found the fork and took another right. There could be no room for mistakes and the less time out in the streets, the better. That said, he was glad to be out in the air again, hot and sharp as it was in these parts.

"Verdugo's Auction House," said Jason, reading the wooden sign on the surprisingly clean-looking building.

It was odd to him that there was no neon sign, perhaps it was a sign of a classier establishment, but he supposed it didn't matter all that much. He tried to open the door, but it was locked. He banged his fist against it and waited, but nobody came to answer it.

"Fantastic," he muttered, "of all days to be closed."

Jason banged his fist on the door once again, this time much harder and louder. To his surprise, the lock clicked, and the door opened.

"What in blazes are you doing bothering me at this time?" asked a middle-aged man with a wispy brown moustache and a dusty bowler hat.

"Are you Mr Verdugo?"

"No," said the man irritably, "I'm Mr Shemp. I'll ask again. What are you doing bothering me? We don't open until three."

"Would you happen to be the auctioneer here?" asked Jason.

"I would, but what's it to you?"

Jason reached into his incredibly light wallet and pulled out five silvers. "I was hoping to have a word with you. This is just for your time, not for any information."

Shemp took the coins and beckoned Jason inside, closing and locking the door behind them. He brought Jason through the quiet building and into a small office where Shemp was organising some paperwork into a dented metal filing cabinet.

"Speak," he said, getting back to work.

Jason had thought long and hard about how he would get the information he wanted and had a plan. "I'm looking for a woman who I believe to have been sold here."

"I don't give information out about purchases."

"Just let me say my piece first. She's wanted in New Dallas for murdering a man named Henry Rolston. She and her sister both fled town a year ago and went on the run. I've been tasked by my employer to track her down and claim the bounty. I've been permitted to offer anyone that sees fit a downpayment for useful information as well as a cut of what's on offer."

Shemp stopped and looked at Jason. "What's the bounty value?" he asked.

"Three hundred and sixty ounces of silver," he said.

"That's some bounty for a young lass, ain't it?"

"That would be a question for my employer, I'm just here to do my job." Jason reached into his wallet and took out another twenty silvers. "I can give you this plus another twenty if the information you can give me leads to her. I'm in Harmony often enough that I have no doubt we'll cross paths again."

Shemp looked at the silvers and then around the room as though someone may have been watching him. He quickly snatched the silvers and stashed them in his pocket. "What's the name?" he asked.

"Lindsay Cooper," Jason said.

"Lindsay Cooper..." said Mr Shemp. "That doesn't ring a bell...nearly a year ago you say?"

Shemp opened a different drawer and pulled out a file filled with handwritten papers. He flicked through them and Jason sat there trying to keep his cool, nervous that it wasn't Verdugo's that Lindsay had come to. Abigail hadn't been able to tell him for certain which auction house it was, and he was afraid he had just wasted most of his remaining silver.

"Ah," he said. "Lindsay Cooper and Abigail Cooper. Do you want them both?"

"Sure, but it doesn't pay extra for the other Cooper girl."

"Well, they were bought by the same person either way. Dan Ryerson, operating on behalf of Ivor Carlisle. Good luck getting Mr Carlisle to let you kill one of his slaves for a sum so paltry to him."

Jason was taken aback. How could it be that Carlisle had bought Lindsay too and Abigail hadn't seen her in

Namaah? Unless...

"New Dallas," said Jason involuntarily.

"Beg your pardon?" asked Shemp as there was another banging on the door.

"Thank you for your help, Mr Shemp," said Jason, giving the man a curt nod. "I'll be in touch one way or another when I'm back in town."

There was then another louder bang on the door and a muffled voice shouting from outside. "Who's bothering me now?" asked Shemp, heading to shoo away the next pest.

Jason followed, hoping to get back to Gunderson's as quickly as he could. He waited for Shemp to open the door, but his heart sank when he saw the man looking to be let in. He was wearing black combat armour with the image of a demon emblazoned on the front. He stood almost as tall as Jason and equally as blonde, but he had wavy hair instead.

"Griffin, what do you want?" asked Shemp.

Griffin of the Fiends, the same man who had captured Jason and sold him into slavery those many months ago. Griffin smiled innocently at Shemp while his four cronies stood behind him, holding a young man who was gagged and had his hands bound behind his back.

"Got some business for you, Shemp," said the mercenary in a warbling, robotic voice. Sniper had told Jason through laughter how he had cut out Griffin's tongue during their last encounter, but it seemed as though Griffin had not learned his lesson.

"Come back at two," said Shemp. "You know that's when I process the new ones for the three o'clock auction."

"Young Marvin can't wait that long," said Griffon, his voice buzzing as a segmented metallic tongue flicked around his mouth when he spoke. "He was telling Sanchez the whole way here that he couldn't wait to have a new master."

Marvin squealed through his gag, terrified of what

was going to happen to him while Griffin's lackey, Sanchez, looked at him and laughed. Jason knew it was risky, but he couldn't let Griffin do to this young man what he had done to Jason. It wasn't right.

"Wait just there a second," he said, pushing past Shemp. "Marvin? Marvin O'Driscoll? I haven't seen you in quite some time, my friend. What have you done this time to get yourself into such a predicament?"

Marvin looked at Jason in confusion, but he didn't dare make a sound. The young man realised that this was his only chance to get out of this nightmare.

"Who are you?" asked Griffon, looking at Jason suspiciously while not recognising his disguised face.

"Name's John Thomas," said Jason, lying once more. "I hail from down near Fort Wood. I met this boy and his mother a fair few years ago. He's gained a foot since then, but good to see he's well fed."

"He's our property until Mr Shemp finds us a buyer," said Griffin.

"Come on now, Mr...Griffin, was it? I wouldn't ask if I didn't know him already, but would you let this one go? He's a good kid and I'm sure his mother misses him dearly."

"I very much doubt that," said Griffin with a sick smile, "considering she was being devoured by a mutant when we last saw her. A shame, but that's the way it goes sometimes."

"That's a shame indeed," said Jason, smiling back.

He pulled out his gun and shot Sanchez in the knee, catching the gang of Fiends off guard. Jason punched Griffin in the throat and bolted forward, dragging Marvin down the street and sprinting as fast as he could.

"Get...him!" called Griffin, spluttering.

Jason heard a gunshot as he ran down the street with Marvin in tow and saw a man no more than two feet to his right collapse as a bullet struck him. Jason grabbed Marvin and dragged him inside an alley. Taking the Camlorn approach, he kicked in a door and ran through the bar, much to the chagrin of the bartender.

They stormed through, past a mixture of curious and uncaring patrons. Once they exited through the front door, the pair were back on the main street and started to weave through the crowds. They did not hear their pursuers, but there was no doubt they would be on the hunt. Jason turned around and pulled the gag from Marvin's mouth, letting him breathe easy.

"Thanks," said Marvin. "Who are you?"

"No time for that, get moving!" said Jason.

There was a sudden bang and a clink as a bullet hit a tin-roofed stall. Jason and Marvin picked up the pace, shoving people indiscriminately out of the way as their very lives depended on escaping the Fiends. A couple of people tried to block them, thinking they were thieves on the run, but Jason tackled them to the ground and leapt back to his feet to get past. Seeing more trouble on the main street than it was worth, the pair headed back into the alleys where they could run unimpeded.

"Split up and find somewhere to hide," said Jason, pulling out his knife and cutting the cables that bound Marvin's hands.

"Who are you?" Marvin asked again.

"It doesn't matter, just go," said Jason, pushing Marvin away and running in the opposite direction.

He didn't know where he was, but he knew he couldn't be that far from Gunderson's Munitions. He weaved through the different alleys and side streets, crossing the main street only when necessary. After a few minutes, he found an isolated corner and slumped against the wall to catch his breath. He couldn't help but let out a laugh in sheer relief to have escaped. Part of him wished that Griffin knew who it was that got the better of him, but that prideful thinking would only lead to more trouble. No, it was best his identity was kept secret. The elusive John Thomas could take the fall.

Once he had the energy to keep running, Jason cautiously wandered back onto the main street. It was the only way he knew he could get back to Sniper and

Abigail without taking hours. He thought it better to go now and be quick rather than be stuck out here where he would be caught eventually.

Bang.

Jason stumbled as a bullet grazed his thigh. He turned to see Griffin approaching him with a look of deathly intent across his face. Jason raised his own gun and shot Griffin in the arm, making him drop his weapon. Jason forced himself to his feet and tried to run, but he was knocked to the ground from behind as Griffin pounced on him. The side of Jason's head hit the road and he heard a crack by his ear as the VM broke and his gun was flung down the street.

Griffin rolled him over and drew back his fist to punch him, but upon seeing Jason's true face he hesitated. "You," he said, shocked to realise who had cost him a sale.

This momentary lapse was all Jason needed. He pulled out a knife from his belt right as Griffin threw his fist forward. The Fiend impaled his wrist upon the blade and he screamed in agony. Jason kicked him aside, pulling the knife free. He stabbed Griffin in the shoulder, where his body armour was thin and climbed back to his feet. He pushed past the onlookers who didn't bother interfering and limped away while Griffin yelled for help from his men.

There was no other option for Jason, he had to hide. He glanced at his leg and was glad that it was not bleeding badly enough to leave a trail. He headed back into the alleys and found an old rusty dumpster. He climbed on top of it and then up on top of the wall. He could see that the rooftop of the house nearby was just low enough for him to reach...if he could make the leap. He breathed deep and checked to make sure no one could see him, then threw himself forward with his hands outstretched. He grabbed hold of the overhanging edge of the roof and pulled himself up. He kept low, crawling along to the flat part, knowing that if he stayed down then he would be hard to see.

"What a day," he muttered, wiping the sweat from his brow with the sleeve of his jacket.

He stared up at the sky as the hot afternoon sun beat upon him. He glanced down at his leg wound and was relieved to see that it was only surface level. It stung, but he would live, and he certainly wouldn't bleed out before getting himself properly to safety. A clean up and a bandage would be enough to take care of it.

Jason was now very much aware of how hungry he was. Right at this moment, Sniper, Abigail and Miranda were probably just finishing their lunch. He wasn't too bothered by it, at least they were safe. However, it wouldn't be long before they would start to worry about him being dead or captured. It wasn't a pleasant feeling to know he was going to put them through that, but he had to wait for night to fall before he could risk going back on the streets. He would be recognised without the VM, but the cover of darkness would obscure him if he stuck to the poorly lit areas.

Jason waited as the hours passed by, trying to find ways to entertain himself. He would count the number of times he heard gunshots—five in total, not as many as he expected—and he even pulled the VM out of the side of his head, examining it to see if he could figure out how it worked; it was a fruitless endeavour when most of what he could see was cracked casing and the stained prongs covered in his brain juice.

At last, the sky turned orange, then purple and finally black. It was time to move. Jason looked over the edge of the roof and jumped back to the wall, then into the alley. It was quiet here, but there was plenty of noise from the crowds nearby. He walked from the alley and looked around, being extra careful that there wasn't someone who even looked like Griffin or his fellow Fiends.

It took him ten minutes of wandering, but he eventually found a street he recognised. From there, he was able to guide himself home. The whole way, he felt as though he was being watched. In fact, he probably was being watched by those who recognised him from his bounty notice. Much to his relief, none of them were bold enough to make any attempt to claim said bounty.

He walked down the street leading to Gunderson's Munitions and spotted the sign that was now very familiar to him. With a final glance over his shoulder, he reached for the door and opened it. He walked inside, but neither a holier-than-thou Sniper nor a worried Abigail were there waiting for him. There wasn't even an excited dog. There was only Miranda and her father. Gunderson himself. And he did not look happy to see Jason.

Chapter 12:
Thick Flesh

24th May 2116: Almost halfway to Dallas and I walk through raider territory. Of course, I do. Idiot, I'm such an idiot. The graffiti in blood should have given it away and I was naïve to think it was years old. Still, what's another twenty dead scumbags to me at this point, eh? One of those morons thought he'd indulge and eat a little human flesh only to get more than they bargained for. How did the Livelong blood taste, you bastard? He's the only one I let live, but I left him with two stumps for hands. At least my flesh will grow back.

*

Jason was stunned to see Gunderson standing there, looking as grizzled and gruff as ever. There was a heavy contrast between him and Miranda, but seeing them side-by-side, Jason could tell that they were father and daughter. Gunderson had a look of anger on his face while Miranda was smiling weakly at Jason as though pre-emptively apologising to him.

"Where is she?" Jason asked.

"Gone," said Gunderson, "and you would have been

too if you were here instead of galivanting around town and making an ass of yourself."

"What do you mean?" asked Jason.

Gunderson's face was sunken into a deep frown. "I got into town this morning and came straight here, as I always do, only to find Felix, Achilles and a girl who claimed to be your sister skulking around upstairs. As luck would have it, a buddy of mine was working the front gate this morning and I was able to get him to let old Snipe and your sister out of town. No questions asked but costing me a favour I was owed. No big deal, no problem."

Jason didn't say anything.

"And of course, the most wanted man in town, who puts my daughter's safety at risk by even being here, is running around and starting fights with scumbags like Griffin over some runt of a slave; a complete stranger. Did you think Griffin wouldn't chase you down? Did you think stabbing him in the hand and shoulder would lower your profile? What in the hell were you playing at, you stupid fool?"

"I wasn't looking for trouble," said Jason, "it just seems to keep finding me in this town."

"Don't play dumb with me!" barked Gunderson. "You should have been laying low like Miranda had told you to do. Frankly, Felix should have tied you to the chair in the back rather than letting you walk out the door."

"I had a lead on my other sister," said Jason. "Was I supposed to skip town?"

"Do you consider me a friend?" asked Gunderson.

"Yes."

"Have I proven to you that you can rely on me and the Black Haze boys to have you back?"

"Yes."

"Then why not pass a message to Miranda?" asked Gunderson, while Miranda avoided eye contact with Jason. "Why not leave me a note saying what I could do to help? You think I wouldn't have done it?"

Jason didn't know what to say. Gunderson was right, of course. He wasn't sure why it hadn't occurred to him, but he thought perhaps he was blinded by the idea of reuniting what was left of his family as quickly as possible that he had let his judgement be clouded.

"I'm sorry," he said quietly. "I wasn't thinking straight."

"You're damn right, you weren't."

"Will you help me get out of town?"

"Of course, you dumb bastard," said Gunderson, "but you have to do everything I say from here on out, you hear? No taking matters into your own hands and absolutely no leaving here without me saying so."

"Yes," said Jason.

"Good," said Gunderson, walking across the room, past Jason and to the door. "I'm going to grab a few drinks. I'll see you both in the morning."

Gunderson slammed the door behind him, and Jason locked it before turning to Miranda, who looked at him and raised her eyebrows.

"He's scary when you piss him off, ain't he?" she asked.

"He's right though," admitted Jason. "After everything you've done to help me, I've done nothing but put you in danger since I got here. I'm sorry."

"Nah, you're all good, sugar," said Miranda with a wink. "If you weren't so pretty, maybe I'd be mad about it."

"Where are the rest of Black Haze?" asked Jason.

"Panther and Henry have gone ahead with Felix and Abigail. You can never have too many eyes on the road, after all. Maiden and Rolston are drinking it up at one of the local dives and Daddy is going to meet them."

Jason walked over to the counter, placed both hands on it and let out a loud sigh. "This town," he said with a laugh. "It's been a wild ride from the day I got here."

Miranda hoisted herself onto the counter and swung her long legs over it. "It's a crazy place, but you get used to it. I find that if you play by the rules then you get by just fine. Best you keep yourself armed though, especially if you're a woman. You'd be amazed at the amount of times I've heard banging on the door at night."

"How do you take care of that?"

"Leaning out the window and putting a hole in someone's foot is usually a good start. It helps to yell that my husband is on his way down there with a shotgun."

"I didn't know you were married," said Jason.

"I'm not," said Miranda, looking into his eyes and giving him a sly grin.

She suddenly placed her hands around Jason's head and pulled him into a kiss. He had no idea what prompted this, but the feeling of her soft lips on his felt good. He started to kiss her back, but only for a moment before he forced himself to pull away.

"What's the matter?" she asked, looking confused.

Jason shook his head. "If there's one thing that's going to make your dad any angrier at me than he is already then it would be kissing his daughter."

"I won't tell him," said Miranda, running a finger up Jason's neck and resting it on his chin. "He won't be back for hours, hun."

"Maybe not, but I can't betray what little faith he has left in me. He may not know, but I would know and it wouldn't sit right with me."

"Suit yourself," said Miranda with a shrug, "but you don't know what you're missing."

"That's what makes it difficult," said Jason with a dry laugh.

Miranda leaned in and gave Jason another small kiss on the lips. "Maybe you can buy me dinner if you ever roll back into town again?"

"I owe you a dozen dinners."

"At least," laughed Miranda, hopping off the counter and walking slowly towards the stairs. "If you're feeling lonely tonight, I'll keep my bedroom door unlocked. Just wake me up if you feel like it, alright?"

She headed upstairs and Jason stood there, feeling a little embarrassed. As beautiful as Miranda was and as wonderful as she had been to him and Abigail over the last few days, he couldn't help but think of Lyra in New Dallas. He wondered what she was doing at this moment and whether the ripples of his chaotic exit were being felt there or had the death of Benedictus already been forgotten by most.

He slumped off up the stairs, exhausted from the events of the day and fell onto his bedroll. He glanced at Miranda's door, but then shut his eyes and drifted off to sleep within a few minutes. That night, he had a completely dreamless sleep.

*

"Good to see you, bud," said Rolston, Black Haze's medic, shaking Jason's hand upon entering the shop.

"Bumpkin," said Maiden with a nod, the brute of a man giving little away with his neutral expression.

"We're going to have a fresh start today, Jason," said Gunderson. "Miranda told me that you spoke to her last night after I left—"

Jason's heart did a backflip into his throat for a moment.

"—and assures me that you've learned your lesson. I like you and don't want there to be bad blood between us, but you're still too new to this world to be able to handle yourself. Not everywhere is as lawful as New Dallas, and I say lawful with a grain of salt even there."

"Understood," said Jason.

"Tell him about Damian," said Miranda, sounding excited.

"Damian?" asked Jason.

"You know that friend I mentioned who was on guard duty?" asked Gunderson.

"The one you said that might not be posted there

again for some time?"

"Well, it turns out that the guard who was meant to take over for the next round of shifts pulled out and Damian has had to fill in for today. It was a lucky coincidence. You couldn't have planned it better if you'd tried."

Maiden and Rolston exchanged sly glances and Miranda tried unsuccessfully to hold back a giggle.

"How lucky for me," said Jason, having a sense that the Black Haze men had interfered somehow. "When do we leave?"

"Now," said Gunderson. "The others have a head start on us and we're going to need to take a different route to reach Highwayland, but we'll get there before too long."

"Why do we need to take a different route?" asked Jason.

"Big Belial is on the prowl," said Rolston, looking deadly serious.

"Big Belial?" asked Jason.

"Erratic toosie," said Maiden.

There were few mutants that Jason feared more than erratics. They were aberrations of aberrations that could act more docile than regular mutants or far more wild. It was an erratic mutant, who Jason's brother Bill had nicknamed Humphrey, that had led the initial siege upon Shackford.

"Indeed," said Gunderson. "He's notorious around these parts for picking off caravaners. Part of what makes him an erratic mutant is that he doesn't like to sit still for too long. He often acts like a rabid dog more than a mutated human. He's occasionally known to flee and show up to trouble someone else another day, but that's only if you're lucky. Fifty different men have tried to kill him, but the tissue around his head is so thick that even headshots don't kill him straight away. You blow it up and it regrows by the next time you see him. A stubborn bastard, he is."

"And best avoided, got it," said Jason.

"Exactly," said Rolston.

"You packed up?" asked Gunderson.

"I can be in about thirty seconds."

"Get it done."

Jason leapt up the stairs, hurriedly stashed his bedroll in his pack and threw on his brown leather jacket. It took a little longer than thirty seconds, but he was back downstairs in no time at all and the three Black Haze members were standing by the door ready to leave.

Miranda walked up to Jason and threw her arms around him. "Sorry for being so forward last night," she whispered in his ear before saying more loudly. "Take care of yourself, hun, alright?"

"Thank you for everything," said Jason and she smiled at him as she let him go. "I mean it. I'd probably be dead twice over if you hadn't given us somewhere to stay."

"Just don't be a stranger if you can clear your bounty," said Miranda.

Jason approached Gunderson. "Ready," he said.

"Got your weapons?" Gunderson asked.

"A pistol and two knives," said Jason.

"What about that revolver of yours?"

"In my pack."

"Get that out too," said Gunderson. "You never know when you'll need a spare."

Jason grabbed his grandfather's gun, Camelot, from his bag and put it in the empty holster on his waist, keeping the pistol by his chest. With a final nod to Miranda, he followed Gunderson outside with Rolston and Maiden sticking close behind him.

"Don't draw any attention to yourself," warned Rolston. "Just keep looking forward and let Gunderson do the talking, alright?"

Jason nodded in agreement, knowing the precarious situation in which he found himself. Each trip outside since he got to Harmony came with its own risks, but having a higher bounty and no VM to disguise himself made him feel that much more conscious of everyone around. He was very glad to have three well-armed friends surrounding him.

The group of four walked to the front gate Jason had entered through. When they arrived, Jason recognised one of the guards as the very same guard Jason had bribed to be let into Harmony in the first place.

"Damian," said Gunderson, giving a nod of greeting to the guard. Jason couldn't believe it was the same man, but he stayed quiet.

"That's who you want taken outside with no questions asked?" asked Damian in astonishment. "You know what happens if we get caught letting Jason Cooper out of Harmony?"

"Good thing you won't get caught," said Gunderson. "You simply scan the three of us through, open the door, then let all four of us walk out of here. Nobody will be asking any questions."

"Son of a..." muttered Damian, shaking his head. "Fine, let's make this quick in case anybody sees. We good, Frankie?"

The other guard silently nodded.

"Good," said Damian.

He took each of the three members of Black Haze to the terminal, scanned the passports on their phones and let them through the gates one by one. Gunderson was scanned last, and he kept Jason close as he walked through and back into the wild. Once everyone was outside, the three Black Haze members lined up behind Jason and moved him forward.

"What are you doing?" asked Jason.

"Covering you in case any wise guy decides to take a shot from a distance," said Gunderson.

"Is that likely?"

"No, but better to look silly than you to be sprawled across the dirt."

"Point taken."

The four kept moving until they were past the ridge that Jason and Sniper had originally approached from and then they allowed themselves to separate and walk more freely. Jason could finally breathe easy, free from Harmony with only mutants to worry about. At least he could trust that *every* mutant would try to kill him and he could prepare accordingly for that.

"To Highwayland," said Rolston enthusiastically.

"Have you been there before?" asked Jason.

"Never even heard of it until Sniper told us about it yesterday. It sounds like a good fortress against mutants, but not so great if raiders show up and blow the support pillars up."

"You try blowing up that much concrete and see how far it gets you," said Gunderson. "That's a lot of resources for a town that may not have that much. You'd destroy half of the good stuff when bringing it down anyway."

"It wasn't a suggestion," shrugged Rolston. "I'm curious to see it anyway. He was saying that one of your buddies from Shackford escaped and made it all the way there. I bet that was a relief."

"Same one that wrote the letter I found in my house," said Jason.

"So I heard," said Rolston, slapping Jason on the back. "I'm happy for you, bud. It's rare someone gets that sort of luck out here, but the kid must have been a fighter."

"He's a lot tougher than he gives himself credit for. I think he's finally starting to realise it."

"West," said Maiden, looking at a compass.

"No sweat," said Gunderson, turning to the left slightly. "Better?"

"Better," confirmed Maiden.

"Could Big Belial have moved West?" asked Jason.

"Could have," said Gunderson, "but we'd have no way of knowing that without meeting him. Sniper or Panther would normally be able to spot him a mile off, but neither of them is here. Even if Felix was here, he'd be without his scope until he's gotten a proper surgeon to take care of it. He's lucky Miranda didn't take his eye out. I love the girl to death, but I wouldn't even let her give me a haircut."

Jason laughed, but Gunderson's silence told him that it wasn't a joke. It wasn't like Gunderson to make many jokes at the best of times, so taking everything he says seriously was the best default position you could take.

The men travelled across the land, not stopping until it was time for lunch. In typical Black Haze fashion, they found a large billboard along the roadside to give them some coverage. Jason volunteered to eat last, climbing up top to keep a lookout until everyone else had finished. He was glad to be outside the walls of Harmony, but the views of the great outdoors of the former state of Texas really put it all into perspective. For a moment, he forgot that he had the looming prospect of venturing out to New Dallas once more where he wasn't so sure he would be welcomed back with open arms even with the favour of King Mercer.

*

"Shit," said Gunderson, looking towards the ridge.

"There's no other way to cross the river?" asked Jason.

"Nope," said Rolston. "Not without taking a twenty-mile detour on foot. This was always going to be a convergence point for us."

"There were more bridges a few years back," said Gunderson, "but they were mysteriously destroyed right around the time raider attacks started to increase. It was just another one of those lucky coincidences."

"Much easier to take out a bridge with explosives than it is an entire highway," remarked Rolston, remembering the conversation two days prior.

The four men stared towards the bridge of concrete and asphalt that stretched across the small chasm.

About fifty feet away from the entrance to the bridge was a large mutant with a head as thick as a tree stump and a barely discernible face from all of the swollen flesh covering it. Its legs were only a foot longer than a regular human's legs, but it was the arms that were its most obvious weapons. Its upper arms were the length of its entire body and its forearms twice as long as that again. It carried itself along with them, swinging forward like a gorilla. Jason was certain that the mutant wouldn't be able to walk without using its arms, its upper body was so grossly disproportionate to its lower half.

"Should we wait until he leaves?" asked Jason.

"We could," said Gunderson.

"Big bounty for Big Belial," said Maiden, holding his rifle up and looking down the barrel.

"That's a hell of a risk to take though, isn't it?" asked Rolston.

"Four thousand silvers ain't nothing to shake your head at," said Gunderson, clearly tempted to take on the devil before him. "If we can get a couple of good shots from here, then we stand a good chance. Split it with the rest of the lads up ahead and we're all walking away with a tidy sum each. We could take a break from the road for a month and still have plenty of dollars left over."

"We've got very little cover," said Jason. "Toosies don't have much trouble scaling walls, never mind ridges."

"Worst case scenario, we jump into the river," said Gunderson. "If we can maneuverer him must right, maybe he'll be the one who drops in the river. Easy target after that if we can keep up with the current."

"You called me reckless before," said Jason sternly. "I think this would be a huge mistake."

"We'll put it to a vote," said Gunderson. "Maiden, what do you think?"

"Kill him," said Maiden without hesitation.

"Jason?"

"Wait until he's gone or take the detour," said Jason.

"Rolston?"

Rolston sighed but didn't answer straight away. He could see how difficult it would be, but the allure of the large bounty was coursing through his mind. "Let's take him out," he said uncertainly.

"This is a mistake," said Jason. "We don't even have a full team here. Do you remember the trouble we had in that town when we left New Dallas? That regular toosie gave us enough of a challenge."

"It was also backed up by lots of wunners," said Maiden.

"If the bounty was one thousand silvers, would you still do it?" asked Jason.

"No," said Gunderson, "but it isn't. It's worth four thousand. This is our bread and butter, Jason, don't forget. We've made it out of more scraps with mutants than you can imagine."

"Ever taken down an erratic stage two?"

"Twice," said Gunderson, holding up two fingers. "One was a particularly aggressive son of a bitch and the other spasmed around like a lunatic. Difficult battles, but I'm still here to tell the tale."

"Fine," said Jason. "I owe you guys in ways I can't repay, so I'll go along with it. At least tell me there's a plan."

Gunderson kneeled and searched through his pack. When he stood up, he was holding four grenades. He passed one to each of the others and then kept the fourth for himself.

"You know how to work these?" Gunderson asked Jason.

"Hold the lever down, pull the pin and throw it," said Jason.

"More or less," said Gunderson. "He doesn't need his legs all that much and his head is well fortified. I think that if we can blow off one of his hands, then that'll cripple him enough that he won't be able to move well. If we can incapacitate him that way, then he should be easy pickings."

"How do you want us to approach, boss?" asked Rolston.

"Some good, old-fashioned bait," said Gunderson, turning to Jason. "Jason, you're the lightest so you can do that. If he gets too close, we'll unload into him."

Jason wasn't too enthused by the plan. "Fine," he said, knowing it wouldn't do much good to argue.

Gunderson talked them through the full plan, what weapons to use at what time, the different angles he wanted each team member to approach from and even tried to pinpoint exactly where he wanted each bullet to strike in case the grenades failed. He was nothing if not good at coming up with ideas on the fly, at least it seemed that way to Jason. Making sure it unfolded as intended was another story.

"Everyone ready?" asked Gunderson.

Jason, Rolston and Maiden all confirmed they were.

"Good, let's move."

They all moved around the edge of the ridge until they found the slope leading down. It was steep, but the jagged rocks and dry grass gave them something to keep their descent more stable. Jason was at the front and he kept the closest eye on Big Belial, who was still swinging around like a demon on drugs. It was almost as though it was playing by the edge of the river chasm. Most mutants would stand still or lie down to conserve energy, but not this one, it seemed as though it was having...fun.

"Men, hang by the rock to your left until Jason's in place," said Gunderson. "Good luck, Bumpkin."

"We've got you covered, bud," said Rolston.

Jason breathed deep and ran straight towards the bridge, not taking his eyes off the swinging erratic. Big Belial was flying around too much to even notice until Jason was almost there already, but when it noticed, it made it known. Big Belial let out a loud screech from somewhere within its swollen face and bounded forward in large leaps towards the young man.

Jason turned and ran alongside the river, as Black

Haze used the distraction to charge forth. Jason glanced over his shoulder and Big Belial was gaining on him. He heard an explosion from nearby and the mutant fell on its face and let out an inhuman roar of pain, but that didn't last for long. Within seconds, Big Belial had pushed itself up and turned towards Maiden, who had thrown the grenade.

Jason winced upon seeing the mutant's back, where the flesh was bloody, raw, and embedded with shrapnel. He began firing at its wrist to hamper its movement, but Big Belial moved too quickly and most of the bullets hit the ground. Jason pulled out his grenade, but Belial was knocked back by a second explosion courtesy of Rolston.

Its head was cocked back and large chunks of flesh were now missing from its face, exposing its mouth to Jason. As with every other mutant, it smiled that hideous smile that chilled him to the bone. He whipped his gun back out and unloaded into its face, while everyone else targeted the arms.

Gunderson ran towards Big Belial and lobbed his grenade onto the mutant's torso, only to be kicked in the chest and thrown twenty feet across the ground as the inhuman beast leapt back to its feet. The grenade detonated and one of the mutant's feet was blown to smithereens, eliciting a screeching wail unlike any other so far. It was a screech so powerful that it made the ground shake.

The erratic spun around wildly, kicking with its remaining leg and lunging with its clawed fists. The men tried to back away, but one large nail pierced Maiden's bulky arm and tore a large chunk of flesh from him. Maiden was knocked to the ground by the mighty strike and Rolston rushed over to pull him out of the way.

Gunderson yelled in fury and unloaded bullet after bullet at the beast, drawing its attention once again. Jason pulled out Camelot from its holster and charged forward. He placed Camelot upon Big Belial's exposed vertebrae and shot four bullets before his foe whipped around, swung its remaining leg and kicked him to the dirt.

Jason crawled backwards over the rough rocks that cut into his hands, but the large mutant leapt over him with that horrific smile and placed its face close to his. He could smell the beast's putrid breath as it opened its mouth to take a bite out of him. Jason shot four more rounds into Big Belial's face that obliterated the mutant's teeth and tore chunks from its cheeks, leaving its mouth a gaping hole that could not close; Jason was out of bullets.

The mutant reared up and reached a hand up high, ready to impale Jason, but he rolled aside in the nick of time as Big Belial's claw pierced the earth. Gunderson and Rolston continued to shoot the abomination while Maiden clutched his arm in agony, but the incredibly stubborn brute was fighting until the last breath, extinguishing the rumours of his tendency to flee. The monster looked into Jason's eyes with its own clouded eyes that were barely visible underneath the drooping flesh that obscured them. Jason knew that this moment would be his last. He was out of options, unless...

Jason holstered Camelot with one hand and hurriedly grabbed the grenade with the other. He pulled the pin, shoved his hand through Belial's ravaged cheek and released the lever. He pulled his hand free and tried to scramble away, but the mutant swung its remaining leg forward and kicked Jason with great force, sending him soaring across the chasm. The last thing he heard before he hit the water was Gunderson calling his name followed by a fleshy explosion as his grenade detonated.

Chapter 13:
Mercer's Mercy

26th May 2116: I met a man on the road today. He was carrying an old guitar, a hefty shotgun, and enough shells to fell a stage three. He said his name was Dawes and didn't give me much more than that. We chatted for a while before I asked him if he knew how to play that guitar of his. He said it was the one thing that kept him sane out here by himself and then played me a few old tunes. Magic. That's the only way I can describe it. There's just something about music that can make all your problems slip away, even if it's just a stranger playing a six-string while sitting on a rock.

*

The Mercer Guard marched forward with their rifles raised, each of them in service to the king who walked amongst them. The midday sun was overhead, bypassing the tallest of tall buildings and beating down upon them all. They walked through the streets of Outer Dallas towards only carnage, ever fearful of what else could be lurking around the corner.

King Mercer ordered them to stop and they broke ranks, making space for the king. He strode past his men while dressed in the best nano cloth that money could buy while sturdy combat armour was fastened over the top for good measure. His rifle was draped over his back, having no need to hold it himself, with two dozen armed and ready men around him.

He surveyed the silent battlefield before him, where one of his most dutiful patrol units lay dead. Amongst his dozen men were the twisted remains of degenerates, albeit there were only four of them. They were more deadly than he had feared and far more durable.

"Sire?" uttered Troy, one of his advisors.

"As expected," said King Mercer.

"Revenants?"

"Revenants," said the king.

He kicked one of the degenerates over, his metal face. The deformed creature had augmented his body with so many cybernetics that it was barely recognisable anymore. Revenants were the most dreaded of the degenerates; they had turned themselves into lethal killing machines at the cost of their very souls.

It was no easy task to fit a degenerate with cybernetics, their biology so warped by the mutations that made them who they were. Devourer of mutant flesh or child of those who had done so, it did not matter. They were no longer fit to be classed as humans, but this...this was beyond even that.

"We will bury our men here and see to it that their belongings are returned to their families," the king told his men. "As for these steel vermin, take whatever they've got and leave what's left of their flesh to rot."

Just then, a degenerate arrived, surrounded by four more of Mercer's men. "You sent for me?" he grunted at Mercer.

"Claude," said Mercer calmly, "you assured me that you have your people in line."

Claude walked up to the revenants on the ground and examined each of their faces. "These are not my men. I do not accept revenants into the fold."

"Is that so?" asked Mercer.

"It *is* so," replied Claude. "My people do not indulge in cybernetics, as per the agreement we have had for years."

"Then perhaps you can tell me whose men these are?"

"I don't know. I've never seen them before in my life. I'll be sure to spread the word amongst my own to be on the lookout for any revenants or revenant sympathisers."

"Do not toy with me, Claude!" yelled Mercer.

"Sire!" exclaimed Claude, taken aback. "I have been nothing but loyal to you and New Dallas. Please, you must believe me, King Mercer."

"It is not about belief! A dozen of my men are dead, their families now without sons, husbands, fathers, brothers, and the best thing you can say is that you'll ask around?"

"I don't know what more I can do."

"You can damn well find out whose men these are if, as you say, they are not your own. It should not be hard."

"Yes, Sire," said Claude, kneeling. "As you wish, Sire."

"Get out of my sight," spat King Mercer as Claude's escorts led him away.

King Mercer stood there silently, looking at the bodies surrounding him. Ever since the death of Benedictus, things had gotten evermore chaotic in New Dallas and it was getting to him. More than once, he had wondered if he should have spared his corrupt advisors just to keep the peace, but he always came back to the same conclusion that the hard times stemming from that brutal execution were the trial he must face to bring back peace and safety to his beloved city.

"My liege," said Troy, the only one brave enough to approach the furious king.

"Do you believe him, Troy?" asked Mercer. "Be

honest."

Troy paused for a moment before answering. "No, sire. I don't believe him."

"Then we are in agreement. Ever since that rat took over from McCoy, he's been trying to undermine me and take over the Admah district. I wouldn't be surprised if he threw McCoy to the mutants himself."

"He answered to Fence before..."

"Before I put a hole in Fence's head? Yes. It is all the more reason to not trust Claude."

"Sire, if I may ask a question."

"Speak."

"Why do you permit the degenerates to live in New Dallas? I have always wondered but not dared to ask."

King Mercer gave a dry laugh. "We should hurry up and deal with this mess, then we can head back behind the walls before mutants show up. I suspect they'll be getting hungry and the last thing we want is a stage two coming down on us. We also need to make sure we let all of our patrolmen know that there are likely still revenants amongst the ruins."

"Yes, King Mercer," said Troy, turning to the men. "You heard the king, let's get to work."

*

"Got him, Pa!" exclaimed Daniel in excitement as the smell of gunpowder filled his nostrils.

"Very good, Daniel," said King Mercer, patting his eldest son on the shoulder.

The boy was only fourteen, but he was already a better marksman than some of the initiates in the Mercer Guard. King Mercer raised his rifle at the mutant chained up between two stone pillars fifty feet away and took aim at the writhing creature.

"Left leg," muttered Mercer as he pulled the trigger.

With a bang and a squelch, the mutant's knee

exploded and it stumbled forward. It pulled itself up by the chains onto its remaining leg and tried to hop towards the king and his son, but it continually lost balance and fell over.

"Why aren't you on the front lines?" asked Daniel, always amazed at his father's remarkable accuracy.

"Because I've got very important business within the city that only I can manage, son."

"Why can't your advisors do that?"

"My advisors are good men, Daniel, but sometimes you have to give the tough orders yourself. It's hard to explain it to you, but one day you will understand."

"You can't just tell me now?"

"You think you're ready to see and hear about hard choices, do you?"

Daniel nodded. "Yes," he said confidently.

"Alright," said his father, "I'll indulge you. Let's say you discover that one of your best friends has been leaking information to spies from the Star Republic, actively undermining you. What would you do to that friend?"

"Am I certain it was him?"

"Yes."

"I would arrest him."

"Alright, he's locked up in a cell, but he wasn't working alone. The network of spies is much larger than you realise and you don't have the resources to declare war on the Star Republic. What next?"

Daniel looked confused. "I thought it was going to be a question about mutants."

"The guns can deal with the mutants," said Mercer, "but a good leader is more than a gun."

Suddenly, Captain Crusoe burst through the door and strode into the courtyard. "Sire, there's an emergency in Admah."

King Mercer sighed. "The Street Cleaners can't deal with it? That's what they're paid for."

"Yes, normally they would, but they reported back to me and I believe you will want to see to this one personally."

"Very well," said Mercer before turning to his son. "Daniel, grab your body armour and a helmet. You think you're ready for the hard choices? Let's see."

"Yes, Pa," said the boy, running off to fetch his things.

Mercer turned towards the mutant who had given up moving and hung limply on the chains. He raised his rifle and shot it through the neck. Its head flopped down and blood gushed from its wound, filling in the gaps on the stone tiles that made up the courtyard floor.

"What's the situation then, Crusoe?" asked the king.

Captain Crusoe looked gaunt as he explained what had happened. As the king listened, he felt sick to his stomach and immediately knew what had to be done, loathe as he was to do it.

*

King Mercer, Prince Daniel and a squad of six men made their way through Admah with the young prince sticking close to his father's sides. The citizens of the most loathsome district of town stared and murmured as the king marched down the street. It was unusual for the king to wander through the city and even more unusual for him to be in Admah.

As King Mercer approached a pair of Street Cleaners holding a degenerate at gunpoint, a crowd gathered round out of curiosity.

"Good day, King Mercer," said the degenerate pleasantly. "I hope it's been as wonderful for you as it has for me."

"Is this sorry son of a bitch the culprit?" asked the king, nodding his head towards the degenerate who bore a disgusting, almost mutant-like, smile. Mercer's cheek started to twitch upon looking at the deformed man.

"This is him, Sire," said one of the Street Cleaners.

"And you're certain of his crimes?"

"Certain. His victims have all identified him and he laughed when we confronted him. He hasn't said a word until you showed up, King Mercer."

"You," Mercer barked at the degenerate, "state your name."

"Name's Gloom," said the degenerate with a twisted smirk.

"Wipe that stupid smile off your face, you worm," said the king angrily, prompting only laughter from the degenerate.

Mercer grabbed his rifle and thumped the handle of it into Gloom's stomach, winding him and bringing him to his knees as he coughed and gasped for air. "Is it still funny, you cretin?" demanded the king as Daniel leapt back in shock. His father was firm with him, but he had never seen him attack another human.

The crowd were all murmuring, asking each other what the man was to have done to deserve the king himself marching down here. Mercer decided to indulge them, for this degenerate needed to be made an example of.

"My dear citizens," he said to the crowd. "Let it be known that King Mercer is a fair and just king, even in the trying times that we all face together. What would you say about a man who claimed to be a humble chef and sold food to his patrons, but spat in it?"

"Disgustin', King Mercer," said one of the men in the crowd.

"Disgusting indeed. Now what would you say if the food he sold was poisoned?"

"Try him for his crimes!" yelled a woman.

"Hang'em," came another man's voice.

King Mercer paced back and forth silently for a moment. "Now what would you say if I told you that this man," he pointed to Gloom, who was smiling once more, "had been feeding people mutant flesh under the guise of it being beef?"

The crowd gasped in horror. Even the handful of degenerates among them looked disgusted by what the king had just claimed. Surely, nobody would be so evil as to do such a thing?

"That's right, dear citizens," said King Mercer. "Gloom here has decided that regular folks like you are just too damn normal. He would rather you be like him! Eleven of your fellow citizens have been fed mutant flesh, each one of them starting to succumb to the same affliction that people like him have no choice but to bear. They're degenerating as we speak, never to be normal again."

King Mercer glanced at Daniel whose face was a sickly green. The young prince already regretted coming with his father to this place, but it was too late. There was no unhearing what he had heard and there was no running away. The king felt an enormous amount of pity for his son, but this lesson would most certainly show him that being a king is not easy; it is suffering.

"You," said Mercer to one of his men, "bring Claude to me and make sure he rounds up a few of his most loyal men. He's never far in this place so it should not take long."

"Yes, King Mercer," said the soldier with a salute before marching off.

"Gloom," said King Mercer, squatting down beside the smirking degenerate, "I'm going to make you wish that you were never born."

Gloom spat in the king's face, shocking the crowd further. The guards behind the degenerate were on the verge of pulling the trigger, but the king held up a hand to stop them.

"No," he said, "we are not to be so easily baited."

Shortly afterwards the guard returned with Claude and a handful of other degenerates. He looked shocked to see Gloom being held captive. "What's the meaning of this?" he asked the king.

"Do you want to tell him what you did or should I?" asked King Mercer.

Gloom started giggling. "Fed a few folks some mutie flesh, boss."

Claude closed his eyes and a look of despair formed upon his ugly face. "King Mercer...I don't know what to say."

"Everyone present here is to stay and witness this," the king called out, looking across the faces of the surrounding crowd. "Lessons are going to be learned today because, clearly, disobedience is running rife in this city. The laws of the land are to be upheld and respected. Basic morals and decency are to be forced in those who they do not come naturally to."

King Mercer walked up to Gloom and started beating the degenerate with his bare fists. At first, Gloom's laughter continued, but it was not long before the laughter subsided. The degenerate's blood was oozing down his face and the cheers of the crowd were fuzzy in his ears as he could only focus on the pain. King Mercer beat him until he started to plead for the beating to stop.

"I'm...sorry," he muttered in desperation as King Mercer once again drew back his now blood-soaked fist. King Mercer froze in place.

"You're what?" he asked.

"I'm sorry," repeated Gloom, now curled into a ball on the ground. "Please...no more."

Mercer turned to the crowd. "We do not hurt people because we want to see them suffer, we hurt them because we want to prevent the suffering of others."

The crowd all murmured in agreement.

"Claude!" called the king.

"Yes, King Mercer?" asked Claude, his voice trembling.

"I asked you to keep your men in line, did I not?"

"Sire, this man is—"

"Is he a Revenant?"

Claude was silent.

"I asked you a question, Claude."

"No," muttered Claude.

"Louder," said the king. "The people need to hear

this."

"No, he is not a revenant," said Claude, dropping to his knees. "He is one of my men. I'm sorry, sire. I'm so sorry."

"Sorry is not good enough, my friend. It is not good enough for him and it is not good enough for you. He's condemned eleven people to a fate worse than death. He is making them just like *you*. My compassion and mercy only go so far and the well has run pretty damn dry, Claude."

Mercer pulled Claude to his feet. "Beat him," he said, pointing at Gloom who lay limp on the ground, his eyes rolling around in his head.

"I...I can't," stammered Claude, looking utterly petrified.

Mercer drew a pistol from the holster on his waist and shot Claude in the knee. The degenerate screamed in agony as his leg buckled underneath him. Claude's men began to move in, but the Mercer Guard all raised their weapons and they started to back off.

"You're his most loyal men," said King Mercer, "it is natural that you wish to defend him. After all, he has done so much for you. But you see, you're all here for a reason. I need to see where your loyalties truly lie. Is it with me and the people of New Dallas or is it with Claude?"

"You, sire," said one of Claude's men without hesitancy.

"Very good," said Mercer with a smile. "What is your name?"

"Me?" asked the degenerate. "The name's Maldonaldo, my liege."

"Maldonaldo," said the king, "I hereby elect you the new overlord of the degenerates, effective immediately. Your first order of duty is to put a bullet in Claude's skull."

King Mercer tossed his gun to the degenerate, who nearly fumbled it. He held the gun shakily as Claude looked up at him, shaking his head. Maldonaldo muttered a quiet apology to Claude as he pulled the trigger, ending the disgraced man's life. King Mercer held out his hand and Maldonaldo passed the gun back over.

"Daniel," said the king, approaching his son who looked like he was on the verge of fainting. "The degenerates are a broken people who can never be like us, but they are still humans in soul. We must pray for these broken people because no one can fix them and *we* are not monsters. Do you understand?"

Daniel shook his head, traumatised by what was unfolding before him. Mercer put the pistol in Daniel's hand and pointed at Gloom.

"I can't do it, Pa," said the boy weakly.

"Son, just pretend it's one of the mutants we use for target practice, alright?"

Daniel nodded and tepidly stepped forward, no longer trusting his aim even at close range. Tears were starting to run down the boy's face as King Mercer ordered the Street Cleaners to pick up Gloom and hold him steady. His vision was blurry, but the degenerate could see the boy approaching. He started to shake his head.

"No," he muttered. "Please, have mercy on me. You're a good kid, right? I'm sorry. I didn't mean to do it. I...I don't know why I did it. I'm sick, you see? There's something wrong with me. I need a doctor or...or something. Come on, please. You gotta believe me."

Daniel looked at Gloom dead in the eyes as he pointed the gun at him. The desperation was real, but there was not even a glint of sincerity in the apology. Daniel unwittingly closed his own eyes and breathed deep. He held that breath for a moment, and then pressed his finger on the trigger. With a bang, Gloom's life came to an end and Daniel heard the thud of his body as the Street Cleaners released their grip on the dead degenerate. He finally dared to open his eyes once more.

The crowd were unfazed by what Daniel had been

made to do, for the criminal was dead. They whooped and cheered. They praised King Mercer and they praised Prince Daniel, the future monarch of New Dallas. One who would do what had to be done. Daniel himself felt empty inside. He knew now that he was not ready and he was foolish for thinking that he was less than an hour earlier.

King Mercer approached the boy and placed his hands on his shoulders. "I'm proud of you, son," he said. "That was not easy and you stepped up to the plate. One day this will all be yours and you must do what's necessary to keep it in order, even if that means getting your hands dirty."

The king ordered one of the guards to take the boy back to his mother, the queen. She would no doubt be very angry with her husband, but he would deal with that hurdle later.

"Those that Gloom condemned," Mercer said to the degenerates, "are to be compensated. Two hundred ounces of silver a head and I will match that personally. They are not deserving of their fates and are to be well taken care of in your community or I will see to it that every last one of you is thrown out of my city. Are we clear?"

"Yes, King Mercer," they said.

"Maldonaldo."

"Yes, sire?"

"Claude did not keep your people in line. Whether that was because he could not do it or he did not want to do it is no longer relevant. I believe I have shown you the new way I plan to operate moving forward. You see what happens when I am crossed."

"I see, sire."

"It is not going to happen again, is it?"

"No, sire, it most certainly is not. I give you my personal assurance of that."

"Good," said King Mercer. "You no doubt know about the revenants on the outskirts of town. Am I correct?"

"Yes, sire."

"You're going to find out who they are and what they're doing this close to my city."

Chapter 14:
Survival

30th May 2116: Back again to this city. I have to say that it's lost a little something since Mercer decided to go scorched earth on criminals. It seemed more orderly before, less tense. I think this is all just temporary. Perhaps once I find Carlisle, I'll be giving Mercer a hand and getting things back on the right track. Stranger things have happened.

*

"You've got to stop swimming in rivers, J," came Bill's voice, followed by his familiar laugh. It was the same laugh that always came after he told a bad or inappropriate joke. "You're just no good at it. You always end up getting washed up along some lost bank."

"What are you doing here?" Jason mumbled without opening his eyes.

"Just checking in on you, little brother. Better get a move on."

Jason was aching all over and could feel that his clothes were soaking wet. His head...had he hit his head? No, he had been knocked off the chasm by the mutant and into the river below. The realisation of whose voice he heard suddenly hit him. He opened his eyes and jolted up, looking for his brother. There was nobody there. Only the full moon watching over him from above. Had he been dreaming or was it God's messenger reaching out to him? Whatever it was, he was grateful to be alive.

"Black Haze," he said quietly while clutching his side and recalling what had happened only a few hours ago.

Jason looked at the river which was flowing before him. He couldn't have floated that far from where he and Black Haze had been fighting Big Belial, surely? The last thing he remembered was an explosion as he fell. There were some faint flashes of him struggling in the water, desperately trying to reach a bank, but had that been real? He wasn't so sure.

Jason turned around and looked at the rock face before him. It was steep, but there were enough grooves and alcoves that he could pull himself up the twenty feet he needed to get out of this small, hidden section of the chasm.

He inhaled deeply and held his breath to try and dull the pain in his side. He squatted down and leapt as high as he could, grabbing onto a jagged rock at the apex of his jump. He pulled himself upwards, the rock cutting into his hand, but he knew he couldn't let go. The more painful his hand was, the harder this would be. He swung his other hand up and grasped onto a thin ledge, then placed his foot in a groove. Little by little, he edged his way up, taking every care not to lose his footing. When Jason's breath ran out and he was forced to breathe normally, the pain returned in full force and he almost lost his grip, but he knew he had to get to Highwayland so Abigail knew he was okay. He knew he had to get back to New Dallas and find Lindsay.

With a final swing of body, Jason threw himself up and over the ledge, onto the sparse grass that covered the dusty soil. He stared at the sky for a moment, admiring the peace and beauty of the moon and stars above him. They didn't care about mutants; they had no attachments to the world. All they had to do was float there in nothingness without worry, without fear, but without anything to love.

"Follow the river," said Jason, climbing to his feet. "I hope there are no more mutants along the way."

His guns. Jason reached down and found that his pistol was missing, but Camelot was still firmly holstered. It would have been lucky, had he any bullets left for it. He reached into his boot and pulled out a knife, the only useful weapon he had left outside of the environment itself.

Jason started to walk alongside the chasm, following the river upstream. He kept an eye out for the taller ridge where he and Black Haze had watched Big Belial. He walked and he walked, the chilly night air hitting the soaked young man. Once he found his friends, he would start a fire and dry himself off, but starting one now with mutants roaming would only ensure that nobody ever saw him again.

An hour later, the ridge came into view. He had expected it much sooner, but he must have drifted further than he first expected. Suddenly, a small memory flashed into Jason's mind of him holding onto a branch while trying to keep himself from being swept along by the river's current, but it faded away not long after.

"Dear God," said Jason quietly, making the sign of the cross upon his body.

Before him was a mess of gore, but within it was the recognisable sight of two enormously long arms. The body they were once attached to was in tatters and its head and legs had been completely destroyed. It was the remains of Big Belial, dead and desecrated. Jason walked up to the beast and stared at it in disbelief. Was it his grenade that finished the job? It must have been for the mutant's head to be so thoroughly pulverised.

"His hand," said Jason quietly to himself while looking down at the monstrosity's arm.

One of the beast's arms had no claw remaining. The edge of the flesh was jagged, and the bone had been snapped. It appeared to have been sawn off, perhaps by Black Haze, who was nowhere to be found. Maiden was injured, but it didn't appear to be life-threatening. Had they been forced to move onto Highwayland or had they turned around and gone back to Harmony? It was certainly closer and if they had Big Belial's hand, they could cash in their bounty.

They wouldn't have left him behind, would they? No, they had to have looked for Jason and not found him. They were good men; they were loyal men. Jason had every faith that after all they'd done to help him, they wouldn't have left him here unless they believed him dead or Maiden's injuries were greater than he first believed.

Jason looked to the bridge and then to the east. He couldn't risk returning to Harmony, so he would have to brave the journey to Highwayland alone. It was a strange prospect to him, being out in the wilderness by himself. He had never been alone in it for this long before with Sniper always around to watch his back. Even when he first fled from Shackford, he was with Cyrus and Kyle at first.

The young man walked over to the bridge and put a foot on the asphalt. He paused and tried to recall the map he had seen Rolston using. From his current position, Highwayland would be to the northwest. No more than six days away on foot. Jason had enough supplies in his bag to last double that if he got stuck, but it was a matter of not getting killed along the way that concerned him. For now, he would have to settle for finding shelter and drying off until morning. Travelling at night was a recipe for disaster.

Jason crossed the bridge, but halfway along he stopped. There was a skeleton here, its flesh completely stripped away and tatters of clothes on the ground. Perhaps this was why Big Belial was swinging around so excitedly before, he had just had a good feed courtesy of this unfortunate soul. Jason looked around and found a torn backpack further along the bridge, its contents strewn across the ground.

"Ammo," he said, pleased to find a small half-full box of 9mm cartridges.

He tried to place them inside his Camelot in the desperate hope they would fit, but he wasn't surprised to find they did not. They would have fit his pistol, wherever that was, but not much good to him here and now. Unfortunately, the skeleton didn't appear to have a gun either. Perhaps it was at the bottom of the river and that was why the traveller had such a hard time against Big Belial.

Jason continued to the other side of the bridge, keeping a watchful eye on what was ahead. Illuminated in the moonlight was the grass from the prairie. It stretched towards the hills that hid behind them, venturing off into the unknown land. There was not a building in sight, nor any sign of shelter. All Jason could do was to keep walking and watching.

He walked and he walked, through the grass and through the night. With each passing minute, the lack of mutants made him that much more expectant of one to stand up from within the grass and flash a smile in his direction. As he walked, the grass started to thin back to dusty soil. He was freezing, he would surely develop hypothermia if he had to continue for much longer.

At last, somewhere to rest as the faint glow of the sunrise appeared on the horizon. There was a lone house that was blown to smithereens by who knows what, but a couple dozen feet from it was an old barn. It had seen better days, but the wooden frame was still in place and the tin roof still covered just enough of the barn to be a shelter.

Jason shivered as he approached the house. He peered around and everything was either destroyed by whatever explosion had occurred here or the elements beating down upon them for many, many years.

There was nothing in the ruins that Jason could use, but something did catch his eye. It was an old ceramic mug underneath the splintered kitchen table that read 'World's Best Dad,' a sentiment that he found quite heartwarming.

The barn was filled with the rusted remains of an old tractor, a vehicle Jason recognised from a pre-collapse book in Shackford. The other tools and contraptions looked much more usable, from shovels to pitchforks and even a brush that he was sure he could have put back together with enough tape or even a couple of small bits of wood for reinforcement.

That was the way of life back in Shackford. If a passing trader had something they considered junk, the people would buy it and repair it however they could. If it was not built to last, they could make it last with just a little bit of wood and a little bit of metal to nail or screw it in place.

Jason closed the one remaining barn door and took an old hatchet to the broken door that lay on the concrete floor. All he needed was just enough of it and he would find a way to start a fire. He knew that he would survive the journey to Highwayland, no matter what it took.

*

They were gaining on him, all three of them. He needed to find somewhere to hide or he was done for. The three stage ones barrelled along, not to avenge their two fallen brethren, but solely to feed on Jason. There were precious few animals here and a diet of plants was not enough for a mutant to grow. That was all they wanted, to feed and to grow. They could never be satiated; they must keep feeding and growing.

Jason ran up the road towards the shack that sat atop a small hill. His lungs were burning and his legs were heavy, but he could not let that stop him. To stop was to die. He didn't need to glance over his shoulder to know where the smiling demons were, they were making no effort to be silent.

Vaulting over the fence, Jason saw a small collection of makeshift graves. There, a shovel. Something he could use. He ran to it and picked it up then made for the shack where he hoped to funnel his foes through the doorway. He sprinted ahead, but they were already too close, leaving him no option but to fight. He held the shovel high and swung, bringing it around in a horizontal arc.

One of the mutants dropped to the ground as the shovel firmly lodged itself in the beast's skull. Jason released the shovel and drew his knife while walking backwards, narrowly avoiding the claw of one of the long-armed freaks. He lunged forward and jammed the knife into its eye socket, then shoved it away from him. Before he had the chance to pull his knife free, he was knocked to the ground by the third mutant.

The mutant bore down on him and he rolled aside as it leapt, its claw scratching the dirt instead of his flesh. The mutant cocked its head and looked at Jason, the constant smile on its face forever unbroken. The human soul trapped within could have been in the most intense pain imaginable, but that smile would still be there. Even when they yelled and screamed, they kept smiling.

Jason tried to scramble away but felt sharp nails digging into his leg. In a moment of desperation, he grabbed a loose rock, bringing the rounded stone down upon the mutant's skull. It grabbed Jason's shoulder, sinking its nails into him. He yelled and smashed it in the head once more. He pummelled the beast with the rock over and over again, until its skull caved in. Even as it fell in a heap, he continued his assault. Once there was barely a remnant of the head, he threw the rock aside and let out a groan as he dropped to his knees. He had done it. He had survived.

He had set out from the barn six days prior and had

a few close calls with mutants, but this was the worst of them. After killing two of the freaks at an old gas station a little way down the road, three more had reared their ugly heads from inside the long-ransacked diner that sat at the far side of the yard. He thought he could take one of them, but upon seeing three together, he knew he had to run.

He felt truly vulnerable for the first time in a long time. In Harmony, the bustling streets and the safe haven of Miranda's store gave him opportunities to hide. Travelling across Texas, he always had Sniper and Achilles to watch his back. Even in New Dallas, he knew that he was protected given that he had the favour of Benedictus for most of his time there. Nobody dared harm Benedictus's property without his say so. There was just something different about being out here in the wilderness alone. It was so open, yet so stifling.

Jason had expected to have stumbled across the road to Highwayland by now, but here he was, still roaming the Texan countryside in search of his destination. He had to be close, but he had no way of knowing just how close he was. He wasn't even sure if he would recognise it on a map, but at the very least a map would have shown him where the old highways were.

Once he had caught his breath, Jason walked over to the other dead mutants and retrieved his knife and the shovel. The latter was a better weapon than his fists, so it was coming along until he found something he could shoot with or bullets for his revolver. He had been kicking himself for days for not thinking to bring the barn tools with him.

Jason approached the shack, but from around the corner, he could see what lay on the other side of the hill and that captivated him much more than the shack. It was a small town if it was even big enough to be called that.

It was unwalled and there was nobody in sight, so it mustn't be lived in. There was an old motel with half its sign missing, a schoolyard with the swings outside still standing, broken houses and shacks aplenty and even an old motorhome sitting next to what appeared to be a bar. The large sign that read Langly Saloon and featured the faded image of a tankard was visible even from here, it was as though it was welcoming everyone to come and have a drink. It was the least dangerous-looking remnant of past civilisation that Jason had seen in days, so he knew he had to see what it held for him. He hoped that he would not come to regret that decision, but roaming without direction wasn't doing him any good.

Jason walked down the hill and along the crumbling old road with its many cracks and holes. He headed straight for the school first, hoping that perhaps there would be a map or an atlas there. This town looked old-fashioned enough that they may have been one of the lucky few places in the Old World that had still used paper and books over screens. It was not lost on him that the buildings were still made of bricks instead of glass panels unlike what could be seen throughout Dallas, New and Outer.

The school itself wasn't very large, likely an elementary school of no more than three or four classrooms. Despite that, it seemed pleasant; it seemed quaint. It reminded him of the school in Shackford that was home to no more than twenty kids at a time, often their ages varying heavily. The children would spend three days a week in school and work around the town the rest of the time. When it was time to graduate at the age of thirteen, it was then then that they took up a full-time job. Jason was relegated to guard duty, but he would spend the rest of his hours helping his family grow vegetables in their small garden.

He pushed open the squeaky, rusty gate and walked towards the nearest window. It was difficult to see inside and even wiping his sleeve on the window just moved the grime around rather than removed it. He kept the shovel held firmly in one hand and approached the door. He pushed it open, listening for any sign of life. Human or mutant, it didn't matter. He could trust nothing and no one out here.

Grimy as the windows were, there was enough light let in that Jason could see clearly. The first thing that caught his eye in the small corridor was a large noticeboard filled with children's drawings. There was everything from drawings of their families to drawings of the town. One child had even drawn an alien descending upon the town that Jason couldn't help but laugh at for its outlandishness.

"Roy," whispered Jason, reading the child's signature. "Same name as Gramps's friend, but he was about thirty when the Old World fell. It couldn't be him then."

Jason walked from room to room, checking to make sure there were no mutants before beginning his search. He was relieved to find not a single monster nor a single soul. The classrooms were filled with computer screens, many of which had been smashed. It didn't fill Jason with confidence as he looked around. Even the teachers' desks were fixed with screens and most of the paper was of such low quality that it fell apart upon picking it up. It looked as though the children's drawings were as much as he would be able to find.

"What do we have here then?" Jason asked, tugging haphazardly on a locked door. He paused, almost expecting to hear a mutant growl from behind, but it was silent.

He smashed the handle with the shovel and twisted the mechanism inside, releasing the lock. He supposed it wasn't breaking and entering if there was no owner to speak of. He pushed the door open and his eyes widened upon seeing what awaited him inside. There were books and lots of them. Maybe as many as three hundred.

Jason poured through the shelves, seeing everything from comics telling wild tales of barbarians to encyclopaedias about everything under the sun. There was even a book featuring maps of Texas. He picked it up and flicked through the pages. This was what he needed. He walked back outside the school and into the sunlight, eager to find somewhere he could sit and rest for a while. Now he could start trying to work out where he was to find where he needed to go.

Jason headed for the saloon, walking past the motorhome. Right as he reached for the door, he heard footsteps coming from inside. Immediately, he ran to the motorhome and dropped to the ground, rolling underneath it. He pulled the shovel in with him, right as the door to the saloon opened.

"Waste of damn time," came a gruff voice. "Y'all said there'd be something here for us and there's nothing. Absolutely nothing."

Jason spotted three pairs of feet walking outside and coming to a stop a couple of yards from the saloon door.

"Shut it, Marcel," came another man's voice. "We do the best with what we got, don't we? How could Mitchell and I possibly know this place was looted to hell and back?"

"Victor's right, Marcel," came what must have been Mitchell's voice. "This place is out of the way enough we thought it was a sure thing. It just so happens we were wrong."

"And now we're out supplies from getting here," said Marcel angrily.

"At least we found that old Cash record," said Victor, trying to calm Marcel down.

"And it's not even one of his best!" yelled Marcel. "You could probably flip that for a couple of silvers to some collector or a bar with a working jukebox, but we're still down a lot of money getting out here. Don't try and hide it."

"Could be some tech up at that school there," said Victor, pointing towards the schoolhouse Jason had just come from. "Worth a shot, ain't it?"

"Suit yourselves," said Marcel, "I'm going back inside and helping myself to that last half bottle of whiskey. It's the least you pair owe me for dragging me out all this way."

Jason watched as Victor and Mitchell's feet disappeared, while the saloon door slammed shut. He was going to wait just long enough for the two scavengers to get out of sight before making a run for it. They may not have been bad men, but he wasn't going to take any chances, especially when they were down on their luck.

Once he was confident, the coast was clear he started to edge out from underneath the motorhome, only to retreat back in quickly. Marcel had brought a chair outside and slammed it down roughly in front of the saloon. He sat down with a bottle of whiskey in one hand and his rifle draped across his knee while staring out into the wild.

Jason had no guarantees that he could get away unscathed. Even his footsteps could alert Marcel to his presence and the young man's silhouette on the horizon could be target practice for the angry scavenger and his rifle.

Jason glanced at the shovel. It would be that easy. With Marcel's backup gone, all Jason would have to do is get close enough to him with the shovel or his knife and he would have immediate safe passage out of the small town. He would be gone before Victor and Mitchell returned and they wouldn't have the faintest idea of where he ran.

No. No, he could not even consider that. It was murder. For all he knew, Marcel could be an innocent man whose biggest sin was a bad temper. It was wrong to have even thought about it and Jason began berating himself for it.

"It's wrong," he mouthed silently to himself. "He lives. It's wrong. He lives. I only kill to defend. Thou shalt not murder. I only kill to defend. Thy shalt not murder."

Jason quietly crawler out from underneath the motorhome with his shovel in hand. He looked around the corner and towards the schoolhouse. There was no sign of Victor and Mitchell. He took his chance and slowly edged around the back of the saloon and ran in the opposite direction until he was safely out of town. No men chased him down and no gunfire followed him. He ran across the grasslands until he found a small collection of trees where he sat down and pulled open the book of maps.

He stared at it but took nothing in. He had been tempted to commit an unprovoked killing. A murder. It was swelteringly hot outside, but he felt a chill all the way to his bones. How easy it would have been to give into darkness, how easy it would have been to taint his soul with such a foul act. To even have considered it when escaping was just as easy for him. He hated what this world was doing to him. He hated the thoughts that had crept into his head all because of desperation. He tossed the book aside got on his knees, bowing his head low. He prayed for salvation and the strength to resist the call of such heinous sins.

Once his prayer was over, he sat with his head in his hands for a while, thinking. He thought about everything that had happened to him since he left Shackford, as he had done many times over. He thought about his first kill, a degenerate named Rubin who had tried to murder him with his gang of thugs. He had every justification for it, but it didn't stop the hollow feeling in his chest anytime he thought about shooting Rubin. Taking another man's life, no matter how evil they may be, was not something to be taken lightly.

"Only when they deserve it," Jason's voice croaked out as he kneeled under the tree. "Only when they deserve it."

*

The sun was setting as Jason walked under the highway with his shovel in one hand and the book of maps in the other. He had spent almost an entire day trying to work out where the abandoned town was and another day trying to make his way to the nearest highway, struggling to get the directions just right, but he had found it. Now he just needed to be sure he was following it in the right direction and taking the right forks.

He found walking under the highway refreshing thanks to the shadows it cast. It had been nearly two weeks on the road and he was tired; without company, it was even more exhausting. Even a mostly silent companion like Achilles would have helped. It was easy to understand how people could go crazy out here when they were in fear for their lives at all times and they hadn't another soul to talk to.

The highway up ahead looked to be broken with a large pile of rubble beneath the drop off. It lay in a colossal heap on the ground. Jason looked up at the long gap above him that kept the two parts of the road separate. If one was to fall from there, it would be the end of them.

"Unless they shot themselves up with Livelong," he joked to himself.

He looked up again, squinting. Surely not? He ran out from underneath the highway and looked up to see a few shacks just over the edge. Was this it? Was this Highwayland? He had been here before. This *was* where Camlorn had jumped from those many weeks ago. He ran along, forgetting his tiredness and headed towards the pillar where the intercom was hooked up. As he pressed the button, he looked up at the hole where people came and went from.

"Hello?" asked Jason, not waiting for anybody else to speak first.

"Who's there?" came a fuzzy voice through the speaker.

"My name's Jason Cooper. I need to talk to Kyle. Is he there?"

Chapter 15:
Welcome Back

1st June 2116: Still no sign of him. I've searched high and low, asked everyone that will still speak to me and none of them know where the Rat King is. If he's not here and he's not in Harmony, then where could he be? My best guess is that he stopped in another settlement along the way, maybe to offer jobs to some of the stronger men and more attractive women. It'd be strange for him to do that personally, but I don't know. Something stinks.

*

The elevator neared its peak. The gears turned and the pulleys pulled as Jason ascended to the top. He was finally safe, yet he could not help but fear. Paul had let him up but said little else to him. Had Abigail reached Highwayland safely? What about Sniper? Panther? Henry? What if they had died on the road? What if not all of them made it here together, the same way Jason had been separated from Gunderson, Rolston and Maiden?

"Jason!" called Abigail, pushing past the barrier,

leaping onto the elevator and throwing her arms around her brother. "I knew you would show up. I knew it."

As Jason hugged her tightly, he spied the smiling faces of Sniper, Panther, Henry and Kyle watching him. Achilles barked excitedly, clearly pleased to see his travelling companion once again. Sniper, Panther and Henry's faces fell once it dawned on them that he was alone.

"The fellas?" asked Panther, adjusting the goggles that rested atop his head.

"I haven't seen them in about ten days," said Jason, releasing his sister and walking over to the group. "We ran into Big Belial—"

"You've got to be kidding!" exclaimed Henry, looking stunned. "We knew he was prowling, but we gave his territory a wide berth."

"Well, he found us and Gunderson made the decision to go for the bounty."

"They're dead then," sighed Panther, looking utterly defeated.

"No," said Jason, "but Big Belial is."

"Who is Big Belial?" asked Kyle.

"Stage two erratic mutant," said Henry. "Like one of the ones that attacked your home."

Kyle's expression suddenly turned from curiosity to terror.

"Out with it!" barked Sniper, growing impatient. "Jason, tell us what happened with that damn mutant."

Jason explained everything about the encounter with Big Belial, from him dancing around by the bridge to the decision to try and claim his bounty. There were audible gasps from Abigail and Kyle while the older men all listened silently, giving only nods and winces as responses.

"And you're certain that the freak's claw wasn't blown to oblivion?" asked Henry.

"Certain," confirmed Jason. "The flesh looked like it had been cut and the bone was snapped. I've dealt with more than enough animals in my time to know what it looks like, even if you have to scale it up a tad for Big Belial."

"I can't believe they would abandon you there," said Kyle quietly.

"There must be more to it," said Sniper.

"Has to be," said Panther. "They probably looked up and down the river for you but had to retreat for some reason. I bet if you had waited by the bridge they'd have shown up eventually. It sounds like you sank more than a fair share of bullets into the big brute, so I get why you didn't hang around."

"The others more than me," said Jason.

"Bumpkin the bait," chuckled Henry, earning a dirty look from Abigail.

"They may have had to take Maiden back to Harmony to treat his arm," said Jason. "Who knows what filth is encrusted under that Belial's nails? It only makes sense to take proof of his death back with them."

"That settles it then," said Panther. "We'll head back to Harmony right away. Find out what the story is and make sure everything's alright."

"You aren't going to wait until morning?" asked Jason.

"No need," said Panther, tapping his goggles. "It's safer to set off when it's getting dark just in case there are...um, less than pleasant humans on the road."

"Villainous scum," nodded Henry. "No shortage of them out there."

"Lower us down, Kyle, would you?" asked Panther.

"Sure," said Kyle, rushing over to operate the elevator.

Panther and Henry stepped onto it. "Glad you're safe, bud," said Henry while Panther gave a small salute.

"Take care of yourselves, gents," said Sniper.

"Find a way to let us know if the others are alright," said Jason.

"Will do," said Henry as they started to descend.

"Thanks for getting Abigail here safely," Jason called

after them, remembering his manners. "I owe you guys."

"Our pleasure," came Panther's voice amidst the rumbling of the generator and the clanking chains of the pulleys.

Jason, Sniper and Abigail headed over to the edge of the highway and watched silently as the two Black Haze members headed off into the sunset. It was too brief a reunion for Jason, but he understood why they had to leave. He was grateful for everything they had done—whatever that might have been—in getting his sister here safely.

"Where's my VM?" asked Sniper, turning to Jason and tapping his finger on the side of the young man's head.

"Yeah, that's a funny story," said Jason, rubbing his neck.

"Hilarious funny or make-me-want-to-punch-you funny?"

"Would you believe me if I said Griffin broke it?"

"Griffin?"

"Griffin," repeated Jason. "I owe you big for the VM. It wouldn't have gotten broken if I hadn't taken it out."

"Doubt you have nine hundred and fifty silvers to pay me for it unless you've suddenly become very wealthy in the last two weeks."

"How much?" asked Jason, stunned that such a little box would cost so much.

"Don't worry about it," said Sniper. "What's this about Griffin then? Still the same old scumbag he was before?"

"More or less. Complete with a shiny, metal tongue and a new hole in his hand after an incident with my knife and a misplaced punch."

Sniper chuckled. "Got that stumpy tongue of his fixed up, did he?"

"I'm sure you won't be surprised to know he's still up to his old slaving tricks too," said Jason, "but that's not the most pressing matter right now. I know where

Lindsay is."

"What?" exclaimed Abigail. "Where? How?"

"Carlisle bought her right after he bought you," said Jason, leaving Abigail perplexed.

"No," she said, her brow furrowed. "No, that can't be right. She wasn't with me at Namaah, not even once."

"Not in Harmony, no," said Jason.

Sniper closed his eyes and shook his head. "She's in New Dallas, isn't she?"

"I'm certain of it," said Jason. "She was probably a few streets away from me the entire time I was there. While I was in The Third Circle, she was in Namaah the whole time."

Sniper shrugged. "No rest for the wicked, eh? When do we leave?"

"We go tomorrow morning," said Jason.

"No," said Abigail. "Not happening."

"Why?"

"Look at you!" she yelled.

"What's wrong with me?"

"You're cut and bruised all over, you look like you haven't slept properly in days, and you're covered in sunburn from what I can see underneath all of the filth."

"I hadn't even noticed the sunburn," said Jason, taking off his jacket and looking at his arms.

"Alright," said Sniper. "We'll rest up for what remains of today and all of tomorrow. We can get ourselves stocked up while we take it easy and head out the day after. A fair compromise?"

"Not really," sighed Abigail.

"The sooner I go, the sooner we get her back," said Jason.

Abigail looked heartbroken at those words. "I know...I know..."

*

It had been over a week of tiresome travelling, but Jason was finally starting to recognise the roads and buildings nearby. Seeing the familiar skyscrapers of Dallas, some in Outer Dallas and some within the confines of New Dallas, gave him a strange sense of déjà vu. He had made the journey here only once before and it felt like a lifetime ago that he was being carted up to the city to be sold, but he knew exactly where he was and which way to go.

"Settled on a plan yet?" asked Sniper.

"Yes," said Jason.

The two had gone back and forth at least fifty times on the journey here. They had talked of infiltration via the old passageway Sniper had used on his last visit, walking straight through the front door using a hefty bribe that neither was in a position to pay and even shooting the Mercer Guard standing at the gate. That last of those options was Sniper's suggestion and Jason didn't dare ask whether it was in jest or not, choosing to presume that it was.

"Care to enlighten me with your bright idea?" asked Sniper.

"We're going to play it straight," said Jason. "Walk straight up to the door and ask to be let in."

Sniper laughed. "Of all the plans we came up with, that's what you're going with?"

"Yes," said Jason, bluntly.

"Fair enough," said Sniper. "We're searching for your sister, so I'll take your lead."

"If you think I'm being reckless, feel free to stop me."

"Sometimes a bit of recklessness is good. If you hadn't convinced me to track down Camlorn, we wouldn't have gone to Harmony. If you didn't agree to help him, you wouldn't have found Abigail. See where I'm going with this?"

"I do," said Jason, keeping his eyes on the road as he walked.

The pair had been lucky enough to only encounter stage one mutants up close on their journey. A single stage two mutant was resting atop a building in a town they had passed by. Thankfully, it had made itself visible enough that the pair knew to avoid the town and get moving quickly. Sniper had complained about his lack of eye scope a couple of times, insisting that having to be extra vigilant would keep them back by at least two days, but Jason thought they had made good time considering their situation.

Achilles had been running ahead the entire way up to Outer Dallas, but he suddenly darted back to Sniper once they reached the perimeter. "What is it, boy?" his master asked him.

Suddenly, a trio of Mercer Guard hailed them from a makeshift outpost cobbled together from broken down old cars and chain link fences that had been torn apart. The soldiers beckoned them over and signalled to holster their guns. Jason, Sniper and Achilles did as they were told and walked over to the men.

"Y'all heading to New Dallas?" asked one of the guards.

"Yes," said Jason.

"You see anything odd on the way here?" asked the guard.

"Nothing unusual," replied Jason.

"Odd in what way?" asked Sniper.

The three guards looked at each other. "Revenants," said the guard who was doing the talking.

"What are revenants?" asked Jason.

"Cybernetically augmented degenerates," said Sniper. "I didn't think they were particularly common in these parts, fellas."

"They didn't used to be," said the guard, looking around. "They've been attacking folks on the road, even us guards. How long has it been since you two were last here?"

"A few months now," said Sniper. "Have things changed that much?"

"It's been a wild time, my friend," said the guard, wiping the sweat from his brow. "Keep straight along the main road, alright? Watch your backs the entire way because we're stretched thin trying to keep things tight both inside and outside the walls."

"Appreciate the warning," said Sniper.

"Thanks, guys," said Jason.

The three guards nodded to them and resumed their watch of the road as Jason, Sniper and Achilles continued on their way to New Dallas.

"That's not normal, is it?" asked Jason.

"No," said Sniper. "No, it is not. I've never seen guards posted this far out. I wonder what Mercer's up to? Revenants attacking people out here? Something's strange, that's for sure."

"What's the deal with these revenants? They're degenerate cyborgs?"

"It's not easy to augment degenerates. Their DNA is too messed up from their condition. It can be done, but it's rare and incredibly painful. Doesn't help that it makes that already aggressive bunch much more aggressive. Revenants are outcasts among outcasts. They're not allowed in New Dallas at all, a full on blanket ban unlike regular old degenerates."

For all its faults, New Dallas was a mostly safe and peaceful place to live and it surprised Jason that anyone, even a subgroup of degenerates, would want to ruin a good thing. In Harmony, there could be a street brawl and the guards would take bets on the winner. In New Dallas, the Mercer Guard would break it up immediately. Respect for the law kept the majority of people in check and ensured that the city ran as smoothly as could be expected.

The men and the dog continued down the road, watching their backs, sides and fronts, but all was quiet as they finally approached the metal walls that lined the city of New Dallas; a city within a city. There were a handful of guards atop the main wall, patrolling back and forth along a walkway, as well as a pair at the gate. One of them held up a hand to Jason and Sniper, prompting the pair to stop.

"You two got passports?" he asked.

"Yes," said Jason and Sniper in unison.

"Alright, come on ahead," he said, as Sniper retrieved his phone and Jason held out his slave brand to be scanned.

The guard connected Sniper's phone first and gave him an odd look, but he didn't say a word to the grizzled wanderer. He scanned it and waved Sniper on through the open gate. He then scanned Jason's hand, giving him an even odder look, but the guard waved him on in.

"Zero tolerance for law-breaking these days, Mr Cooper," said the guard. "Consider it a friendly warning, not a threat."

"Understood," said Jason.

"Enjoy your time here as a free man," said the guard. "No need to scan your brand anymore, a passport has already been added to your digital wallet."

Jason thanked him and then followed Sniper and Achilles into New Dallas where the familiar long street and the many side streets of Renaissance—the entrance district—filled Jason's eyes. He felt almost nostalgic for the city he had been bound to by slavery, yet he had known order here in a world of chaos. There was something comforting about it, yet it was not something he wished to return to.

"Where to first?" asked Jason.

"The bank," replied Sniper. "I need to see just how broke I am thanks to you. I'll need to use the blockchain bridge to move my silver from Fort Wood and Harmony to New Dallas otherwise we're even more screwed."

Jason and Sniper walked up the street and moved among the people. It was a strange feeling to be back in this city for both of them, neither having intended to ever return after their last visit. As the two walked through the busy street and towards the bank, the crowd parted at just the right moment for Jason to spot her.

Lyra. She was standing at her stall, talking to a customer while stirring the rice in her wok. Her ashy blonde hair captured her face perfectly and her sparkling blue eyes were visible even from a distance. Jason stopped and stared at her, wanting to go over and talk to her, but he knew it was better to let her get on with her life.

"Go on over if you want to," said Sniper, nudging Jason.

"No," he replied, shaking his head. "I don't want to have to say goodbye again."

Sniper nodded understandingly. "There are plenty of other women out there," he said. "Miranda seemed quite keen on you."

"She did?" asked Jason, feigning ignorance.

"Yeah, but you were too dense to notice. There must be something about the gormless look of someone naïve to the world that women like. Come on, let's get moving."

The two headed towards one of the public banks, walking past the armed guards who stood outside. Achilles remained on the street. Sniper knew that the dog, well-behaved as he was, wouldn't be permitted inside.

The interior was near indistinguishable from its former Old World self. The marble floor was polished to perfection and reflected the ceiling. The wooden frames of the tellers' desks were admittedly chipped but had a clean coat of varnish that kept them looking new. Jason was about to approach a teller, but Sniper redirected him to a set of terminals attached to the wall.

"I don't want to deal with bankers," said Sniper. "Let's keep it digital where we can help it."

Jason and Sniper hooked their phones up to the machine and their jaws both dropped when they saw their balances.

"Where did this come from?" Jason asked.

"You too, huh?" remarked Sniper.

Jason tapped on the transaction history and saw a hash dated the day before yesterday. It was for five hundred and seventy-one silver ounces. He looked over at Sniper's screen who was looking at the same thing, but the transaction time was showing as a minute later. Jason glanced back to his own screen and noticed there was a memo alongside the transaction that simply read 'BB' and nothing more.

"BB..." muttered Sniper.

"Big Belial," said Jason, excitedly. "Gunderson, Maiden and Rolston must be alright. They're back in Harmony."

"Well, I'll be..."

"The bounty was for four thousand ounces of silver. Split that seven ways between the five Black Haze men along with you and me...that must be it."

"Why did Gunderson cut me in? That wasn't necessary when I'm not a full-time part of his crew."

Jason shrugged. "Maybe he thought the money would be useful to us without any funds for New Dallas. Gunderson's a good man. Doesn't let his friends being split up stop him from lending a hand."

"I'll take this newfound boon and write that off from your debt to me."

"Sounds good to me," laughed Jason. "You can't say I didn't earn this silver, that's for sure."

Jason and Sniper departed from the bank after withdrawing a good handful of Dallas dollars and walked over to the entrance to Admah, the entertainment district. This is where Jason knew he would be least welcome, especially now that Carlisle had a bounty on his head. In any case, he was sure that even if the bounty carried weight this far he was still safe enough on the main streets.

The two men were scanned through the gate, both receiving that same unusual look from the guard here that they did from the one at the New Dallas entrance. The two men didn't say anything to each other until they were well out of earshot of the guard.

"I don't like that look we keep getting," said Sniper.

"Nope," said Jason, glancing over his shoulder. The guard wasn't watching them. "I don't like it a single bit."

"What do you reckon they're up to?"

"Who knows? My details are probably flagged on their system after what happened a few months ago. You're probably on the system for aiding and abetting me, or maybe because you're ex-Mercer Guard."

"I hope it's that straightforward," said Sniper before calling over an urchin boy who was kicking a can along the sidewalk. "You," barked Sniper.

"Eh?" said the dirty-faced boy.

"You heard of Ivor Carlisle?"

"Of course! Everyone knows him around here."

"He still alive and kicking?"

"Last I heard, he was."

"Any big shootouts happen at Namaah?"

"No...I don't think so."

"Good," said Sniper, flipping him a quarter dollar. "Scram."

The boy caught the coin and ran off excitedly.

"What was that about?" Jason asked.

"Trying to get a gauge on what Camlorn's been up to," said Sniper. "If there's been no chaos at Namaah and Carlisle is still alive, then either Camlorn hasn't reached New Dallas or he hasn't found Carlisle."

"Maybe Carlisle isn't here."

"Hard to say," said Sniper. "We'll get ourselves geared up first and worry about that later."

They made their way through the streets, careful to keep an eye on their surroundings in case anybody had dared follow them. To their relief, all seemed clear as they headed into Kim's Arms and Deals, where a Caucasian man greeted them.

"Annyeonghaseyo," said Mr Kim nonchalantly before realising who had entered his place of business. "Felix Creighton. Seeing you twice in one year is not something I would have expected given your departure not too long ago. I almost didn't recognise you with both your real eyes on display."

"Devon," said Sniper with a courteous nod while scratching Achilles' ears. "This here is my friend—"

"Jason Cooper," said Kim. "We've met once before. I never did get that nano cloth back from your old boss before you went and splattered his brains across the wall of his office. Lost me some good business there, you know."

"Sorry about that," said Jason.

"Don't be. Benedictus was a scumbag and the only thing he was good as was a generous pit of silver. With all the craziness since, the Mercer Guard has been keeping me in business. Granted, it would be nice if I wasn't paid mostly in tax breaks."

"And what craziness would you be referring to?" asked Sniper.

"Revenants," said Kim. "A lot of those half-metal, half-mutant nasties running about. Word is, a couple of them made it into town and caused some havoc before being put down. The Street Cleaners had a field day hunting down who was responsible for helping them get in."

"Street Cleaners?" asked Jason.

"Not the sort of folks who pick up trash," said Kim, smiling and shaking his head. "Well, in a sense they do. They waste a few badduns, then pick them up and take their corpses to The Drop."

"Sounds like we need some protection while we're in town," said Sniper, gesturing towards the wide assortment of guns, gadgets and body armour around the shop. It was even more plentiful than what Miranda kept back in Harmony, but she had a few select items on full display that Kim no doubt kept hidden out the back.

"Planning on killing another crime lord?" asked Kim, with a shrewd look. Jason and Sniper glanced at each other while Kim laughed at his own joke. "What is it you boys need?"

"Ammo," said Sniper, pulling out his pistol and rifle. "Lots of ammo."

Jason took out a replacement handgun that Kyle had given him in Highwayland along with his grandfather's old gun. He set them on the countertop for Kim to take a look at.

"My, my," said the arms dealer. "Ain't that a fancy piece. A real antique that one, you don't see many of them around. Eight rounds in the chamber, if I'm not mistaken."

"You've got bullets for it?"

"The gun is an antique, but the bullets are commonplace," said Kim. "Step into my office, gents. I'll get you sorted at a discount on account of you being friends and all. Two percent off all wares except for specialty items."

"Got any more nano cloth?" Jason asked.

Kim smiled slyly as he gestured towards the back room where he kept a mixture of contraband and his most high-tech equipment.

*

"That'll be one thousand three hundred and eighty-five ounces," said Kim, tallying up everything the men had purchased. "Want to pay together or separately?"

"Separately to account for the different ammo and my goggles."

Kim looked at his sheet of paper and tallied everything up. He brought each of the men over to his terminal in turn and accepted the digital transfer of their coin. Jason was almost broke once again, but at least now he had the means to survive in New Dallas and a trek across the wasteland should things get ugly.

Secretly, Jason knew that Sniper had a much healthier stack of silver than he let on, having accidentally spied his friend's account balances for at least seven different towns in the bank earlier. Sniper often claimed to live frugally to get by, but he had no need to considering his hidden wealth.

"It's been a pleasure, Devon," said Sniper. "If we don't see you around..."

"Then I'll know you've had to go on the run again," chuckled Kim.

"Thanks for the discount," said Jason, knowing that the two percent Kim had offered them was understating it. The discount was probably closer to twenty-five percent.

Jason, Sniper and Achilles left Kim's and headed back to the main street of Admah. No sooner had they rounded the corner than a man tripped on the ground in front of them.

"Please!" he said, looking at them desperately, but a bang and a blood splatter from his head later and he was dead.

Jason and Sniper looked around to see a man wearing a black duster over body armour. He kept his handgun pointed at the dead man before them. A couple of civilians cheered and applauded the man before he walked towards the corpse and dragged it along by the foot.

"What the hell was that?" a stunned Sniper asked a passerby.

"Street Cleaners just doing their job," said the woman with a smile.

Before Sniper could ask anything else, a man in much finer body armour that bore the white lion of King Mercer approached them along with two of his men. Jason recognised the guard; he was there at the raid on Benedictus's after he had passed the message about the Livelong dealings on to King Mercer.

"Jason Cooper and Felix Creighton?" asked the man.

"Yes?" replied Jason.

"My name is Captain Crusoe and I work for King Hector Mercer. I would like for you both to come with me."

"Is that an order or a request?" asked Sniper.

"It's a request," said Crusoe, "but if you refuse the request then it becomes an order. If you comply, no need to turn over your guns. We'd like to keep this on a good faith basis."

"Alright," said Jason. "Take us wherever you need us to go."

Sniper gave Jason a look of uncertainty, but he said nothing. Crusoe led the pair and Achilles back into Renaissance, waving them through the gate without bothering to scan their passports. As they walked towards the gate to Loyalty—the governmental district where King Mercer resided—they passed by Lyra's stall.

She looked up as Jason walked by and the two locked eyes. Her jaw fell open in shock and she dropped the plate of rice she was about to set on her countertop. No sooner had they seen each other than Jason was on his way again.

Chapter 16:
The Audience

2nd June 2116: The headaches are getting worse and more frequent. I've spent all day trying to remember Angie's birthday, only to get nowhere. I remember our wedding day, I remember the day we met, but I just can't put my finger on her birthday. I've had a few lapses of memory before, but nothing like this. Can't lie, my paper friend, but it's got me spooked. It feels like it's truly beginning now. I thought I had six months, but I now believe I'll be lucky to have three.

*

The buildings of Loyalty were much more cared for than the ones in the rest of New Dallas, but they still bore the mark of the end of the Old World with their extensive chips, scratches and cracks. Most of the broken ones were ugly metal frames coated in glass, many of which were missing panels, while the stone buildings remained standing tall, bruises and all.

Jason and Sniper were brought up a small stone staircase where three arches sat at the top, all leading to doors to take them into King Mercer's palace. It was a marvellous building with many peaks and spires, yet not what Jason would have expected a palace to look like. A clock sat near the top of the large central spire, showing the time as a little after midday. The two guards standing outside the doors saluted Captain Crusoe and his men as he led Jason and Sniper inside while Achilles was left outside with the guards.

"Up here," said Captain Crusoe, bringing them to a staircase that took them to a small landing which then forked to the left and the right.

Crusoe guided them up the staircase, taking the left fork, and through the corridors which eventually led to a fairly unremarkable doorway where a flag hung on a pole beside it. The right side of the flag had a horizontal bar of white up top and one of red down below. The left side of the flag was a thick blue vertical stripe bearing a white lion within it. It reminded Jason of the old Lone Star Flag of Texas that Mercer had since made his own to represent New Dallas in all its glory. He had seen the flag a few times in his previous stay here, but the white lion emblem alone was much more common to see.

"Mr Cooper, you first," said Crusoe.

"Not without me, no," said Sniper, stepping forward. "You say you want this to be in good faith, yet you tell us nothing."

"I'll be alright," said Jason. "I'll shout if I need you, bud."

Crusoe opened the door and then closed it once Jason had entered. The room before him was painted a dull green that had no doubt faded from a more pleasant shade over the years. There were half a dozen large windows on the right-hand wall, each topped with an arch. There was some grime at the top of the windows, but they were mostly kept clean which let the early afternoon sun shine through. The room decked with chairs and at the far side sat a podium that had been broken apart to make way for a much grander chair than the others, upon which sat a man in robust combat armour. He had lightly tanned skin with a dark beard and dark hair. King Mercer.

"Jason Cooper," he said with a smile. "I've longed to meet you, my friend."

Jason approached the king but stopped a few feet from Mercer's chair. "King Mercer," said Jason, bowing his head.

"No need for that here, Jason," said Mercer. "You aren't in service to me, my friend. I'm in service to you. It was you who helped me weed out some of the traitors in my midst. It was you that spurred me to action after letting myself grow complacent over the years."

Jason stood there silently, not knowing what to say while Mercer gazed upon him.

"Thank you," said the king.

"You're welcome," said Jason, unsure if this was the right response.

"Why is it that you've come back? With Felix Creighton, no less."

Jason decided it was best to be honest. "I'm here looking for my sister. Her name is Lindsay Cooper and she was purchased by Ivor Carlisle of Namaah. I believe he's brought her to this city to work for him as one of his...his girls."

"A noble intent, no doubt, but how do you suppose you'll find her and get her out of the city? Slavery is not illegal here, as you know. Non-citizens brought in from outside are fair game in New Dallas."

"I know," said Jason, "but I'll do whatever it takes to reunite what's left of my family."

Mercer nodded. "I suppose you're wondering why I've summoned you here. Shall I tell you?"

"If you would, King Mercer."

"Very good," said the king. "It seems that we continue to find common enemies, Jason. First, it was Mr Benedictus. Now, it's Mr Carlisle. Much like your former master, he's part of the Livelong trade that continues to plague my wonderful city. He's also very well protected and keeps himself distant from solid proof of his wrongdoings. There's only so much I can do in ignoring my own laws, even if it's to the benefit of the people. They respect it for now as the streets are being cleaned up, but if it continues they'll start to fear for their own safety over the slightest of infractions. An unfounded fear for the vast majority, but it could lead to some problems down the road. Carlisle also employs too many people to be disposed of by my men without repercussions, particularly now that he has taken over The Third Circle too."

Jason said nothing, content to hear Mercer out and see where the king was going with this.

"There has been a war for power in New Dallas and I'm trying my best to keep it out of sight, but it continues to creep into view. There are powerful elites, of which Carlisle is one, who I had let get away with too much for too long. No more. I've killed most of those who wormed their way into my government, purging the ranks quite effectively. I've even forced the degenerates to take new leadership. What do you make of this?"

A thought suddenly struck Jason that he had never considered before. "Are these elites working with the degenerates and revenants?" asked Jason.

"To my knowledge, yes," said the king.

"Sire, have you heard of The Regressionists?"

King Mercer burst into laughter. "The Regressionists?" he said once he had calmed down. "That lunatic cult who believe that mutations can be reversed?"

"Yes," said Jason, his face deadly serious.

Mercer's curiosity was piqued. "What of them?"

"If the degenerates and the revenants were working with Carlisle, what would it take to buy their loyalty?" asked Jason.

"Money, food and security. That's usually what they go for. It's how I've kept them in line for so long. Mostly the latter two."

"What about the promise of turning them into normal humans? It may be too late for the augmented revenants, but for the average degenerate..."

King Mercer paused and thought intently about the question before speaking. "No, surely they would not be so dense..."

"Dense or desperate?" asked Jason. "What if The Regressionists had promised them the opportunity to regain their humanity for destabilising your city? What if they're prepared to put their lives on the line for a chance to be normal? No longer outcasts in society."

King Mercer pondered this idea for a moment. "Regardless of whether that's the case, how would you suppose that be stopped?" he asked.

"I'll eliminate Ivor Carlisle for you," said Jason. "Cut the head from the dragon and see if the attacks stop. You can pin it all on me and give me safe passage out of town if I'm right. Fake my death or whatever you need to do to relieve yourself from any of the blame that may come should I be wrong."

"You're a bold young man," said Mercer. "You remind me of myself when I was twenty years younger. You still have that spark of hope and naivety that I had at that age."

"What do you say to my proposal, King Mercer?" asked Jason.

Mercer smiled. "Captain Crusoe, send in Mr Creighton," he called out.

The door at the far end of the room opened and Sniper walked up the path between the chairs and stood beside Jason. He looked upon Mercer, his face still and his eyes cold. It was taking him an enormous amount of effort to hold his tongue, considering the lust for revenge that he had for all these years. Even knowing that it was one of the king's men and not the king didn't quell it as it should have done.

"Felix Creighton," said King Mercer. "May I express my long overdue condolences over what happened to your wife and son?"

"You may," said Sniper, through gritted teeth.

"I have seen to it personally that Nathaniel Ezra met his end in mid-March."

"I know."

"Yet you don't seem pleased with this?"

Sniper smiled a forced smile and shook his head slowly. "I'm rosy as can be, King Mercer. Got nothing else to say about the matter."

"Very well," said Mercer, his brow furrowed and keeping an eye on Sniper's hands. He had seen looks like this one too many times. "Your friend, Mr Cooper, has an idea that he has just relayed to me that he will no doubt fill you in on. I'll see to it that the pair of you have carte blanche here in New Dallas to do whatever it is that you need to do to find Jason's sister, but that comes with a condition. You must make sure that Ivor Carlisle is dead."

"You can't make your goons take care of him?" asked Sniper.

"Not without backlash that I would prefer to avoid," said Mercer. "Do you agree to the terms?"

"If Jason agreed, I agree," said Sniper coldly, struggling to hide his disdain.

"Very good," said Mercer. "You're both free to go. Speak to Captain Crusoe should yo—"

"King Mercer," said Jason abruptly. "Where can we find the leader of the degenerates?" he asked. "You said there was a change in leadership."

"Maldonaldo? He'll be skulking around in the degenerate area of Admah, much like the others."

"Come with us," said Jason, prompting a confused look from both Sniper and Mercer.

"Come with you?" asked the king.

"Just for this," Jason replied. "Let's find out if my theory about the degenerates and the revenants is correct. That way you don't need to just take our word for it if I *am* right."

Mercer laughed. "You don't shy away, do you son? Fine, I'll come with you. Let's see if you're as bright as you seem to think. I will say that I certainly hope you are."

Mercer stood up and walked towards Jason and

Sniper; the latter averted his gaze. The king led them from the room and he beckoned Captain Crusoe and his men to follow him. They moved along silently, the captain not daring to ask where they were going. They walked through Loyalty and back into Renaissance, picking up two more of the Mercer Guard along the way, all of whom surrounded the king. All the while, the people cheered upon seeing their king walk amongst them. He was loved by his people, there was no question of it.

They moved along into Admah and casually strolled through the district, every one of the party with a gun in hand. Without fear or hesitation, they walked up to a house the king guided them to and Captain Crusoe threw open the door. The degenerates standing guard here scrambled to draw their own weapons as the king held up a hand to calm them down.

"We're hoping there won't be any trouble today, gentlemen," said Mercer. "Where's Maldonaldo?"

The two degenerates looked at each other uncertainly. "Upstairs," one of them said after a moment.

Captain Crusoe led the way and everyone else followed, including the two degenerates. They no longer saw the need to stand guard by the door, not that they had been particularly effective at it either way.

"Who's there?" came Maldonaldo's strained voice from behind a locked door. Captain Crusoe gave it a heavy kick and it flung open.

Maldonaldo was sitting behind a desk while a young woman with a face as messed up as his own was kneeling on the floor. He jumped to his feet and adjusted his trousers, dragging the girl up with him.

"Pardon me, sire," he said to King Mercer.

"You," said Mercer to the girl. "Out."

The girl ran from the room, thoroughly humiliated before the king of the city as Maldonaldo tried to compose himself, equally as embarrassed by the position he was caught in.

"What can I do for you, sire?" he asked, walking around from the table and kneeling before King Mercer.

"Jason, you're the one with the bright ideas, aren't you?" asked Mercer. "You deal with this as you see fit. Maldonaldo, you're to answer him honestly or you'll feel my wrath."

Jason stepped forward as Maldonaldo rose up. Jason looked at the degenerate straight in the eyes. This man may just have been his ticket to securing Mercer's full faith. If he could do that, he knew he would find Lindsay. The king had to hear what Jason knew was the truth from one of the degenerates themselves.

"Maldonaldo, wasn't it?" asked Jason.

"Yes," replied Maldonaldo.

"My name is Jason Cooper," he said. "I've no doubt that you've heard of me."

"We've met before, Mr Cooper," said Maldonaldo. "In passing, at least. You hid in one of our secure areas after you killed Benedictus."

"Good, then you know who I am," said Jason. "Were you born this way, Maldonaldo?"

"What way do you mean?"

"With this affliction you bear."

"My mutation?" asked Maldonaldo, affronted to be asked, but he wouldn't take it any further in front of the king. "No, I was a normal child until I was about twelve."

"So you remember what it was like? Before you transformed."

"All too well."

"Do you miss it?"

Maldonaldo stared at Jason with disdain in his eyes. "You know damn well I do," he said, "but there's no going back for me. Nothing can undo this...this curse."

"What about the rest of them?" asked Jason, gesturing towards the two door guards in the room with them.

One of them moved to speak, but Maldonaldo held up his hand. "I see where you're going with this, Cooper.

No, I'm not part of The Regressionists, if that's what you're asking. I see their pack of lies for what it is."

"And the rest of them?" repeated Jason.

"I can't speak for them."

"No, but you can silence one," said Jason, pointing towards the guard who had attempted to speak.

Maldonaldo sighed. "Fine," he said, looking to King Mercer and then back to Jason. "I suspect I'm a dead man anyway at this point, so tell me exactly what it is that you want to know?"

"You're not allied with The Regressionists but are other degenerates within the city?" asked Jason.

"Yes."

King Mercer whistled in amazement. "Would you look at that," he muttered with a frown.

"And the revenants?"

Maldonaldo closed his eyes. "All in service to The Regressionists. Every last one of them in Outer Dallas."

"Ivor Carlisle?"

"One of the lead bankrollers of the whole thing. Keeps his name off of all documents, used to send his goons over here to hand over the money he owed my brethren. It's an open secret that he's one of the lead financiers of everything that the turncoats and the revenants are up to."

Jason looked at Maldonaldo pointedly.

"I don't know what it is they're up to," he said, "but more than enough of my people buy their crap. What would you give to not be a pariah in a world filled with little hope? As soon as King Mercer put me in charge, I've kept things clean. It doesn't mean everyone is going to agree with me or do what they're told. Being on the straight and narrow creates its own set of problems when people are constantly working to undermine you."

Mercer walked forward and stood a foot from Maldonaldo, looking directly into his eyes. "Do you believe him, Jason?"

Jason looked at Maldonaldo who didn't break eye contact with the king even with such a powerful man right up in his face.

"I believe him, King Mercer," said Jason with full sincerity.

"Then you should be thanking Mr Cooper, Maldonaldo," said the king, "because he just saved your life."

Maldonaldo breathed a sigh of relief as he slumped his shoulders.

"Thank him," said King Mercer. "And make it sound like you mean it."

"Thank you, Mr Cooper," said Maldonaldo with a pained smile. It was the same smile Sniper had used when speaking with Mercer in his chamber. "Thank you very much."

"Last question for you," said Jason. "Where does Carlisle keep himself? Namaah?"

"He hasn't been to Namaah since he arrived here almost two weeks ago," said Maldonaldo. "I don't think he's even come into New Dallas at all."

"Oh, he hasn't, has he?" asked Mercer, stepping back from the degenerate leader.

"No," said Maldonaldo, "but you'll never get to him if that's what you're planning."

"Why would that be?" asked Mercer.

"That lab of his is well fortified," said Maldonaldo. "Protected by some of ours, some of his and some creatures you'd rather steer clear of."

Jason and Sniper looked at each other. "Lab?" they asked in unison.

*

"Camlorn had to have known about the lab," said Sniper when he, Jason and Mercer arrived back in the king's chamber. "Why didn't he tell us?"

"Who is Camlorn?" asked King Mercer.

"He's a former Regressionist, turned Regressionist

hunter," said Sniper.

"He knew there was a laboratory," said Jason. "He told me I was barely scratching the surface back in Harmony. Whatever they're up to is much more sinister than just injecting people with Livelong."

"Injecting people with Livelong, you say?" remarked Mercer quietly. "Now why doesn't that surprise me? And I'm sure they're selling the fake cures right back to them?"

"That's to start with," said Jason. "Who knows what else they're doing."

"Camlorn knows," said Sniper. "We need to find him."

"What's his full name?" asked Mercer. "What does he look like?"

"Eric Camlorn," replied Jason. "Clean shaven fella with jet-black hair that he keeps short. Tall man with wide shoulders and he can take a few bullets before getting right back up again. Camlorn injected himself with Livelong to give himself the strength and durability he needs to hunt down the rest of The Regressionists."

Mercer walked to the corner of the room and slid open a panel in the wall, revealing a terminal. He turned it on and tapped a couple of passwords onto it, granting him access. He started searching for something in silence while Jason and Sniper watched on, unable to see clearly what was displayed on the screen.

"This him?" asked Mercer, moving aside and pointing to a picture of a man.

"That's him," said Jason.

"Eric Camlorn," said Mercer. "Born in the year 2083 AD in Farrow, within Star Republic territory. Received his New Dallas passport papers about seven years ago along with his wife, Angela Camlorn. She died over a year ago—"

"His wife is dead?" asked Jason.

"Sadly, yes," he said. "No cause of death listed here and it only gives the month as June with no specific date."

Sniper looked distraught to hear this. Nobody knew better the pain of losing his wife than he. He had been the one to give Camlorn the hardest time since he and Jason first met him, but he suddenly looked incredibly sympathetic and regretful to the man he had been so wrong about.

"Do you want the good news?" asked King Mercer.

"Good news?" asked Jason.

"That's what I said."

"Of course."

"He's been moving around the New Dallas districts for the past few days. Most of his time is spent in Fairfax, but he scanned into Admah about thirty minutes ago. We must have just missed each other."

"We need to go find him," said Jason.

"Do as you will," said Mercer. "Carte blanche, as I said. You had my trust before, but now you've got whatever you need from me."

Jason thanked Mercer and rushed from the room, not realising that Sniper had stayed behind.

"Something I can do for you, Mr Creighton?" asked Mercer, closing up his terminal and concealing it back behind the wall panel.

"Did you order my exile from New Dallas for refusing to follow orders all those years ago?" asked Sniper.

King Mercer looked at him and then walked on over to face him properly. "Yes," he said.

"Did you give the order for the attack on my family all those years ago?" Sniper asked him.

"No," said the king. "Killing a man's wife or child in front of him is an atrocity that I would never condone. I didn't find out the full details of what happened until I heard that you were the one who had left New Dallas with Jason. I had my men do a little digging and that's when I learned of it. And, if it makes you feel any better, I didn't approve of Ezra's harsh tactics in making the settlement you were trying to bring on board give me its allegiance. You were right to refuse to carry out your orders, I'm just sorry it cost you so much."

Sniper nodded. He kept eye contact with King Mercer and held out his hand. The king looked down at it and then back to Sniper before accepting the handshake.

"I'm sorry I blamed you all this time," said Sniper.

"I'm sorry that I robbed you of your vengeance," said the king. "Truly."

"It's probably for the best. That's what Jason would say, I'm sure."

"He seems to be a good friend."

"He is."

"True loyalty is rare. Make sure you watch each other's backs."

"We do."

Sniper bid Mercer a silent farewell and rushed off to find Jason, who was waiting at the entrance to the palace with Achilles, both of whom were eager to go. Jason had an impatient look on his face, but he couldn't help but notice that Sniper looked lighter.

"What took you so long?" Jason asked his friend.

"I had to have a word with Mercer," replied Sniper.

"You didn't punch him, did you?"

"No," said Sniper. "I figured it was time to let go and speak to him properly. No fists, no bullets."

"And you feel better?"

Sniper nodded. "Can't change the past so it's best to move forward. He said he didn't put the order out to kill my family and I chose to believe him."

"I'm glad," said Jason. "He doesn't strike me as a liar."

"Enough about him," said Sniper, not wanting to talk about the conversation in any greater detail. "Let's go find our old friend, Camlorn."

"I know someone who might be able to help us find him quicker," said Jason.

"Who could that be?" asked Sniper, badly feigning ignorance.

Jason, Sniper and Achilles headed straight from

Loyalty and into Renaissance, but they did not turn to their right at the gate to make their way towards Admah. No, they headed straight on towards a stall where a girl was cooking up some armadillo for her customers.

Chapter 17:
Release the Hounds

3rd June 2116: I'm starting to think it may be time to give up on Carlisle for now, but I fear that if I track down a few other names I've skipped on my list that I'll not be myself by the time it comes back around to him. If I storm Fantom, I'm certainly a dead man. If I leave New Dallas, I could be gone for months by the time I track down some of the more significant players. I thought that removing the lynchpin would destroy the machine, but it looks like I'll have to just smash it so thoroughly that having a lynchpin doesn't make a difference.

*

Sniper hung back with Achilles as Jason approached Lyra's stall where she was busy working. She passed a helping of rice and grilled armadillo to her customer latest; a middle-aged man who appeared to be blind, but he had no trouble finding his way around the plate with a knife and fork.

"It's even better fresh," he joked.

"You get it fresh more often than not," said Lyra

before suddenly noticing Jason approaching.

"Hello," he said, feeling stupid for forgetting every other word in the English language.

"Hi," she replied, her voice suddenly meek.

"Who's behind me?" asked the customer.

"Nobody, Cormac," she said.

"Cormac?" he laughed, accidentally spraying rice everywhere. "Why the devil are you calling me Cormac, girlie?"

"Why did you come back?" asked Lyra. "How?"

"I'm looking for my sister and King Mercer gave me a pardon," said Jason. "I'll still need to watch my back while I'm in town, but it's been smooth enough so far. How have you been?"

"Your sister?" asked Lyra in shock. "She's here in New Dallas? Both of them or...or...what?"

"Lindsay is here, yes. Abigail is not. She's safe in a town about a week to the east."

"You found both of them?" asked Lyra, in a state of disbelief. "You have to tell me everything."

The customer swung around and held out his hand for Jason to shake. "You must be the guy who set chaos into motion in this town," he said. "Cormac McConnell. Lyra's father."

"That's me," said Jason, shaking Cormac's hand. "A pleasure to meet you, Mr McConnell. Your daughter kept me sane during my extended stay here."

"Sane?" laughed Cormac. "Ain't nothing sane about what you did, Jason. It took a lot of guts. The guts of a madman, but I'm glad you did it. Too many damn cowards in this town and they were letting scum get away with everything under the sun. Not anymore, my friend. Not anymore."

"Your sisters?" asked Lyra, ignoring her father.

"I'll tell you everything when there's more time," said Jason, "but I need your help finding someone."

"Lindsay?"

"No."

"I thought you said you were looking for your

sister?"

"I'm looking for someone else and I think he can help me find the man who has my sister."

Lyra looked confused. "I'm not sure I follow."

"I'm looking for a man named Eric Camlorn. Tall fellow with—"

"Eric Camlorn?" asked Lyra. "Isn't he one of them Regressionist wackos?"

"You know him?"

"Not well, just in passing. He's eaten here before and talks a lot, but I tend to tune him out."

"Have you seen him recently?" asked Jason. "Please think hard, it's important."

"No...I don't think so," said Lyra. "Not in a few months at least."

"Do you have any idea who he knows in town or where he might be?"

"I'm sorry, I don't."

"What about where The Regressionists around here hang their hats?"

"Admah," said Lyra with certainty. "A small dive called The Trough. I don't know if that's where all of The Regressionists go, but I've heard of a couple of them hassling people there on more than a few occasions."

"Thank you," said Jason sincerely before rushing to Sniper. "I'll explain everything when I can. It was a pleasure to meet you Mr McConnell."

As Jason, Sniper and Achilles headed towards Admah, Jason heard Cormac say something about him being a nice young man. A smile flickered across Jason's face for a second before his mind refocused on the task at hand.

"You hear all that?" Jason asked.

"The Trough," replied Sniper.

The three headed through the gate and Jason asked one of the Mercer Guard for directions to the bar, which the confused guard gave after a moment of hesitation. Jason remembered the street names well, moving through them with ease. He hoped that he was going to the right place and that Camlorn hadn't already made his way to Namaah and caused chaos. Frankly, it was a miracle that he'd been here for days and not caused any trouble.

"That's it," said Jason, pointing out the sign up ahead.

He and Sniper walked up to the bar while a particularly gruesome-looking degenerate lay outside unconscious and covered in his own vomit. Jason tilted his head to the side, worried the disfigured man would choke if he threw up again. Sniper laughed in amazement at Jason before pushing open the door to the bar.

"What's so funny?" asked Jason.

"That's why you're different, bud," replied Sniper, looking around the bar. "Son of a bitch, there he is."

Camlorn was leaning against the bar with a beer in his hand, swirling it around with a look of defeat on his face. Jason and Sniper approached him and he was so lost in thought that he didn't even notice them until they were right beside him.

"Gentlemen," he said glumly. "Fancy seeing the pair of you here. Chasing me across the state again, are we?"

"Why are you so miserable?" asked Jason rather bluntly.

"That bastard Carlisle," said Camlorn. "Haven't seen head nor tail of him since I got here. Been looking for days and there's zero. As best as I can tell, he never arrived. I doubt we would be so lucky for him to have met his end on the road. He always travels by wagon with a minimum of eight armed guards by his side at all times."

"Wouldn't it be nice if your guardian angels turned up to save the day?" asked Sniper.

"You've got my attention," said Camlorn, sitting upright with a curious look on his face.

"What do you know about a lab outside the walls? Somewhere in Outer Dallas."

Camlorn chuckled. "Oh boy, you've been digging

deep, haven't you?"

"You know it then?" asked Jason.

"Fantom Research Centre," said Camlorn, nodding slowly. "I know it alright. You think Carlisle is there?"

"According to the leader of the degenerates around these parts."

Camlorn looked perturbed. "Never in my days have I seen or heard of Carlisle going anywhere near that place. Something serious has to be going on for him to be in that lab."

"Would a power grab in New Dallas be enough?" asked Sniper.

"Maybe," muttered Camlorn, "maybe..."

"What's the story with this place anyway?" asked Jason.

"I've earned your trust at this point, haven't I?" asked Camlorn.

"Enough that I would believe whatever it is that you'll tell me about it," said Jason while Sniper nodded in agreement.

"Fantom Research Centre is where the experiments that the Regressionists perform take place. It's well-funded and it's well-secured. Their supposed cure for Livelong? Fantasy it may be, but many attempts were made to create it. You know what isn't fantasy? The other Human Improvement Drugs and technology that they're working on and continuing to experiment with to this day. It's the sort of stuff that would make some of the horrors you hear about in the Star Republic look playful."

"And these HIDs work, do they?" asked Sniper.

"Some of them do," said Camlorn. "Some of them work for a short time before killing those who take it and others just kill people outright because their bodies can't handle it."

"Are the revenants that have been causing problems for New Dallas coming from there?" asked Jason.

"Almost certainly," said Camlorn. "There's a HID that can be used to temporarily calm the unusual mutation of Livelong that courses through a degenerate's bloodstream. It won't undo anything about their mutation, but it allows them to be turned into cyborgs with much less risk."

"What are we waiting for then?" asked Jason. "If Carlisle is there, it's where we need to be."

Camlorn set his beer on the counter and stood up. "It's a suicide mission, you both understand that right?" he asked with a deadly seriousness in his voice that didn't suit him.

"If it means I can find my sister while helping you stamp out Carlisle's evil, I don't care," said Jason.

"And how about you, Patch?" asked Camlorn.

"You're owed vengeance for *her*," said Sniper.

Camlorn's eyes widened, but only for a split second before his expression changed to a calm smile. "Let's burn the entire place to the ground, gentlemen. Make it so that there's nothing left and everything The Regressionists have worked for is reduced to ashes."

*

Jason, Sniper, Camlorn and Achilles walked through the streets of Outer Dallas, keeping their weapons drawn at all times. Every so often a mutant drew close and one of the men would shank it with a blade. Camlorn was a fan of using his Livelong-enhanced strength to snap its neck, which naturally led Sniper to calling him a show-off.

"Going swimming, jackass?" retorted Camlorn, mocking Sniper's new goggles.

The Mercer Guard they encountered at various outposts along the way would try and warn them off, but that didn't deter the men. The guards would shrug and call them lunatics, and maybe they were right, but they had to see the task at hand through to the end. Jason refused to return to Highwayland without Lindsay, and

Carlisle was the key. Setting foot inside Namaah was certain death, but if there was nobody to pay the wages or own the slaves, then the establishment would fall apart.

"Revenant," whispered Camlorn, pulling the two men into an alleyway. Achilles stuck close to his master's side and also hid from view.

"Enhancements," said Sniper, pulling down his goggles to read the heat signature of the patrolling revenant.

"No eyepieces, so I doubt he knows we're here," said Camlorn.

Jason held his finger to his lips and hurried quietly through the alley as Sniper tried to pull him back. Jason made his way around the building and found what he had hoped for—an exit back onto the main street. He watched as the revenant walked by. The human monstrosity had a face that looked like it had been boiled in acid and one of his arms was replaced with a prosthetic limb tipped with a machinegun. He was strolling along, looking for anyone he could make his next victim.

Jason held up his handgun and took careful aim. He breathed deeply as the revenant walked away from him and up to where Camlorn and Sniper were waiting. Forcing his eyes to remain open, Jason pulled the trigger and the bullet erupted from the barrel and tore straight through the revenant's skull. The creature fell to the ground, dead. It was painful to Jason, even though the revenant had almost nothing left of his humanity. There was no doubt he had murderous intent, so Jason buried his shame about his dishonourable kill.

Sniper, Camlorn and Achilles emerged from their hiding spot and ran down the street towards Jason.

"Reckless," said Sniper, pulling his goggles up.

"Not at all," said Jason. "Did you want to face him head on or is shooting him from behind guaranteeing our safety?"

Sniper let out a dry laugh. "Got me there," he said as Camlorn smirked.

"We're close," said Camlorn, looking around. He pointed further down the street towards a dilapidated apartment block. "We should be able to see it from there."

The four headed into the block, not letting their guard down as they sought out the staircase leading up. They almost stopped on the fourth floor with Camlorn being certain that they were high enough to be able to see it clearly, but Sniper insisted they head up to the sixth. Camlorn kicked in a door and the three men approached the dust-covered window.

"Perfect," said Sniper, nodding as he strained to see outside.

"Doesn't look perfect," remarked Jason.

Sniper took the butt of his rifle and rammed it into the window three times, smashing it into a dozen shards. Most of the shards fell to the ground below where Jason faintly heard them shatter into many more minuscule fragments.

The men ducked down and looked outside. The lab was as unmistakable as the Crown Pharmaceuticals facility Jason had infiltrated under Benedictus's orders months ago. It had all the hallmarks of the newer buildings of the Old World, a metal frame covered by glass panes from top to bottom. It was no more than four storeys tall, but from here Jason could see a road leading underground. It wasn't the structure of the building that concerned him, however, as there were stage ones lurking around. Most of them were sitting or standing around lazily, but a small gaggle of them were running towards the shattered glass down below.

"Don't shoot," said Camlorn, holding up a hand. "We want to strike at the same time so that they don't know we're coming. The people inside run the lab on nuclear, so they have more than enough power to keep their cameras on. Once we make a scene, they'll know we're here."

"Won't stop us," said Jason confidently.

"Do you see that?" asked Camlorn, pointing towards the road to the underground that Jason had noticed. "It's the subterranean parking lot and it's where they'll be letting the mutants out from. Most of their operations are based in the basement floors of the facility, but they're not stupid enough to keep active mutants running around with them. The glass windows are easily shattered so if the door is sealed, we're still good. Once we're inside, we'll make our way down."

Jason nodded. "Sniper, as discussed, you'll pick the mutants up from above once Camlorn, Achilles and I are in place. If any guards or mutants come out after we clear the area, we'll take care of them while you run down and join us."

"Right," said Sniper, pulling an eyepiece of the goggles over his left eye, leaving his right eye exposed. He crouched down and took aim with his rifle at a mutant lurking outside the front door of the lab.

"You sure you can aim that thing without your zoom scope?" asked Camlorn, half-jokingly.

"You'll find out," said Sniper nonchalantly.

"Wait for our signal to come down," said Jason. "If anybody tries to sneak up on us, waste 'em. These are evil people, no mercy."

"I'm less bothered by that than you," replied Sniper, keeping his eyes focused on the building. "Go shred those stage ones down below and let's get this show on the road."

"Good luck," said Jason.

"Likewise," said Sniper.

Jason, Camlorn and Achilles headed back through the door and down the stairs. As they neared the ground, they slowed their pace to keep themselves quiet. Jason kept his knife in one hand and his pistol in the other, while Camlorn carried only a knife. They crept up to the edge of the doorway and glanced outside. Three mutants were sniffing around, trying to locate what had broken the glass.

"Go," whispered Camlorn, nudging Jason.

He and Jason ran out and each stabbed a mutant through the eye socket as the unexpecting creatures turned to face them. The third mutant lunged for Jason, but Achilles leapt at it and sank his teeth into its leg. The hardened hound growled viciously as he tore the mutant's calf muscle to shreds, giving Jason an opening to finish the job. Camlorn threw his dead mutant aside, dashed to the remaining mutant's back and grabbed it by the head. With a forceful twist, he snapped its neck and tossed it onto the concrete slabs upon which they stood. For good measure, Camlorn slammed his foot down on the dead mutant's skull, crushing it against the sidewalk with a gruesome squelch.

Jason, Camlorn and Achilles ran towards the glass building, alerting the mutants. The two men held up their guns, aiming for the closest foes and pulling their triggers. As they fired, mutants in the background started dropping dead, one by one, as Sniper removed them from play. Two dozen mutants were cut down to eighteen, then twelve, but a sudden grinding from somewhere nearby distracted Jason. The grinding was followed by a venomous barking that sent shivers down Jason's spine.

"Oh damn, they're unleashing them already," said Camlorn, laughing. "They must want rid of us good and fast."

The barking grew louder as a pack of hulking canines, almost the size of a cow, bounded up the road from the underground. They were hairless and hideous with swollen bodies and stretched skin. Their salivating mouths were contorted into an expression somewhere between pain and ravenous hunger. Dogs, they were no longer.

"Here come the mutemutts!" called Camlorn, turning his attention to the hounds.

Jason and Camlorn unloaded round after round into the ferocious beasts charging towards them while Sniper and Achilles focused their attention on the stage ones. The mutated dogs did not fall as easily as the mutated humans, taking three of four headshots each before they dropped.

"Damn," said Jason, dropping a magazine as he scrambled to reload.

He whipped out Camelot right as a mutemutt leapt through the air at him. He pulled the trigger five times in rapid succession, the barrel of his gun following the mutt's corpse down to the ground as it dropped. He holstered Camelot and grabbed his magazine from the ground then loaded his gun.

As he stood up, he saw Camlorn wrestling with one of the mutemutts. Jason ran towards him, killing another mutated dog that was running for him before taking careful aim at Camlorn's foe. He shot the dog in the neck, distracting it enough for Camlorn to break its jaw and throw it aside. The former Regressionist finished off his would-be devourer and rejoined the battle.

As the last of the stage ones fell, Achilles turned towards his fallen former brethren and sank his teeth into the neck of one of the much bulkier canines. He tore its throat open and Camlorn delivered a powerful kick to the mutemutt's head, snapping its spine and ridding the group of what they thought was their final foe. There was a loud bang as Sniper shot one of the seemingly dead mutts that had stirred.

"Inject Livelong...into a dog...and this...is what you get," panted Camlorn.

"I thought it only...worked on humans," replied Jason, his chest heaving.

"These old Rovers would have been dead...within a year of their injections," said Camlorn. "They mutate more rapidly...but their bodies reject it."

The front doors to the lab slid open with a whoosh and four revenants appeared, all armed to the teeth and covered in metal from head to toe. One of them with a cybernetic eye pointed a rocket launcher at the apartment block and fired, but Camlorn shot him in the leg just in time to throw off his aim. The rocket careened upwards and exploded on contact with the top floor of the apartment block, raining bricks and debris down on the street.

In the chaos, Jason ran towards the nearest wall for cover while shooting at the revenants who fired back relentlessly. Camlorn was undeterred and charged at the revenants as they shot at Jason, tackling one to the ground and beating him to death this his fists.

As another revenant turned on Camlorn, Achilles leapt at it. The revenant caught the leaping hound and tossed him aside, while Jason leaned around the corner and landed a lucky shot right on the metal dome of the rocket-launching revenant, leaving just a large enough dent in the side of his head to take the machine freak down.

Camlorn dove aside as one of the revenants removed his hand, revealing a long, sharp blade that he brandished like a sword. The revenant lunged forward to stab Camlorn, who dropped his gun as he scrambled away from his attacker. Livelong or no Livelong, he didn't fancy being stabbed. Jason shot at the revenant, but the metal plating covering his body took the bullets with the revenant barely stumbling.

Achilles meanwhile was back on his feet and sank his teeth into the other remaining revenant's body armour. The dog gnawed and gnashed as the revenant tried to pull Achilles away, but his mighty jaw was gripping too tightly. The revenant pulled out his gun and shot the dog in the side. Sniper appeared right as his faithful pet fell upon the concrete.

"Bastard!" he called, raising his rifle and firing bullet after bullet. Even when the revenant dropped dead, he continued to furiously shoot the brute's corpse. "Die! Die!" barked Sniper as he shot the pulverised corpse of his enemy.

Camlorn yelled as he took the final revenant's blade to the arm. Jason reloaded his gun as quickly as he could manage and shot at Camlorn's attacker. At the same time, Camlorn grabbed his own gun from the ground and fired. The revenant took the bullets, barely fazed. Jason ran forward and tackled the revenant, knocking him over as he tried to retrieve his blade from Camlorn's arm.

Camlorn pulled the blade free himself and pushed Jason aside before thrusting the blade into the revenant's throat. The dying revenant coughed and spluttered in his dying moments.

"H-help," he uttered pathetically, knowing his death was imminent.

Granting the cyborg a final mercy, Jason put his gun under the monster's chin and pressed on the trigger.

"Tough sons of bitches, ain't they?" asked Camlorn with a look of relief, but then he spotted Sniper kneeling over Achilles. "Good grief..." he muttered, much less chipper.

"He's still alive," said Jason, running over to the dog and throwing his pack on the ground. He pulled out a t-shirt and hurriedly cut it into strips with his knife, then wrapped it tightly around Achilles. "Get him back to New Dallas."

"We need to get into the lab," Sniper said, his voice weak but certain. "If we don't, they may double or triple security efforts. It would take bringing in Mercer's men and leaving the city vulnerable to even dare a second try if they're as armed as Camlorn said."

"Take him to New Dallas," insisted Jason.

"I'm not letting you do this without me," said Sniper.

"Achilles has been with you through thick and thin," said Jason. "He's family to you. Take him to New Dallas. We'll handle this."

Sniper looked to Camlorn, who nodded. "Take the dog and get him fixed up, Patch. Time's a-wastin', my friend," he said.

Sniper hoisted Achilles over his shoulder. "Watch your backs," he said to his friends.

"Watch yours," said Jason.

Sniper ran away from the facility with Achilles

whimpering as he was carried, leaving Jason and Camlorn alone. The pair looked at each other and walked over to the doors, which did not slide open for them as they had done for the revenant militia.

"As I said, there's an easy fix to this," said Camlorn, punching the glass, which caused it to shatter. "After you, Jason."

Jason stepped inside the building, pistol in hand, ready to face the dangers within. One way or another, he would find Carlisle and make him pay for his crimes. He would get revenge for his sisters, and he would find a way to bring Lindsay to a new home.

Chapter 18:
Uncovered Evil

4th June 2116: I decided I would be a respectable gentleman and shave today, only to find that it took a slight tug to pull the hairs straight out of my face. There was surprisingly little resistance and no pain whatsoever. That wasn't going to work for me, so I shaved with my knife as I always do. I'm going to cherish these mundane chores while I still can, which doesn't seem like it will be for long. The time of judgement approaches and I fear it. I fear it because I know exactly what I've done and I know exactly where I'll be going.

*

Camlorn followed Jason inside the Fantom building. It was as bland inside as it was outside, the sterile white walls and pale grey carpets having just enough contrast to be distinguishable from each other. The reception desk at the front was empty and the old plastic flower pot stood empty and undecayed in the corner. As they stepped, Jason and Camlorn's feet crunched the glass that had sat within the front door until moments ago.

"Welcome back, Eric," came a man's voice over an intercom, "it's been a while since I've seen you. You look well, but I would much appreciate it if you would leave and not return."

"Good afternoon, Dr Millar," said Camlorn, giving a mocking salute to the camera nearby. "Mighty rude of you to ask an old friend to leave."

"When that old friend slaughters his way through my people, I think that rudeness is justified."

"Your twisted games and experiments end today, Millar," said Camlorn with disdain in his voice.

"Leave now and I won't unleash any more of our pets. They're getting hungry so they'll be extra violent today."

The intercom emitted static for a moment before falling silent. Camlorn casually walked down the hall, spinning his gun around his finger. Jason followed more cautiously, but Camlorn turned around and let out a loud whistle. He took his gun and started banging it against the doors in the corridor before laughing to himself.

"What are you doing?" Jason asked him.

Camlorn turned around to look at Jason with a sly grin on his face. "That slimy old fool is bluffing," he said. "The rest of the revenants must be in Outer Dallas or busy trying to infiltrate the city. We've caught him off guard."

"Does it matter where the revenants are if he's got other freaks ready and waiting?"

"I'm starting to doubt that he *does* have them ready and waiting. He let loose no more than a dozen mutemutts and there were already a bunch of stage one lurkers. I'm starting to think this siege on New Dallas has The Regressionists more spent than Millar would like us to believe."

"You sound awfully confident about that," said Jason. "You willing to bet your life on that, Camlorn?"

"Doesn't matter if I am or not, does it? We're going deeper either way."

"After you," said Jason, gesturing ahead.

Camlorn strolled ahead and towards a door. He flung it open and walked over to the stairs, but suddenly bent over and clutched onto the handrail. He grimaced for a moment, letting out a couple of stifled grunts before standing up and walking on down the stairs. He and Jason both knew what it was, the mutation of his mind and body was occurring slowly but surely. Time was running out before he lost himself. It might not be today or tomorrow, but it was coming, and it was inevitable.

"Want me to take point?" Jason asked.

"Nah, I'm peachy," said Camlorn.

They continued down three flights of stairs until they reached a door. Camlorn tried to push it open, but it was secured tightly. There wasn't even a glass panel to peer through to see what lay on the other side, which told Jason that this was the place they were looking for.

The intercom on the wall beside the door buzzed and Millar's voice came through. "This is your final warning, Eric. There are armed men that won't hesitate to slaughter you and your friend if you don't retreat right now."

"Open the door, Millar," said Camlorn. "The boogeymen are here, and you don't want to piss them off now, do you?"

"It's your funeral, Eric," said Millar before the intercom fell silent.

The door suddenly clicked and Camlorn kicked it open and walked on inside. Jason moved to follow, but a barrage of bullets rained upon them and Jason threw himself back into the stairwell, having taken a couple of nasty grazes to the arm. If it weren't for his nano cloth armour taking the worst of the firing squad's assault, he would have been dead. Camlorn, however, was less lucky having been front and centre during the attack. He lay bleeding out on the floor as the four armed men who attacked them ceased firing.

"One down," came Millar's voice through the

intercom. "I tried to warn you both, but you just wouldn't listen. A real shame, but you have only yourselves to blame."

"Where is Carlisle?" demanded Jason, backing away.

"Mr Carlisle is otherwise engaged, Mr Cooper," said Millar. "You think I don't know who you are after what you did to Mr Benedictus? Do you know how far you set us back and how hard we've worked to ramp up our efforts? Between you and our late friend on the floor, the damage caused has been immense. I hope his death was painful."

Jason ran up the flight of stairs behind him and ducked low, pointing his gun through the railings. He had come too far to retreat and he would face the guards no matter the outcome. He quietly muttered a prayer aloud as the door swung open and he fired at the guards, taking one of them out and forcing the others back. As the door swung back to a close, more gunfire broke out. Seconds later, Jason heard a voice calling to him.

"Clear," grunted Camlorn.

Jason couldn't help but laugh as he walked back down the stairs and entered the room. Camlorn was lying on the floor with his gun in his hand, surrounded by the corpses of the three guards he had just killed. The formidable man was covered in blood from head to toe, some of his own and some from his enemies. He had bullet holes throughout his arms and legs with many more grazes across them. There was also a single graze on the side of his head from a bullet that had come dangerously close to killing him.

"You alright?" Jason asked, helping Camlorn to his feet.

"Absolutely fantastic," said Camlorn, forcing himself to smile. "It's pretty good this Livelong stuff, ain't it? Side effects notwithstanding. They should mass produce it."

"Who wouldn't want to take twenty bullets and get back up?" asked Jason mockingly. "Is it still painful?"

"Oh yeah," said Camlorn. "It's like being stung by a

hornet and having it wiggle its stinger around for an hour or t—"

Camlorn winced again and clutched his head.

"You wait here and I'll go on alone," said Jason.

"Nah, I'm good...I'm good. It'll pass."

Jason kept Camlorn propped up and the two pushed ahead into the next room. It was a large room and they were ten feet above the ground on a long metal walkway. Jason's eyes widened with horror and his jaw hung open as he saw what lay below.

"Welcome to The Regressionists," said Camlorn upon seeing the look on Jason's face. "You're now seeing what lies beneath the surface."

There were dozens of rows of giant test tubes, some the perfect size for humans and others big enough for larger animals. Connected to countless wires and suspended in a pale green liquid within were mutants at various stages of their transformations between human and stage one. Beyond that there were more mutemutts, but even worse were the other animals. Some of them, Jason could not identify, but others had clearly once been bears which were on the verge of bursting from their tubes. There was a bobcat which would have given Big Belial a run for its money and even a badger with claws so sharp and long that they were almost swords. Each of them was fleshy and hairless with strained looks upon their comatose faces. This place was sick; this place was twisted.

"Dear Lord," muttered Jason, "please give me the strength to end this."

The walkway ahead forked in two and, from the left side, came a man in a stained white lab coat. He had brown hair and a thick beard, both of which had a fair number of grey streaks. He held up his hands as he walked to the centre of the fork and faced Jason and Camlorn.

"Please," said the man, who Jason immediately knew to be Millar, "don't come any closer and just hear me out."

"Where are your friends?" asked Camlorn.

"It's just me," said Millar, approaching cautiously.

Camlorn raised his gun and shot Millar in the knee. The scientist cried out in pain and dropped to the ground, shakily clutching his leg in pain. "Eric, you piece of shit," he said.

"Foolish of you to come any closer," said Camlorn. "What did you think would happen? You think we would let you saunter on up to us, stab us in the back or inject us with one of your concoctions? No way, you idiot."

"Carlisle!" demanded Jason. "Where is he?"

"I will not tell you," said Millar as he writhed in pain.

Camlorn pushed himself free of Jason and used the railing to drag himself towards Millar. The scientist reached into his jacket, but Camlorn grabbed his arm and snapped his wrist, forcing him to release a vial of orange liquid. He tossed it into the sea of experiments down below where it clinked against the glass of a mutemutt's tube.

"You've lost, Millar," said Camlorn. "Maybe try doing the right thing for once and we'll consider showing you some mercy."

"What have you done to yourself, Eric?" asked Millar, seeing the bullet holes in Camlorn's arms and legs.

Camlorn looked at Millar scornfully. "I took a dose of Livelong just so I could see to it that each and every one of you in your rotten organisation pays. I've maybe got a couple of good months left before I join those creatures in the vats below, but it's been worth it just to see the looks on the faces of your men as I killed them. Mutants are your bread and butter, aren't they? You should be pleased that I'm well on my way to becoming one of them. Maybe I'll make you drink my blood and let you become a degenerate. How's that for showing you mercy?"

"If the mutation hasn't fully taken hold, that won't work," said Millar.

"You're the man who would know," said Camlorn, reaching into his jacket and pulling out a vial of purple liquid. "Perhaps I'll let you join me in becoming a regular old mutant then. You love them so much, don't you?"

"Please...no," said Millar, looking desperate.

Jason walked up to Millar and stomped on his knee, making the scientist cry out. "Where's Carlisle?" he demanded once again.

"I'll show you," said Millar quickly, letting out a long sigh. "I'll do it...I'll show you."

Jason pulled Millar onto his feet and supported him as he had done for Camlorn, who was now able to unsteadily walk by himself again. He clung onto the handrail for good measure as Millar directed them down the left path of the fork, where he had come from a couple of minutes ago.

The door at the end opened automatically and led them into a small room with a large grey and white pod of metal and plastic, connected to a dozen different apparatuses with wires thick and thin. There were two other men wearing lab coats in here, monitoring the machines. They reached for guns strapped to their waists, but Jason and Camlorn were quicker off the mark.

"Don't touch them," said Jason.

"Listen to him," said Millar softly.

Camlorn shot both of the scientists and Millar called out. "They had surrendered!"

"Whoops," said Camlorn.

"You're a monster...an utter monster, Eric."

"I am, but it's you who made me this way."

"She would be ashamed of you," spat Millar.

Camlorn grabbed Millar and threw him to the floor. He walked over and jammed his thumb into the wound on Millar's knee and twisted it. "Hurts, don't it, Millar? This is the same pain I've had in my heart since you took her from me. Since you...since you killed her."

"I did what I was told!" screamed Millar as Camlorn

continued to torture him.

"You should have disobeyed!" shouted Camlorn. "All you had to do was treat her injury, but you inject her with some of your experimental bullshit. I had to put her down. I had to make sure she was laid to rest before...before she became..."

Camlorn trailed off and took his thumb out of the bullet hole. He walked backwards and leaned against the wall before slumping to the floor. He clutched his head as tears streamed down his face. He wept for a few seconds before pulling himself together and then he pointed at the pod.

"What...what the hell is this?" he asked.

Millar was breathing deeply, trying to recover from the intense pain that Camlorn had inflicted upon him. "You wanted to know where Mr Carlisle was," said Millar. "Well, he's in there."

Jason dragged Millar to his feet. "Explain yourself," he said.

Millar looked Jason dead in the eyes. "When you caused your little scene in Harmony, Mr Carlisle opted to return to New Dallas. Everything was going smoothly until he and his entourage reached Outer Dallas. They were on their way to the gates when a pack of revenants, our own revenants, attacked him. They mistook him for a traveller, would you believe? The four guards you both killed...those were the last of Mr Carlisle's company who had escorted him to me in desperation."

Jason pulled Millar over to the pod. "Show him to me."

Millar pressed a button and the pod separated, the outer plates widening and the top one raising itself up, revealing Ivor Carlisle. He was a man in his fifties, tall and stocky, but already much more sallow than he no doubt was before the attack. His whole body had been shaved, at least what was left of it. His left leg was amputated just above the knee and he was missing his left hand and several fingers on his right. His eyes darted about his head, looking from Millar to Jason and back again, but the rest of his body remained motionless save for his punctured chest heaving up and down with assistance from the tubes that had been fed down his throat and into his lungs to keep him breathing.

"His eyes are moving," said Jason. "Is he of sound mind?"

"Yes," said Millar. "He needs constant care and we're waiting until he's stable enough to be fitted with the cybernetics that we can use to save his life."

"Is that really him?" Jason asked Camlorn.

"That's him," said Camlorn, nodding his head.

"Good," said Jason, shoving Millar to the ground. "That one's yours."

Camlorn walked over to Millar with his knife held high as Millar pleaded for his life. "No, please!" cried the doctor. "You said you would show mercy."

"I'll make it quick," said Camlorn. "That *is* your mercy."

With that, Camlorn stabbed Millar through the eye socket as he would a mutant. The doctor lay dead on the ground, no longer a threat to New Dallas, no longer a threat to the remnants of the world. Camlorn walked over to Jason and Carlisle then stared into the pod at the fallen man who stared back at him, kept alive by machines.

"After all this time hunting him," said Camlorn, clutching his leg and leaning on the edge of the pod to keep himself stable. "He got himself killed."

Carlisle eyes were filled with fear. A man with all of the resources to try and steer the world away from the evil that had spread throughout it, yet he chose to continue the cruelty for his own gain. He thought he could live forever, become an emperor among the ruins like so many other Regressionists who wanted to use the power of Livelong without the drawbacks. Their pride and vanity had cost them everything and they would pay the eternal price.

"He deserves this," said Jason.

"Such a pathetic state to spend your final moments

in," said Camlorn. "It almost makes you pity him, don't it?"

"No," said Jason, raising his revolver and pressing it against Carlisle's head whose eyes begged him to put the gun away. "Burn in hell, scumbag. You had your chance."

Jason pulled the trigger, killing Carlisle instantly and cutting one of the last ropes that held The Regressionists up. Without Millar to lead their experiments, without Carlisle to fund their operations and with their manpower decimated thanks to Camlorn's relentless assault on them, they were done. All that remained was the lab and the remaining experiments it held. The Regressionists could never recover.

"You think there are any others left in this place?" asked Jason, looking around.

"If there were, they would have shown up by now," said Camlorn. "I think Millar was being honest for once when he was telling you about the immense damage we caused. The assault of the revenants was a last-ditch effort to grab some power after Benedictus was killed and, with Carlisle on the verge of death thanks to his own hapless minions, it was doomed to fail. Talk about death by hubris."

"So that begs the question of what we do about the lab," said Jason, getting the feeling that Camlorn already had an idea in mind.

"Burn it to the ground," said Camlorn.

"Did you bring anything to burn it to the ground with?"

Camlorn shook his head. "No need," he said. "There are fail-safes in place for if the mutants get a bit too rowdy or the experiments break loose en masse. They've never had to be used because there used to be dozens of armed guards here at all times, but I trust the one I want will still work."

"Explosives?"

"Lots of explosives," said Camlorn.

He walked back to the door and grabbed onto the railing outside as Jason followed him to the walkway. He moved straight ahead, taking the other path of the fork. He entered one of the rooms along the way where there were several terminals set up. He started tapping on the screen of the largest and navigating through the menus.

"They let you know how to set the self-destruct sequence?" Jason asked him.

"Nah," chuckled Camlorn, "but Mr Benjamin Burnside was kind enough to give me his password in exchange for his life. The man knows his electronics and he helped rig this place years ago."

"Burnside?" Jason asked. "The man from Carson Robotics?"

"Yes indeed. I was lucky enough to find him in Harmony shortly before I ran into you. He swore to me that he had parted ways with The Regressionists and looted some of their best equipment for that robot girl of his. Good thing too, he may have had Carlisle fitted with the cybernetics already if he was hanging around here. For his faults, the man is a genius."

"You let him live?" surprised that Camlorn had shown any level of compassion to a Regressionist.

"He chose a different path than many of the others," said Camlorn solemnly. "All of this could have been avoided if they had truly wanted to help the world, but they decided the world as it is now worked for them."

"It saddens me to think about that," said Jason.

"Likewise," said Camlorn, finishing tapping on the screen. "I've set it on a five-minute timer. That should give us enough time to get out of here."

"Did you think about the mutants that might have gathered up above after hearing our shooting match earlier? We weren't exactly quiet."

"No...no, I did not think about that."

"Then it's best we get moving right now," said Jason.

Camlorn put his arm around Jason's shoulder and the two made their way out of the room and down the walkway. Jason didn't even spare the tubed experiments down below a glance. The poor humans and beasts would be set free in death, the only option left for them. The two men ascended the stairs and walked back to the entrance and out of the Fantom building.

"Three of them," said Jason, holding up his gun alongside Camlorn.

The two crippled the fast-approaching mutants by aiming for their knees, not wanting to get drawn into a longer fight. They probably had no more than a minute before the Fantom building blew and they wanted to be well clear of it. As the men moved down the street, a loud explosion burst out from behind them and the unmistakable sound of cascading rubble hitting the ground followed it.

The job was done at last and The Regressionists were no more. It was only a matter of time before the lingering members realised it and had the chance to choose a different path ahead. Whether they did or not was up to them.

*

Later that night, Jason and an almost fully healed Camlorn walked towards Namaah surrounded by Captain Crusoe and a number of Mercer Guard with the moon hanging high in the sky above them. The seedy building sat a few streets away from The Third Circle and was reminiscent of its Harmony counterpart, albeit less grimy on the outside and without the glowing neon sign. The wider and more open streets of New Dallas made each and every building stand out on its own without the need for the extra flair.

One of the two door guards outside moved to stop Captain Crusoe upon seeing the large group of armed men approaching. "What's the meaning of this?" he asked.

"You're hereby relieved of your employment," said the captain. "Your boss was killed by revenants a few hours ago and I suspect you'll receive no wages if you continue to stand around here waiting for payday. What you will receive, should you interfere with our business, is a visit from the Street Cleaners. Do you understand me?"

"Yes, sir," said the guard, looking distraught at his sudden unemployment. He and his fellow guard walked away, not sure whether what the captain had said was true or not, but the thought of a visit from the Street Cleaners was more than enough to spook the pair.

The group walked inside Namaah and Captain Crusoe put his index finger and thumb between his lips and whistled loudly. The customers all stopped drinking, the servers stopped serving, and the dancing girls stopped dancing.

"Mr Ivor Carlisle is dead as of a few hours ago," once the music had been cut. "He met his end at the hands of revenants in Outer Dallas and will no longer be running this show. I suggest that once we're through here, you all clear out or throw one last party at his expense."

The crowd murmured in disbelief, but a couple of the customers moved to leave only to be stopped by the Mercer Guard.

"Not one person is to leave until I say so," ordered Captain Crusoe. "I strongly suggest you take me seriously or there will be consequences. Now, is there a Lindsay Cooper here?"

"She's in the back," called a gruff bartender, nodding towards a door in the corner of the room. Jason's heart jumped in his chest. She was alive. She was here.

"Bring her out," said Crusoe.

The bartender shrugged and slumped out from behind the bar and through the doorway. Less than a minute later, he returned followed by a confused blonde girl of eighteen whose expression grew fearful at the sight of the guards who had seemingly come for her.

"She looks a lot like you," murmured Camlorn as Jason stared at his sister, still not believing he could be so lucky as to find both her and Abigail alive. They had been separated for so long in such a cruel and unforgiving world, but they had been given a chance.

"D-did I do s-something wrong?" Lindsay stammered, looking at the captain.

Jason moved past Crusoe and walked out into the open. Lindsay gasped and her eyes filled with tears at the sight of the brother she hadn't seen in almost a year. She rushed over to him, jumped into his arms and bawled loudly.

"I-I knew you would...come back for me," said Lindsay. "Am I...free?"

"Yes," said Jason, barely holding himself together. "We're all finally free."

Chapter 19:
Reunion

5th June 2116: It's done. Carlisle is dead and dawn is breaking over New Dallas. The Regressionists will take a little time to peter out, but I'm sure most of them will be gone by Christmas. I can spend my final days in peace without worrying. I know there isn't much time left, but at least I can enjoy a few laughs and smiles on the way. Jason, if you're reading this diary later, then remember this. The things we do, we do out of love and not out of hate. You're not too far gone and, knowing you, you never will be. Your future is bright and filled with hope. Take care of yourself, bud. – Eric Camlorn

*

"How're you feeling, boy?" Jason asked Achilles as the sturdy German Shepherd gingerly sniffed around the young man's feet, moving in such a way as to navigate around his painful wound.

"Going to need to put him on a wagon to get him to Highwayland," said Sniper, "but he'll be fine. As I said, no vital organs hit, he just needs to not tear his stitches."

It had been three days since Sniper had brought his

dog to the clinic for treatment. The master had not left his canine companion's side the entire time and Jason had visited them a couple of times to fill him in on everything that had happened with The Regressionists and Carlisle, but most of his time was spent with Lindsay.

"Are you Mr Creighton?" asked Jason's sister, walking forward nervously to greet Sniper.

"That's me," said Sniper, holding out his hand for her to shake. "I'm glad to see you're safe and sound. You know, your twin sister was awful worried about you."

"Abigail worries about everything," said Lindsay, smiling brightly and waving her hand dismissively, but Sniper could tell that she was trying to brush over a brutal nine months.

"Gentlemen and lovely lady," said Camlorn, coming between Jason and Lindsay and putting an arm around each of them. "It's a beautiful day outside and the wild, wild wasteland is calling to us. Should we perhaps get a move on before Mercer's men get impatient?"

"Mercer's men?" asked Sniper, looking at Jason. "What's he talking about?"

"Mercer agreed to lend us four of his men to see us to Highwayland safely," said Jason. "He said it's the least he can do after everything."

"Mighty good of him," said Sniper. "Fewer people to keep an eye on until I get my scope reinstalled. He's alright, Mercer, isn't he?"

"Standup fella," said Camlorn with an exaggerated smile, "now let's go before my face gets stuck this way, I lose all my hair and start trying to eat you all."

"The man's got a point," shrugged Jason as Sniper gave a faint nod of agreement.

"What does that mean?" asked Lindsay.

"We'll tell you later," said Sniper. "Best to stay in the dark on this one for the time being."

The group left the clinic, keeping their pace slow so Achilles didn't need to run to catch up with them. They headed down the street and Jason sent them on their way towards the exit to Outer Dallas where the Mercer Guard would be awaiting them.

Jason looked over, seeing alone Lyra at her stall as she stared out into the world. As he approached, she turned to him and waved.

"Howdy, stranger," she said pleasantly.

"Morning, Lyra," said Jason.

"You never did come back to explain our last conversation," she said. "I thought maybe you'd skipped town without saying goodbye."

"Better thinking that than thinking I was dead, right?"

"I'd be more offended if you'd skipped town," giggled Lyra. "But I'm glad you're safe."

"I'm glad I'm safe too," said Jason.

Lyra nodded towards Jason's group. "Is that Lindsay?" she asked.

"That's her."

"She looks a lot like you," said Lyra, flicking Jason's hair with her finger, "I think it's the bright blonde locks."

"We take after our grandfather on Dad's side. Abigail looks more like our mother with her red hair and all."

Lyra smiled, but there was a sadness in her eyes that Jason could see. "Is everything alright?" he asked.

"I'm just having a hard time letting go, I suppose," she said. "You've only just gotten back, and this is only our second conversation...and it's almost over."

"I'll come and visit," said Jason. "I can't say how often, but I promise I will."

Lyra breathed deeply and looked down the main street of Renaissance and then into Jason's eyes. She reached out and took his right hand, holding it tightly. She breathed deep before exhaling and uttering in a weak voice. "Ask me again."

"Ask you again?"

"Yes."

Jason stared back at her silently for a moment, not sure if she had meant it. "Come with me," he said.

"Come with me and leave New Dallas behind."

"Alright," said Lyra, her lip quivering as she smiled at him.

"What?"

"Alright," she repeated. "Let's go."

"Your father?"

"He said he would come too. I'm not sure if he was joking or not, but I'm going to hold him to it either way."

"Go grab your things and meet us by the door," said Jason. "We'll wait for you both."

Lyra tossed Jason a small bag from underneath the stall counter. "Grab the silver and non-perishables," she said while walking away. "I'll be back soon."

Jason started to laugh and dragged his hand across his face. He couldn't quite believe that she was going to come with him. They would finally have a chance to start over somewhere far away. Somewhere safe.

*

"...and then, bang!" said Cormac as Lindsay listened attentively. "Blew up half the damn street! Little pieces of debris flew right into my eyes, and everything since has been a murky white blur."

"I can't imagine," said Lindsay, not knowing what to say.

"It's not all that bad," said Cormac rather cheerfully, "but it'd be nice to see something other than a blur."

"Cybernetics are always an option," said Sniper.

"Nah," said Cormac shaking his head vigorously. "I want to see with my own eyes rather than having digital images beamed into my brain. It may work for some, but something about it gives me the willies, my friend."

Camlorn scratched his head as he walked alongside the horses just up ahead. "There are other methods for healing body parts, but I can't say I'd recommend them," he called back.

"You think that there Livelong would fix my eyes after so long?"

"Daddy!" called Lyra angrily.

"Just curious," said Cormac, holding his hands up to reassure his daughter. "I like having hair, being able to frown and all that other good stuff."

Jason and Lyra were walking alongside the wagon with Camlorn so as not to burden the horses too much. They had been on the road for a couple of days already and Camlorn had insisted on serving as their navigator, so none of the sights were familiar to Jason this time around. Sometimes in this wasteland, places that were completely different felt the same while other times things that were similar felt completely different. It was hard to put his finger on why, but Jason thought about it often and he couldn't explain why it continued to crop up in his mind.

"I hope we don't run into any more mutants," said Lyra, looking away from the road and over to the large stretch of dry grassland to her left.

"If only we were so lucky," chuckled Jason. "We'll be just fine. These guards know what they're doing, Sniper and Camlorn are veterans out here and I'm not so bad a shot myself."

"It's strange to see," said Lyra pensively. "The mutants, I mean. I've seen them from a distance lurking around Outer Dallas, but never up close...at least not from what I remember. There's just something about them that makes me sick to my stomach, yet sad at the same time. To think that they were once people...I've known it from when I was young, but I never quite accepted it fully."

"My brother Bill used to make up stories about the mutants. He would give them names and talk about all the different things they got up to before they turned into what they are today. He would have the tallest of tales, let me tell you. One of my favourites was about a private detective called Hugo Jones who solved crimes with a hammer."

"How did he solve crimes with a hammer?" giggled Lyra.

"I'd rather not say," said Jason, laughing at the memory of Bill telling the story around the dinner table. He would always say his entire tale with a straight face.

"He'd smash in the kneecaps of anybody who wouldn't cough up the information he wanted," called Lindsay from the wagon.

"Yeah, I kinda read between the lines there," said Lyra with an awkward laugh.

"Quite the character this brother of yours," said Cormac trying to contain himself through his laughter. "I'm sure we'd have gotten along famously."

"I don't doubt that for a second," said Jason.

It was nice to be out on the road with this group of people, regardless of whether there were mutants lurking over every other hill looking to cause trouble. To Jason, it felt like they were one big family and that was a feeling he sorely missed. He was excited for what Highwayland would bring for them all. He was excited to reunite Lindsay and Abigail. He was excited for a future with Lyra by his side.

"We got a live one!" called Creed, one of the Mercer Guard. "It don't look too alert."

"Leave it to me," said Camlorn, running up the road with his knife in his hand.

Everyone watched as Camlorn approached the stage one which was lying against an abandoned car that had rusted far beyond salvage. As he drew close, the mutant stirred, but Camlorn was too quick and jammed his blade into its skull without remorse. He wiped it clean on the rags that were what remained of the mutant's jeans and waited for everyone to catch up.

Lyra shuddered as they passed the dead mutant. She clung close to Jason, terrified that it would spring up and attack them. "Eugh," she said, looking away and closing her eyes until they were well past it.

"You get used to them," said Sniper, "but you can't ever let your guard down when you're on the road. We'll make sure you're a crack shot in no time, don't worry about that. Means you're prepared should things ever take a sudden turn for the—"

"You don't half know how to spoil a mood, do you?" asked Camlorn. "Maybe keep it light for the ladies, Patch."

"Always better to be prepared," said Sniper.

"Not my point, my friend," said Camlorn. "Not my point."

The two bickered for a while before Jason told them to shut up, for which the rest of the company was most grateful. Every now and then they would happen upon another mutant and the men—save for Cormac—took it in turn to deal with the wandering fiends.

"I'm not sure I'll ever get used to this," said Lyra as Jason ran back to the party after skewering one of the mutants that had crept over a small hill to their left.

Jason smiled at her and then looked to the road ahead. "His name was Marvin Phelps," he said as Lindsay rolled her eyes and Camlorn let out a hearty guffaw. "He was once a travelling spice salesman from Georgia before the fall of the Old World and, boy, did he have a temper if you didn't pay up on the spot..."

*

The wagon pulled up to the concrete pillar just below the entrance to Highwayland. Camlorn stayed well back, knowing that even after everything that had happened with The Regressionists and with Jason and Sniper to vouch for him, he still wouldn't be welcome after killing Johnny and shooting one of the guards. He didn't say it aloud, but Jason could see why the Highwayland residents would think that way.

"It's Jason Cooper," said Jason after pressing the intercom button. "We've got nine people, a dog and two horses. Four of the people are resting for the night and the rest of us are here to stay for the foreseeable future. Will you let us up?"

"I'll have a word with my superiors," replied Kyle jokingly.

Shortly afterwards, the elevator began to noisily descend towards the ground. Once it arrived, it carried the wagon with the horses up while Lindsay, Lyra and Cormac rode with them. The four Mercer Guard members were to go up next, so Jason and Sniper walked over to Camlorn who was sitting on the ground, looking off towards the hills in the distance. He looked calm; he looked peaceful.

"You good?" Jason asked him as he approached.

"Peachy, Jason," Camlorn replied, looking up to the sky. "Just peachy. Nice day out, ain't it?"

"Leave you with a nasty burn if you're out here for too long," said Sniper. "Can you still get those?"

"It's never even crossed my mind with everything else going on," said Camlorn.

"I suppose not," said Sniper.

"Listen, fellas," said Camlorn, standing up. "I wanted to thank you both for giving me a hand with my list. There are still a few stragglers on there, but with Millar and Carlisle dead and no more lab to speak of, they'll disappear soon enough. Maybe they'll play around trying to convince people to take some Livelong, but I'm sure it'll peter out once they realise their support network is gone."

"I should be thanking you," said Jason, holding out his hand for Camlorn to shake. "I wouldn't have found either of my sisters if we hadn't met."

"I'm an optimist, Jason," said Camlorn, clasping Jason's hand firmly. "I think the Lord would have steered you in their direction sooner or later."

"Sorry I tried to shoot you," said Sniper, also shaking Camlorn's hand once Jason had finished.

"What do you mean tried?" chuckled Camlorn.

"Fair," laughed Sniper.

"So where are you heading next?" asked Jason.

Camlorn looked around, taking in the hills, the grass, the highway and even the ascending elevator that was now carrying the four men into town. He closed his eyes and inhaled through his nose then out from his mouth as a smile crept across his face. "I think I'm ready to die and this seems like a decent place to go out," he said, sounding satisfied. "This is where we part ways for good, fellas."

"Can't say I didn't see this coming," said Sniper, while Jason looked on aghast.

"You've still got time!" Jason protested.

Camlorn's face fell. "Did you know I forgot my own middle name this morning?" he asked. "Such a simple thing, but everyone knows their middle name, don't they? Mine is Martin and it took me over an hour to remember it. The headaches are getting worse and they're getting more frequent, even when I'm not recovering from some sort of injury. Each night, I wake up in a cold sweat and have to pull myself together. It's getting closer...too close for me to be around other people."

"We can set up a watch until things get worse or something..." said Jason, trailing off. He didn't want Camlorn's life to come to an early end, but he couldn't force the man to keep living when his very being was changing into something demonic.

"I'm tired of death," said Camlorn, his voice heavy. "I'm tired of all the killing, tired of all the suffering. I'd just like to go out while I'm still me and on my own terms. Maybe I'll be blessed enough to see my Angie again, even if it's just my life flashing before my eyes as I fade away. I don't think heaven will be waiting for me for going out like this, but I suppose it wouldn't be waiting for me if I go out a mutant either. Who knows?"

"Don't you want to at least say goodbye to the others?" asked Jason.

"Nah," said Camlorn. "I want you to see the looks on their faces when you go up that elevator. Priceless, I'm sure. In all seriousness, I do have one request before I go."

"What is it?" asked Jason.

"Bury my body and say a prayer for me. Nothing fancy, it would just be nice to have something to send me off."

"Of course," said Jason. "I pray for you every night, Camlorn. I pray for all of us. I'll do it."

Camlorn reached for his pistol and spun it around before putting it up to his temple. "Have a good one, boys," he said with a smile. He held his gun steady and closed his eyes, but his hand began to quiver and he brought it back down again. "Damn pussy, ain't I?" he chuckled and dropped his gun on the dry soil.

Jason slowly reached for his own gun and raised it, pointing it straight at Camlorn's forehead. "It's been a pleasure, Eric. Mostly."

Camlorn laughed and closed his eyes. "Don't you dare miss and hit me in the throat, Jason. You hear me?"

Jason's hand was shaking and he was worried he would do just that when...bang. Camlorn hit the dirt with a hole in his forehead and a smile still on his face. Sniper lowered his smoking gun then walked over and pushed Jason's gun down.

"Couldn't let you do it, J," said Sniper. "It'd eat you up inside for the rest of your life even if it's what he wanted. Me? Eric Camlorn and Felix Creighton have a lot in common so it's only fitting that I'm the one who puts him down. Besides, I've shot him before so I'm not exactly breaking new ground here, bud."

The pair stood there quietly for a moment as Jason tried to steady his shaking hand. He thought that after everything, he would have a moment of serenity. This should have been a happy time, but now he was faced with the death of another person he cared about.

"I'm tired too, Sniper," said Jason quietly. He clutched his chest, right over his heart. "Each and every one of them, I feel it. Stefano. Benedictus. The degenerates, the revenants. Even Carlisle. I feel it and I hate what this world has done to me. What it's forced me to do just to keep myself going. To keep the ones I love safe."

"Death ain't pretty," said Sniper, putting a hand on Jason's shoulder. "Even if we think it's right or necessary. Worst part is you get desensitised to it after a while. It becomes second nature out here, where mutants aren't the only problem...but it's over now."

Jason looked towards Highwayland where his sisters, Kyle, Lyra and her father were all waiting for him. Every time he thought he had made peace with killing, it came back around and kicked him in the head. He knew it was something he'd have to wrestle with over and over again but, with any luck, would never metastasize and grow into a cancer of paralysing fear. Perhaps, out here he could find a life close to the one he had in his old home. Free of killing other men.

"It's worth it, isn't it?" Jason asked Sniper, his eyes still fixed on Highwayland. "If it's for them, right?"

Sniper nodded. "We're the men, Jason. We do things we don't want to do without complaint so that others don't have to. We put ourselves through hell so that those we love don't suffer. We put it on our own backs and we keep on walking."

"And we still lose sometimes."

"That we do...that we do. Still, we keep walking into the sunset with our burdens because that's what we have to do. At least we know that one day the sun will rise and we'll feel a little lighter, at least until the next day is done."

Jason stood there staring into the distance quietly while Sniper walked over to Camlorn's body and placed his hand on his dead friend's face. He muttered something quietly that Jason couldn't make out before closing Camlorn's eyes. Sniper picked up the discarded gun and wedged it in his belt while checking their surroundings for any mutants that may have heard the shot. All seemed clear for now, but the view from the town above would give him certainty. Once he had that,

Eric Camlorn could have a proper sendoff.

"What's your purpose now?" Jason asked.

"My purpose?"

"Since you've made peace with Mercer."

"Right now?" replied Sniper with a faint smile on his face. "My purpose is to bury our friend, just like he asked us to. Come on, bud, let's get a shovel and break the sad news to the others."

Sniper walked towards the old highway that he could now call home, while Jason remained standing with his grandfather's old gun in his hand. He looked at it for a moment and then holstered it. For now, he would share Sniper's purpose and see to it that Eric Camlorn was buried and he received his prayers.

After that, Jason would find a new purpose, whatever that may be. There was still a longing inside him to push through the darkness so that he could see the light. There was still a spark left in him that kept him from giving into despair. It was something kept alive by his friends, his family and his faith.

He still had hope.

Other Works by Jordan Allen

Mutagenesis: The New World (2021)

A post-apocalyptic sci-fi novel set in Texas decades after hordes of mutants wiped out civilisation. It's a tale of survival, adventure and coming to terms with misfortune.

Hollow Kingdom (2023)

A sword and sorcery tale of a prince trying to reclaim his kingdom and solve the mystery of his father and brother's fates.

Ashes of the Necropolis (2023)

A mercenary seeks his missing companions in a city filled with the undead and at the mercy of a wicked lich.

Moonlit Soul (2023)

The tale of a soul-seeking assassin and the valiant paladin he's targeting on their separate journeys that are destined to converge.